Goodnight
Moo

Books by Mollie Cox Bryan

Goodnight Moo

Mollie Cox Bryan

KENSINGTON BOOKS
www.kensingtonbooks.com

KENSINGTON BOOKS are published by

Kensington Publishing Corp.
119 West 40th Street
New York, NY 10018

All Kensington titles, imprints, and distributed lines are available at special quantity discounts for bulk purchases for sales promotion, premiums, fund-raising, and educational or institutional use.

Special book excerpts or customized printings can also be created to fit specific needs. For details, write or phone the office of the Kensington Sales Manager: Kensington Publishing Corp., 119 West 40th Street, New York, NY 10018. Attn. Sales Department. Phone: 1-800-221-2647.

Kensington and the K logo Reg. U.S. Pat. & TM Off.

First Kensington Books Mass Market Paperback Printing: September 2020
ISBN-13: 978-1-4967-2134-1
ISBN-10: 1-4967-2134-9

ISBN-13: 978-1-4967-2135-8 (ebook)
ISBN-10: 1-4967-2135-7 (ebook)

10 9 8 7 6 5 4 3 2 1

Printed in the United States of America

Cast of Characters

Brynn MacAlister—cheesemaker, dairy farmer, sleuth

Becky MacAlister—Brynn's sister

Nathaniel and Hannah Scors—Wes's parents

Wes and Max Scors—Nathaniel and Hannah's sons and Nancy's grandsons

Josh O'Connor—honey farmer and president of the Shenandoah Springs CSA

Chelsea O'Connor—Josh's daughter

The O'Reilly family (Miriam and David, and their children, Frank and Tillie)—owners of the local apple orchard

Willow Rush—organic vegetable farmer

Mike Rafferty—fire marshal

Schuyler Rafferty—vet-acupuncturist

David Reese—owner of the tractor shop

Charlie—the IT expert

Roy—student, hacker, friend of Wes

Cast of Cows

Buttercup—one of Brynn's three Red Devon milking cows, docile and sweet

Marigold—the shyest of the cows

Petunia—vocal and stubborn, in mourning for her lost calf

Jewel—shy, orphaned Scottish Highland cow

Chapter 1

Brynn MacAlister preferred fall, but summer in the Shenandoah Valley in Virginia ran a close second. Spring wildflowers hung on throughout much of the season and Brynn and her cows enjoyed the honeysuckle, bluebells, and pink lady's slipper in the fields. Brynn didn't appreciate the humidity and heat, but she cherished the way the community gathered its resources for one of its biggest events of the year—the Shenandoah Springs annual fair. This year, Buttermilk Creek Farm was sponsoring for the first time a local cheesemakers' shed and contest.

She had visited the fair last year as an outsider and it was part of the reason she fell in love with the place. Most of the locals were still family farmers and now they were micro-farmers, specializing in products like honey, Christmas trees and pumpkins, and organic vegetables. Shenandoah Springs was a haven for the organic, local farm movement. And the fair provided a perfect place to gather and show off their hard work.

She recalled the stalls of homemade food, such as

pies and cakes, and canned goods, gleaming jars of tomato sauce, pickles, deep crimson pickled beets. The craft display building was her favorite, with the many quilts, afghans, and lace items—last year, a stunning intricate red lace tablecloth won best in the show.

But this year, she was a part of it—and couldn't be happier. She sat at her kitchen table and gazed out the window at her small farm with her three cows and Freckles, the Saint Bernard–collie mix puppy, hanging out together.

"Do we have all the labels we'll need?" Wes, her assistant, asked as he placed a plate of cucumber sandwiches in front of Brynn.

She slid a small box toward him. "Yes, I ordered more."

He gazed out the kitchen window at the darkening sky. "It will let loose any moment." He motioned to the seal-gray sky. The dark clouds had been gathering all day—it was a pattern over the past few weeks. The afternoon storm. Petunia, her most sensitive cow, always ran into the barn at the first crack of thunder.

"As of this morning, we have eight local amateur cheesemakers entering the contest," he told her.

"That's plenty for the first year. Don't you think?"

He nodded. "Try the sandwich. The spread is new. Thoughts?"

Wes was a creative cook, baker, and, as it turned out, cheesemaker. Of all the things Brynn had done in her life, agreeing to allow him to move into the guest house was one of the best decisions she'd ever made. He helped her out, and in return, she taught him how to make cheese and other dairy products.

She bit into the thin sandwich and a light, refreshing flavor exploded in her mouth. "Mmmm."

"Lemon and dill," Wes said. "With my Greek-style yogurt as a base."

Brynn swallowed her first bite. "I love it!"

"I've got a few more things to perfect, but we might consider adding this to our offerings."

"It's delicious and perfect now," Brynn said, reaching for another tiny sandwich.

The first boom of thunder sounded and Petunia shot across the backyard field toward the barn. With all of her cow heft, she moved with grace, and her ever-loyal dog companion, Freckles, followed. The other two cows, Marigold and Buttercup, paid no attention to the thunder.

Brynn chuckled watching Petunia head for the barn. She turned her attention to the list in front of her on the table. Buttermilk Creek Farm was the sponsor of the cheesemaking shed and Brynn wanted to ensure this first year was fabulous. She had visions of it growing into a state competition. "Do we have everything?"

Wes glanced over her shoulder. "If by that you mean everything but the kitchen sink, yes, yes, you do."

Brynn laughed, just as her phone buzzed. She picked up to uneven heavy breathing.

"Oh my God, Brynn, there's been a terrible accident." The voice on the other end was a scratchy, tense whisper, but she recognized it.

Brynn's heart leaped in her chest. "Willow? Are you okay? What's going on?"

"I'm on my way to the hospital. Accident . . . tractor . . . it's horrible."

"Willow? Who? Who was in the accident?"

Wes had been fussing with cucumbers on the counter and spun toward Brynn.

"Josh. Driving the tractor and I'm not sure . . . It was a hired guy. It's bad."

"Josh?" His face flashed in her mind. The honey farmer who had been in farming since he was a kid. A tractor accident? "That doesn't sound right."

"It's strange." Willow sobbed.

"Where are you, Willow? You aren't driving, are you?"

"On my way to the hospital. My dad's driving me."

"Thank God for that. You're too upset to drive."

"I was there," she said. "I saw the whole thing. It was a nightmare!"

A sudden urge to rush to her side prompted Brynn to stand. "I'll come to the hospital."

"No," Willow said. "I need you to pick up the quilts for me today."

"Quilts?"

"Yes, for the quilt display. There are about twenty. I'm e-mailing you the addresses now."

"What am I supposed to do with them?"

"Put them in the hall and I'll take care of the displays."

Brynn's first thought was to run to the hospital, but she was eager to help Willow out in any way she could. "I'm happy to do it," Brynn said. "Please keep me informed and stop by when you can."

"Will do. Thanks. I gotta go." She clicked off.

Brynn's mind raced. Tractor accident? She never liked tractors, but they were a necessary evil if farmers wanted to get things done with efficiency. She didn't own a tractor but had rented one for the field where she planted special food for the cows.

Poor Willow, having seen the accident. What exact horror had she witnessed? Brynn shivered.

"What's going on?" Wes sat at the table.

"There's been a tractor accident. Josh hit some-one."

"What? That sounds weird. If anybody knows his way around a tractor . . ."

"Accidents happen." Brynn recalled the fire that stole Nancy's life. She had assumed Nancy's death was an accident, but it turned out not to be. "Wil-low's on the way to the hospital. She's shaken. She saw everything."

Willow had been one of the most friendly people to Brynn when she moved to Shenandoah Springs. She was the backbone of the Community Supported Agriculture program and showed Brynn the ropes, filled her in on the best places to eat and the local gossip. When Nancy died, they became even closer.

"Can you hold down the fort? I've got to pick up about twenty quilts."

Wes cocked his eyebrow. "That's not on your list."

"It's for Willow. She won't be able to get to it today."

"I can hold the fort down, but you may need help. Quilts are heavy and twenty of them will be very hefty. It will be much faster with two of us. We need to get back to our own list."

Once again, Brynn remembered what a good move it was to partner up with Wes, Nancy's grandson, whom she didn't even know before her death. Their friend-ship had blossomed through their love of cheese and Nancy, even though Brynn would turn back the clock if she could have just one more nice hot cup of Earl Grey with her friend. Wes was the next best thing.

"Is Josh okay? I mean, what happened? Did he fall off the tractor? Tip it?"

"No, I don't think so. He hit someone, one of the summer helpers. At least I think that's what Willow said."

"How awful!"

Brynn slid her laptop across the table, cracked open the lid, and pressed the switch. The e-mail from Willow was already there. She hit print. "Let's get these quilts delivered so we can go to the hospital."

Chapter 2

Delivering twenty quilts to the fairground was not as easy as it had sounded. First, as Wes predicted, they were heavy. Second, a few of the quilt makers had such specific, painstaking instructions that Brynn tried not to roll her eyes. When she thought of everything her own quilts had been through—quilts were pieces of art, yes, but they were also sturdy, reliable ways to keep warm.

The fairground edged outside of Shenandoah Springs proper. The fields were coming alive with tents and buildings and carnival rides. As Brynn pulled up the car to unload, she noted a crew of men hanging lights around a small stage. She exited her car and Wes followed. They scooped the quilts up out of the back seat.

"We must make a few trips," Wes said.

Even folded, the quilts were colorful and impressive, and as she carried them Brynn thought about the hours the quilters had put into them. Such patience.

She and Wes delivered the first batch to the craft hall and traveled back for more. She spotted Tom Andrews, another member of the CSA and a neighbor, talking with a younger man, dressed to the hilt. Tom looked up at her. "Hey, Brynn. Wes."

"Hi." Brynn stopped walking in front of a broad, tall man, probably in his forties. He wore his graying hair with bangs; Brynn tried not to stare at the bangs falling across his forehead.

"This is David Reese. He owns the tractor shop off Route 240," Tom said.

Brynn extended her hand. He shook it. "Nice to meet you." His eyes scanned the length of her, prompting Brynn to fold her arms. Wes stepped forward, offered his hand, and they shook.

"We're in the middle of delivering these quilts, so we don't mean to be rude, but we have to keep moving. I need to get to the hospital."

"Hospital?" Tom asked. "Everything okay?"

"You haven't heard? There was a tractor accident. Josh. I know nothing else. I'm sorry."

Tom paled. David shifted his weight. "He bought a tractor from me. I best get over there and see what's going on myself."

"Let me help you with the rest of the quilts," Tom said, following Brynn and Wes.

When Brynn first met Tom, she didn't know what to make of him. First, he called her sweetie, which she didn't like; second, he attempted to ruin one of her business connections. Attempted. But after she confronted him and they had a talk, they'd gotten along well. She understood she was an outsider and in a place like Shenandoah Springs that used to mean something. But the trend was clear—more and more people were coming to farm, craft, and enjoy a community of like-minded people. It was difficult for locals to see change.

"Thanks, Tom," Brynn said as they dropped off the last quilts.

He opened his mouth as if to speak, then closed it. He nodded.

Brynn changed the subject. "How are the pies coming?" Tom's wife, Elsie, was in charge of the pies for the fair—both the ones for selling and serving fair attendees and the ones for the pie contest—the crown jewel of every country fair.

"She's busy. Some people take their pie very seriously."

Brynn laughed.

"I know I do," Wes said with a grin.

Tom cleared his throat, tucked his thumbs into the front pockets of his jeans. "I can't imagine Josh having an accident. I mean, I know accidents happen, but . . ."

"He knows his tractors, doesn't he?"

"He's been driving them since before he should. I remember when he was a kid." Tom looked off into the distance. "He always scored high with the tractor pull, too."

"The what?" Wes asked, wide-eyed.

"It's a contest. We hitch a trailer on the back and load it up with people on it and see who can pull the most. It's a lot of fun."

Brynn was not a mechanical, tractor person. But she conceded it sounded like fun.

"I'll check it out this year, if I can. I'll be so busy with the new cheese shed."

"Can't wait for that," he said, grinning. Tom had become one of her biggest fans, which Brynn considered a victory of sorts.

After they said their good-byes, Brynn and Wes hopped into the car and headed for the hospital to see Willow and check on Josh.

"Tom's turned out to be cool," Wes said.

Brynn nodded. "Sometimes first impressions aren't accurate."

"Sometimes I imagine him and my gram in the same room together, though, and it makes me laugh."

Wes was the grandson of Nancy, the woman killed in the church fire a few months ago. Nancy was Brynn's closest neighbor. She'd planned on renovating the church and turning it into an upscale farm shop, but it burned and Nancy died. Brynn swallowed the grief creeping into her throat. She missed Nancy and their daily teas.

"She did have a problem with a few locals, but she never went into detail about which ones." Brynn stopped at the stop sign, looked both ways, then lifted her foot from the brake.

"I wonder what she'd think of what they are doing to the church now."

Brynn shrugged. "If she were here, it'd be a hopping farm shop."

"She despised organized religion."

"I remember." Brynn turned into the hospital.

She drove around the crowded, zigzag parking lot and found a place to park.

When Brynn and Wes found Willow, a man had his arm wrapped around her. Her head was tucked in the crevice between his neck and shoulder. When he studied Brynn, it was almost as if she were gazing at a male version of Willow—same mocha skin, brown eyes, and high cheekbones. He must be her father.

Brynn lifted her chin to him. "I'm Brynn. How is she?"

Willow didn't lift her head.

"She's in shock." Her father tucked a blanket closer to Willow. Her brown hair covered most of her face. "But she's asleep now. So that's good."

His eyes skirted behind Brynn to Wes.

Hospitals were odd places to meet people for the first time. He looked askance at Wes and Brynn wondered why.

Brynn moved forward, keeping her voice down. "What can I do to help?"

Willow's father looked up at Brynn. "It'll take time for her to get over this. But in the meantime, pray for Josh." He was a big, hulking man, and the word "pray" coming out of him only endeared him more to Brynn.

Brynn's heart sped. She'd thought Josh was fine. "Is he okay?"

"Oh yes, he's fine. But he may face murder charges."

Brynn's hand covered her mouth as she gasped.

"The young man he hit died."

Chapter 3

Murder? Did Brynn hear that right? She gazed across the room at a painting of a farm scene as if it held answers.

"It was an accident," Wes said, after a few moments. "Surely not murder."

Willow's father's eyes told another story. "I hope you're right."

"Josh wouldn't hurt anybody," Brynn said more to herself than anybody else.

Willow's father frowned and tucked his daughter in closer to him.

Brynn sat down next to them. "Where's Josh's family?" Josh had a big, supportive family. Where were they? In another part of the hospital?

He shrugged and Willow stirred, sitting up. "Brynn. When did you get here?"

"A few moments ago."

Wes sat on the other side of Brynn. The chair creaked with his weight.

"The quilts?" Willow asked.

"All delivered." Brynn paused. "What else can I do for you?"

"Thank you. That's a big relief."

"Can I get you coffee or water?" Wes asked.

"Water please," Willow said.

"Nothing for me," her dad said.

Wes took his leave and the three of them sat in silence. A nurse passed. Another group of people entered the waiting area and sat huddled in a corner. Brynn's eyes barely left Willow, pale and glassy-eyed.

"Do you want to talk about it?" Brynn didn't know what else to say.

Willow shuddered. "I can't. Not yet."

Brynn wished she'd brought along a jacket, as someone must have set the temperature to "frozen." She eyed the waiting area, appointed with brass lamps, wood coffee tables, and glossy magazines. The hospital featured the works of local artists on its walls. One of the best things about it was the artwork, but if it was meant to distract from bad news, it didn't work. It was pleasant, but not magic.

Josh was a good guy. He'd been in farming his whole life. But farming was a profession fraught with danger. Accidents happened, no matter how cautious you were. How did he hit another person with his tractor? That was the odd thing that Brynn couldn't wrap her mind around.

Why was anyone even near a moving tractor? Who was this young man, anyway?

"Who got hit? Did you know him?" Wes asked as he brought the bottled waters to them.

"It was Evan," Willow replied.

Wes's eyebrows shot up. "Whoa! Does Roy know?"

Roy was a young man who'd been hanging around

with Wes from time to time. He was a hired hand at the O'Reilly farm and a computer major at James Madison University. Brynn had only met him once. She gathered Roy and Evan were friends. Brynn also figured the whole group of summer help must have been socializing a great deal. She didn't have time for it—but she was glad that Wes did. After all, he was young and should have a social life.

Willow opened her water and shrugged. "I have no idea."

"Was Evan a hired guy?" Brynn asked.

"At first, yes. Then he dated Josh's daughter," Wes answered.

His words hung in the air and Brynn's eyes shot over to Willow's dad, who nodded at her. "Okay, that complicates things," she muttered. "But Josh would hurt nobody. I know that. We all know that."

Another pause in the conversation.

"He went crazy when he found out Chelsea was dating him," Willow said. "She's only sixteen. I'm not sure of his age. . . ."

"Too old for her," Willow's father finished. "That's how old he was."

A wave of respect washed over Brynn. Willow's father was a good dad. Willow's stories about him were heartwarming. He was involved in her life even though Willow's parents split up years ago. Brynn was sorry she'd not met him earlier, but he was a busy guy and she was busy herself.

Wes shifted in his seat. "It'll devastate Josh's family."

Willow's hand covered her face, and she nodded, sniffed.

A nurse walked into the room. "Willow?"

"Yes."

"I've informed his family. You're free to go." The nurse walked closer to her and crouched in front of her. "Go home and please take care of yourself."

"I'll see to that," her father said. "Thank you."

For Brynn, walking out of the hospital felt like leaving a battle scene. She couldn't say why. She figured she'd gotten there at the tail end of the situation and didn't want to pry. They had informed the young man's parents of his death. Willow's father was taking her in hand to make sure she'd be okay. There was nothing here for Brynn to do—unless Willow needed her.

"We're parked over there," Willow said. "Thanks for coming."

Brynn opened her arms and Willow fell into them. "If you need anything, holler at me. I'm serious. I'll be checking on you."

Willow looked resolved. "We have a fair to put on."

"I'll take care of your part."

"Me too," Wes said.

"It might be good for me to keep busy."

Her father wrapped his arm around her shoulder. "Your mom texted me. She's at the house, made chicken noodle soup for you."

"Okay, well, let me know what you decide. I'm happy to fill in for you or not," Brynn told Willow.

"Thanks, Brynn."

She and her father walked off to another section of the parking lot.

"What did she witness?" Wes asked as they walked toward their car.

"The whole thing," Brynn said. "But who knows what went down. I can't imagine Josh hitting someone with a tractor." She slid the key in the door, flipping the unlock button.

Wes opened the door and slipped in. "In some countries in the world, he'd be celebrated and justified for killing a man who'd been sleeping with his underage daughter."

Brynn's heart stopped. "What did you say? He'd been sleeping with Chelsea?"

"Oh yes." He nodded. "It was not a healthy situation at all."

She turned the ignition and flipped on the AC. Wes was more tuned in to the local gossip than Brynn. Especially with the younger people. Her stomach tightened. A father whose young daughter was sleeping with an older man working for him. A father who had killed the same man, albeit by accident.

As much as Brynn hated to admit it, the situation for Josh seemed bleak.

Chapter 4

When Brynn and Wes arrived at home, it was time to bring the girls in—Petunia, Marigold, and Buttercup. Brynn had taken Marigold out of the milking cycle, as Marigold was now expecting a calf. It concerned Brynn because Petunia had lost a calf and it took a long time for her to get over the loss. She selected Marigold because her vet advised her to give Petunia's body time to replenish and recover. But even so, Brynn wondered if the other cow having a baby would affect Petunia.

The sun was dipping low against the mountain and splayed out soft Creamsicle orange and pinks. Brynn paused in appreciation. She opened the barn door, and the girls filed in, with the ever-growing Freckles tagging along. When would she stop growing? A Saint Bernard–collie mix, Freckles was getting bigger by the minute.

After the evening milking, Brynn rambled back to the house where Wes was happily cooking dinner. The place smelled of fresh tomato sauce, crafted with just-picked tomatoes and oregano from the garden.

Wes stirred the sauce. "I can't get Josh off my mind. Or Evan. What a messed-up situation."

"I agree." Brynn reached into the cupboards and pulled out a few plates. "I'm sure there's a lot more to the story than we grasp."

"Must be." He held up a spoon. "Taste?"

She took the spoon from him and blew on the sauce, then slid it into her mouth. Swallowed. Her taste buds came alive. "Heaven!"

Wes grinned. "Good. The pasta is almost done."

Brynn set the table, all the while enjoying the aftertaste in her mouth. "Fresh tomatoes make such a difference. I can't believe it."

"Yeah, fresh everything is best." He strained the pasta and placed it in a bowl on the table.

Brynn took in the table—sauce, pasta, bread, grated Parmesan cheese, wine—an Italian feast. Her stomach growled. As she thought about it, she realized she'd not eaten since breakfast.

"Man, I'm hungry." She sat down. Wes followed suit.

In the middle of their supper, Brynn's phone rang. "Damn. I need to get this. It's a contestant." She wiped her mouth. "Hello."

"Hi, Brynn, I've a quick question for you."

Brynn recognized Freda's voice on the line. "Sure, Freda."

"Is it okay if I switch my cheese?"

"What do you mean?"

"My cheddar soured. I don't know what happened. I'd like to enter my farmstead cheese."

"No problem," Brynn answered.

"Okay, thank you."

"Sure."

"I heard about that awful tractor accident. Do you know anything about it?" Freda asked.

Brynn's pulse escalated. "Not really. I'm sorry." The grapevine was already humming. "Have a good evening."

"Thanks, you too." Brynn hung up the phone.

"She switched cheese, then asked me about the accident," Brynn told Wes before returning to her plate of spaghetti.

"People love to gossip." He grinned. "I know Gram did."

Brynn laughed. "Yes, she did."

"She knew everything about everybody in our hometown. I assume she was like that here, too."

"Yes. Well, she tried. She found the people here puzzling. She couldn't understand why they didn't like her plans for a farm shop."

Wes twirled his spaghetti on his fork. "She'd have been all over this Chelsea business."

"Do you mean about her sleeping with the older guy?" Brynn took a sip of her wine.

"Yeah, she had strong feelings about young women. But Chelsea . . . well, I've heard that she was no innocent."

Brynn thought a moment. "I guess it doesn't matter. It's still considered statutory rape, right?"

He shrugged. "I have no idea. And in any case, it was definitely on him. He should have known better, I suppose."

Brynn wondered if he was thinking about Tillie, one of their neighbors. She decided not to pry. She knew the two of them had become good friends. But Tillie was young and busy with school and her band and they didn't see each other often. It was comforting to learn he had strong feelings about the Chelsea situation.

Brynn remembered having crushes on older boys. None of them gave her the time of day. Which was just as well. High school was fraught with enough drama to last a lifetime and her parents were strict with her, which would have added to the drama.

Her ex-fiancé was a few years younger. They met while learning to make cheese and soon formed a partnership, which culminated in finding the farm. Then they broke up because he cheated on her. She kept the farm and said good-bye to him.

Her phone buzzed. "Hey, Schuyler."

"Hey, got a question for you." Schuyler was not one for pleasantries, a spitfire of a petite redhead who practiced veterinary acupuncture.

"Okay," Brynn said.

"Can you take another cow?"

"What?"

"Yeah, there was this old woman living up in the hollow. She recently died. She had this cow. I'm trying to find a home for her. It's a Highland cow. You know, one of those shaggy cows? Can you foster her until I can find a her a home?"

Brynn's first reaction was yes, but then she thought about her own cows and wondered how they'd react. "I have the room for her. I'm not sure how my girls will take it, though."

"We'll introduce her slowly and see what happens. How does that sound?"

"Good."

"Okay, I'll bring her by tomorrow."

"Tomorrow?" Brynn said loud enough that Wes's eyebrows shot up in interest.

"Yep. See you in the morning." Schuyler clicked off.

"What's going on?" Wes asked.

"We're getting a new cow tomorrow."

"You can't say no to Schuyler." He grinned and shook his head.

"Can anybody?" Brynn said, shrugged, and laughed.

Chapter 5

Brynn finished processing the morning milk and turned to find Schuyler behind her. She gasped.

The petite redhead grinned. "Sorry. Didn't mean to scare you."

Brynn placed her hands on her hips. "Then why did you sneak up behind me?" She laughed and hugged her friend.

"It's good to see you," Schuyler said. "How are you doing?"

"Just busy with the fair."

"Yeah, me too, but my business has exploded. There was an article in the paper about veterinary acupuncture and I've been incredibly busy ever since."

The two of them walked out of the milk parlor and Freckles, the dog that Schuyler found and Brynn adopted, greeted them. Schuyler crouched down and rubbed Freckles, tail and hind end wagging, as Brynn scanned the area. Her three girls were grazing. She didn't see a furry Scottish Highland cow anywhere. "Where is she?"

"She's still in the trailer." Schuyler stood and walked toward the driveway and Brynn followed. Freckles sauntered off with her cow friends.

Schuyler stopped. "She's shy. And while she's free of disease that would harm your cows, she's not healthy looking. I wanted to prepare you. She's thin. The woman who died had been ill for quite some time and I guess couldn't take care of her."

Brynn's heart sank. *Poor thing.*

Schuyler opened the trailer and slipped inside. She exited leading the small cow. Brynn opened the gate to her field and turned to see the furry creature. "Thin" was not the word for it. This cow needed food—and plenty. She reached over to her and the cow backed off.

"Shy," Schuyler said. "Give her some time."

Brynn nodded. The cow's big eyes met hers and Brynn saw the fear in them.

"How will she be with the other cows?"

"It's hard to say. But I've seen cases like this and it just takes time. She'll keep to herself awhile and your girls will respect that. Then, one day, they will all be buddies. Thanks for putting up the portable fence. That was a good idea. That way, they can all get used to each other for the day and still stay safe. I don't expect any problems. Your girls are so well adjusted." Schuyler wiped her forehead. "It'll be another humid day. I hate this heat and so does she."

"All that fur, she must be hot."

"Yeah, and as you're aware, cows hate the heat."

"I need to read up on this breed."

Schuyler walked toward her truck. "It's an ancient breed. They are a beautiful animal, aren't they?"

Brynn had seen the shaggy cows before in photos, usually in Scotland perched in a picturesque, grassy landscape. She'd never seen one in person. This skinny cow was not a good representative of the breed, but Brynn saw the beauty in her.

"What's her name?" Brynn asked.

"Jewel. If you fatten her up, I should be able to find a good home for her." Schuyler attracted strays and found good homes for them. She said it was a gift. Brynn believed her.

Freckles ran along the new fence and sniffed at the strange creature. Jewel backed off into the far corner. As if sensing her fear, Freckles wandered back to the crowd of cows on the other side of the field.

"Do you want to come in for coffee? Breakfast? Wes has something cooking, I'm sure."

Schuyler stopped. "I wish I could. I'm needed over at the O'Neil place. One of their horses is sick."

"Have you heard from Willow?" Brynn asked as Schuyler opened the door to her truck.

"Yes, she's doing better. It's Josh we need to worry about." She heaved her tiny self into her truck. "He's in trouble."

"I don't understand what happened," Brynn said.

"Nobody does. Josh knows tractors. Been around them his whole life." Her amber eyes flashed. "But he says he lost control of the tractor."

"What?" Brynn's heart thudded against her rib cage. "How can that be?"

Schuyler shut the truck door, the window still open. "Your guess is as good as mine."

"It's an awful situation. I don't understand it." Brynn tried to imagine it, yet she didn't want to.

"I know. But that girl of his, Chelsea? She's got issues. Always has. It's sad. A young girl like her hopping into bed with everybody she can."

"What?" Brynn was shocked.

Schuyler nodded. "Low self-esteem, anybody?" She turned the ignition. "I'll touch base later."

Schuyler drove off waving.

Brynn turned to watch the little furry cow. She stood in the field, awestruck. Brynn wanted to comfort her but figured it was best to wait. She didn't want to frighten her any more than she already was.

Brynn made her way into the house, where cinnamon scent wafted and drew her into the kitchen.

"French toast this morning," Wes said as he put the plates on the table.

"Yum," Brynn said. She moved to the kitchen sink and washed her hands, even though she'd already washed them in the barn, and then sat down at the table and checked out the food. "That's an odd-looking French toast."

"It's stuffed with ricotta cheese I made," he said as he sat down across from her.

"Fresh ricotta cheese! You're getting to be quite the cheesemaker."

He flashed a grin. "That's what I'm here for."

"Have you heard from Max?" Brynn asked as she cut her stuffed French toast.

He nodded. "Yes, he loves his internship. Says he's learning a lot and having a great time in New York." Wes's brother, Max, was a business major and was enjoying the whole college experience. Wes had had a hard time with it and had wanted to be a chef, but his parents weren't thrilled. Brynn counted his confusion as her blessing. When he saw her cheesemaking operation while he stayed with Brynn during his grandmother's funeral, he fell in love with the place and being a cheesemaker. His parents supported his move—he was failing school and wasting their money. When Brynn bit into the stuffed French toast, her taste buds exploded with joy. She swallowed. "God, Wes, that's delicious."

"Thanks. Glad you like it. Tillie and Roy tried it out the other day and liked it, too. How's the new cow?"

She swallowed the next bite. "She's very skinny and very shy." The cow's sweet, shaggy face played in Brynn's mind. "But I think she'll be okay."

"Busy day ahead," Wes said, sliding over a sheet of paper containing the list of action items for the fair.

Brynn put down her fork. "First things first. We need to inspect the cheese shed to make sure the re-frigeration's correct."

"I can do that. Why don't you take care of calling all the contestants for the last-minute check-in?"

Brynn nodded. "Sounds good." They had also volunteered to make pies to sell. "When should we bake? Tonight?"

"I've gotten two peach pies baked already. We need to make the chocolate ones."

"Great," Brynn said, and lifted a bite to her mouth. "We'll make the chocolate ones tonight." They planned to bake them last night, but she and Wes had gotten the call about the accident. A knot formed in her stomach. She tried not to reflect on the tragedy. But, with each passing moment, it was getting harder. None of it made any sense.

But then again, accidents never did. Did they?

Chapter 6

In between phone calls, Brynn took quick breaks and peeked out of the window to check on Jewel. She'd been standing in the same corner for hours. The dog had startled her. Not all cows liked dogs. Brynn had worried about that with her own cows, but the stray had wormed her way in, especially with Petunia. In fact, she'd made a huge difference to the grieving cow. People said animals weren't sensitive beings. Those people needed to spend time on a small farm, like hers, and get to know them and their quirks.

Now Brynn witnessed the sweet little Highland cow eating the grass and hay mix Brynn placed there for her. That was a good sign.

A rolling hillside swooped up, over, and behind her backyard field, on the other side of which was the church that had burned down. A group of locals had formed a country church foundation and were raising funds to rebuild the place. And it was coming along.

The house Brynn lived in was the old rectory from

years ago. The church hadn't been active for generations, which was why her friend Nancy bought it, lived in the basement, and planned to renovate it into a farm shop. That didn't work out and Brynn was still mourning the loss of her good friend Nancy.

Revitalizing the church was a good idea—so much better than living next to an empty building.

A phone call from Wes interrupted her thoughts. "There's a problem with the shed. There's no AC, and I specifically asked for it."

"Can we get it at this late juncture?" Brynn asked, glancing out the window to her grazing cows.

"I hope so. I've raised enough of a fuss. But the contestants are bringing their cheese here by tomorrow at noon. They won't be able to install the AC until tomorrow morning."

"Can we get a few window units on our own?"

"It's against the contract."

"What?"

"Yeah, only the rental company can install window units. Insurance or some excuse like that. Let's remember this next year and find another company."

"Absolutely." Brynn didn't want to go into the whole rigmarole of trying to find a shed rental company that would even talk about bringing a shed to the Shenandoah Valley. It'd add to the stress of the moment. "Well, let's hope they mean early in the morning."

"I've told them that. If they don't, I say we don't pay the whole rental fee. They've screwed this up."

Brynn agreed. But she also believed in giving people chances. "Let's give them the benefit of the doubt for now. If they don't get it done early, I'll have words with them."

"I ran into Willow." Brynn heard the car door open.

She walked over and sat back down at the kitchen table, where her list of cheesemakers sat. Two more calls left on the list. "How is she?"

"Not good. She's still shaken." He paused. "I've heard strange rumors. Like that Josh had threatened Evan. I can see a father stepping into this situation. But Josh? He'd not intentionally hurt anybody. I don't get it."

Brynn thought of her own father during her teenage years. He went a little crazy about the boys visiting the house for her, though there weren't many. She didn't date much. She often wondered if she'd dated and gotten serious with someone in high school how her father would have reacted. "Dads can be overprotective."

"As they should be," he said. Brynn heard the car door shut, and the car started. "I'm a guy. I know." He laughed.

"You're one of the good ones," Brynn said.

"Thanks." He laughed even more. "Not sure my parents would agree."

After they hung up, Brynn called Willow. "You should come over tonight for some of the best tomato sauce I've ever eaten in my life."

"Just tomato sauce?" Willow said.

"Well, no, over pasta. We ate it last night and talk about a foodgasm."

Willow paused. "Well, who can pass up a foodgasm? Besides, I can use the company tonight."

"You know you don't need an invitation, right?" Brynn said with a more serious tone than she meant.

"I know, but . . . I hate to barge in on people.

Schuyler's got the market cornered on that." She laughed.

"Yes, but you can't help but love her," Brynn said. Perhaps she'd invite Schuyler, too. Maybe not. Maybe Willow needed to eat and have a quiet dinner with friends, relaxing. Schuyler would inject another brand of energy. Not that Brynn didn't love her. But Willow might need some extra care.

"How's the craft hall shaping up?" Brynn asked.

"Not bad. There are some talented people around here. How do they find the time to quilt and crochet and all of that stuff, let alone do it so well? Listen, I've got to go. I'll see you tonight."

"Great," Brynn said, clicking off.

She remembered the Parmesan cheese she'd had aging in the basement. Tonight would be a perfect night to try it.

She hoped tonight would help Willow forget about the hideous accident she witnessed—even if just for a little while. Good food, wine, a special cheese to go along with it all, along with the relaxing company, should help Willow's spirits. At least Brynn hoped it would.

Chapter 7

Brynn opened the makeshift pen for Jewel. The other cows were curious and had followed her to the corner of the field where the new cow stood. Freckles kept a respectful distance. The new cow was different looking—smaller, shaggy—and Freckles had tried to make friends once and must have sensed the cow's fear. In any case, the dog would not push it. Brynn was glad.

The cow sniffed at Freckles and made her way through the small group onward to a shady patch of the field. She was hot. Brynn sympathized. The girls followed behind her.

Relieved it was going as well as she expected at this point, Brynn turned and moved into the house to clean up and see about supper. Willow would be here any minute.

When she arrived, Brynn saw that she still had a haunted air about her. Pale and forlorn-looking, Willow's normally beautiful mocha skin held a hue of shock or sickness. "My God, it smells good in here!" She entered the kitchen with a bottle of red wine.

"Wes has been busy making this incredible tomato sauce from fresh tomatoes. It's amazing." Brynn reached into the cupboard and pulled out plates. She set the table, glancing out the window at Jewel, off alone in the shady corner, sitting on the ground. The others weren't ignoring her, just going about their own business.

Willow stood next to Wes at the stove. She drew in the scent. "Heavenly. My mom used to can tomatoes and make a sauce from it. She stopped when her arthritis got to be too bad. But it makes a world of difference."

Brynn pulled down wineglasses from the cabinet and set one at each place. "Have you seen the cow Schuyler dropped off?"

"What?" Willow turned and walked over to the picture window and gasped. "That's Jewel! Oh my gosh!"

"You know her?"

"She belonged to Lucy Rhodes. Lived up in the hollow. She was a friend of my mom. She was a schoolteacher and kept cows and chickens but then got sick after she retired."

"She died and left Jewel behind." Brynn set the last glass on the table. "I guess she couldn't take care of her. I'll fatten her up and help Schuyler find a new home for her."

"Pasta is done," Wes said, bringing the bowl to the table.

"Oh, let me help you," Willow said.

"I got it," he replied. "Please, just sit down."

The dinner conversation shifted from food and cows to Lucy Rhodes's English class. It was as if they were tiptoeing around the elephant (or cow) in the room. Brynn didn't know if it was good to discuss the accident or talk about other things to keep Willow's mind off what she'd witnessed. She figured it was best to let her friend take the lead. Willow had been such a good friend to her, introducing her to the community, especially the members of the CSA, which Brynn had become a part of, and she filled Brynn in on all she needed to understand about the locals. She was the most helpful person Brynn had met when she'd moved to Shenandoah Springs.

And when Nancy died, Brynn didn't know what she would have done without the support of both Willow and Schuyler, not to mention Wes and Max, Nancy's grandsons.

"You're a lot like your grandmother," Willow said, smiling at Wes.

Startled, Wes grinned. "What?"

"She was a great cook and embraced the farm to table movement. She must have influenced you in a fantastic way."

He batted his eyes as a winsome look played over his face. "You know . . . you're right. I'd never thought about it. But I was close to my gram. Some of the best memories I have of her are when we were in the kitchen together. She even tried to make Pakistani food and did a good job. Though we were adopted when we were babies and I don't remember anything about the place, she thought it was important that we maintained some cultural connection."

Willow nodded. "I get that. I barely recognize the Native American side of my family. But my mom always cooked traditional dishes for me. And then there are the other things. The stories. The mythology. All of it."

"Yes, Mom always made sure we were aware of Pakistani culture, though I'm an American, not Pakistani. I don't remember anything about Pakistan. It's kind of weird." He shrugged.

"Would you like more cheese?" Brynn asked, holding up the finely shredded Parmesan cheese.

"Yes! Are you kidding?" Willow beamed. She took a sip of her wine.

They each took more cheese and sprinkled it on their pasta.

"This is so nice," Willow said. "I can't tell you how much it means. I don't mind living alone most times. But these days . . . it's good to have company."

"How are you doing with everything?" Wes asked.

"When I close my eyes at night, I still see the accident playing in my mind. Josh on the big green tractor. His arms wildly trying to steer the tractor, yelling at people to get back. And Evan caught beneath the wheel."

"Why was he so close to the tractor? I don't understand." Brynn twirled spaghetti around her fork.

Willow stopped buttering her bread. "I'm not sure. I think he dropped something. He was crouching over into the dirt."

"It makes no sense. Why would he get that close to the tractor when Josh was yelling for people to get away?"

"I've asked myself that question a million times," she replied with a somber tone.

"And also," Brynn said after swallowing her spaghetti. "Why was he telling people to get back? What was going on?"

"He said he lost control of the tractor," Willow said, her eyes meeting Brynn's. "That's one of the hardest things for me to swallow. He's been driving tractors since he was a kid. He knows tractors."

"Perhaps there was something wrong with it," Wes said, and sipped from his wineglass.

Brynn remembered the emotion that played out over the tractor salesman's face at the fairground. "It was a brand-new tractor, evidently. I met the guy who sold it to him at the fairground when we took the quilts over."

"The new tractors are amazing. They're sleek, sophisticated machines," Willow said. "It's hard to imagine him losing control. The older ones are harder to manage."

"I'm sure the police will be all over that tractor," Wes said.

Willow reached for more bread. "I hope they find something wrong with it. Or else our friend Josh is in deep trouble."

A shiver moved up and down Brynn's spine. Difficult to imagine Shenandoah Springs with one of its most vital community members in prison for murder.

Chapter 8

The next morning after taking care of the cows and eating breakfast, Brynn and Wes parted. Brynn went to the fairground and Wes headed to several homes to pick up last-minute craft, pie, or cheese entries.

Brynn strolled through the fairground, pleased by how it was coming together. She remembered when she was here last with her ex-fiancé, Dan, and how much they enjoyed it—a real country fair, with displayed crafts, baked goods, animals, gardening, and tractor contests. All in good fun.

She walked by the colorful carnival trucks. A crew scrambled setting up the Ferris wheel, which was one of the most popular rides. Banners lined the fairway, with lights attached. A radio blared country music as she walked by, finding her way to the cheese shed, with a basket of linens. When she walked in, frigid air met her. *Holy smokes!* The place had ice on the wall!

She dialed Wes as she opened her basket.

"Yes, Brynn?"

She laid the table linen on the shelves. "Did you speak with the shed people?"

"Yes, I asked them to lower the temperature because it was too warm in the shed," Wes answered.

Brynn took a breath. "Well, they did exactly as you asked. But it's too low. There's ice on the walls." She smoothed over the linen on each shelf and shivered.

"What?" Wes asked through the receiver. Brynn heard the car door slam in the background. "Did you say ice on the walls?"

"Yes, I did. I'll give them another call," she said, exasperated. Two more shelves to line with her linen. She hurried to get it done.

"No. I'll call them. Let me deal with them."

Brynn hesitated, only because he was so busy running around today. "Are you sure?" She placed the linen on the next shelf.

"Yes, positive." He paused. "I have two more stops to make; then I'm done."

She finished as fast as possible. She couldn't stand another minute in the freezing shed.

"Well, you're moving right along, aren't you?" She stepped out of the shed, shut the door, and locked it. "We need to set up tomorrow. The fair starts in two days."

"It will be okay."

"Are you sure about that?"

"It's the first year this has ever been done here, right? Nobody has anything to compare it to. Whatever we do they will love," Wes said firmly.

Brynn smiled. "Okay, whatever you say." But she was more concerned with the health and safety aspect of eating cheese not stored at the right temperature. It could get funky. She shivered as her body warmed up to the heat outside of the shed. "See you soon."

"Okay," Wes said, and clicked off.

She walked around the corner and saw a trailer with horses inside. A man walked by them and opened the door of the trailer. He smiled up at Brynn. She smiled back, sad for the horses on this hot day. She was certain he was leading them into the barn, though, where there was probably a great deal of water and it was definitely cooler than in one of those trailers.

Brynn walked by the tractor tent. At least five tractors were there already. Colorful and shiny. Not the old, clunky tractors she recalled, but those tractors ran for generations. Old and clunky—but sturdy.

The dealership had several signs displayed about financing, sales awards, and information about their tractors.

"Can I help you?" a voice said from behind her, startling her.

"Oh! No, I was looking at the sleek new tractors. They're very pretty," Brynn said, and smiled.

"Thank you. I'm David Reese. I think we've met, a few days ago."

That's right. The day of the accident.

"Are you in the market for a tractor?"

"Not this year, no. I have cows. The only growing I do is hay and grass for them. I hire someone to help with it. Cheaper that way," Brynn said.

"The new tractors are amazing," he went on. "I've been in the business thirty years and used to fix anything. I had to send my son to school to learn the new stuff. All computerized."

Josh had lost control of the tractor. Could something have gone wrong with the engine, with whatever computerized version of it was popular now? Brynn didn't see how to approach the subject with the man, who she was sure the police had already questioned.

"Hey, Brynn!" Another voice came up behind her. Willow reached over and hugged her. "Come and see the craft hall. It's amazing, if I do say so myself! Hey, David, how are you?"

"Good, and yourself?"

After they exchanged pleasantries, Willow dragged Brynn to the craft hall, which was buzzing with activity. Shelves and shelves held crafts of every kind—crochet, pottery, jewelry. The quilts were displayed at the end of the hall. Brynn stood a moment to take in the breathtaking sight. The colors, patterns, fabrics reached out to her. People made these things with their hands.

"They are all hand quilted. It's the rules. No machine quilting allowed." Willow gestured. "Look at this one." It was a red one-piece blanket with a pattern quilted onto it. "This is an Amish technique. Simple with the one piece of fabric, no piecing. But look at the stitching."

Brynn was astounded. "Must have taken forever. Look at those little stitches. And they are so even."

Brynn's phone buzzed. She looked at the screen. It was Wes. They'd just spoken. What could he need or want?

"Sorry, Willow." She answered the phone. "Hello, Wes. What's up?"

"I need you to meet me at the sheriff's station," Wes answered.

"What did you say?"

"Sheriff's station. I need you to meet me there."

Brynn's heart thumped hard. Why would she need to meet Wes at the sheriff's station? Was he in an accident? "Are you okay?"

"I'm okay. But I just found a dead body."

Chapter 9

Brynn tried to focus on driving the speed limit. Every stop sign felt like an assault. She needed to get to Wes. She needed to find out what happened. How did he find a dead body? Who was it? Was it someone they knew? Poor Wes! What a horrible thing to stumble on. He was such a softhearted, good young man.

The drive was a blur, and when she walked into the small station, the lights snapped her back to reality.

She scanned the four-seat waiting area and looked for a person to answer her questions. There was nobody behind the desk. She spotted another door. Should she open it and move forward? Her heart thudded in her chest. What to do?

"Can I help you?" a woman said as she entered the room.

"Ah, yes. I'm here to see Wes Scors."

She smiled and nodded her head, as if she'd never heard of Wes.

"He called and said to meet him here. Said something about finding a . . . a . . . body."

The woman's smile vanished as her mouth formed an O. "Yes, I realize who you mean. I'll let them know you're here." And she left the room.

Once again, Brynn was alone in the tiny waiting area. She waited several minutes, checked her phone for messages, and then sat down in the least comfortable chair she'd ever sat on.

The door opened. It was Sheriff Edge, dressed in his brown uniform, with no hat. She'd met him a few months back when they were investigating the fire at the church.

"Brynn, good to see you." He smiled a stiff smile, rimmed in dimples. She'd not realized how handsome he was underneath the huge hat he usually wore.

"Sheriff," she said. "How is Wes?"

"Come on back," he said. "It's complicated."

"Complicated?" Brynn followed him back into an open area with desks scattered haphazardly. Two offices sat off to the side.

"Yeah," he said. She continued to follow him into an office where Wes sat, pale, frightened.

"Wes? Are you okay?"

His eyes watered and he shook his head. He opened his mouth, but nothing came out.

"He's a little shaken," Sheriff Edge said.

"As anybody would be, I suppose," Brynn said. "You don't run into something like that every day."

"You can take him home," the sheriff said, turning to Wes. "But as we talked about, please don't go anywhere out of the area."

Wes nodded.

Brynn was confused. "Well, of course not; he lives here, works here. Why would he leave?"

The sheriff frowned. "Right now, Brynn, he's our only person of interest."

Brynn frowned. "Come again?"

"I'm sorry, but it's true. He's not quite a suspect, but you understand we have to look at everybody who's come into contact with the scene." He spoke slowly and calmly, as if he was attempting to soothe her with his voice.

Brynn felt a little better. *Of course. That makes sense.* Her stomach settled. "I understand. I'm sure the more you investigate you'll find he had nothing to do with the death. Who was it? Who did he find?"

"Donny Iser. He was a summer helper at the Hardy place."

Another summer helper dead?

"That's strange. That's the second summer helper who's died," Brynn said.

The sheriff nodded with grim acknowledgment.

"Was he killed? I mean, how did he die?" Brynn asked.

"Let's just say, it's more than suspicious." Sheriff Edge used air quotes around suspicious.

What was going on around here? First the tractor accident where a good man supposedly ran over a helper and now this? Brynn wanted to go home and crawl in bed beneath her warm quilt.

Brynn turned to Wes. "Are you ready to go?"

He looked at the sheriff. "Is it okay?"

"For now, but like I said . . ."

"I won't go anywhere. I've got nothing to hide," Wes said, his voice hushed, as if breathless. He stood. "Let's go home, Brynn."

He swayed. Brynn caught him by the arm. "Are you all right?"

He nodded. "I stood up too fast. I'm fine."

And it's not every day you're a person of interest in a murder.

Brynn held his elbow, and they walked out of the cramped office into the larger room.

"Can they really imagine I killed a man?" Wes said as they drove away from the station.

"Of course not. They need to investigate every lead. You found the body. I don't know this to be true, but I've seen on TV that sometimes killers will call the police and pretend they found a body."

"Well, that's stupid."

"It's a cat-and-mouse game," Brynn said. "Deep down, they want to be caught."

He paused. "I've never watched those shows. I don't like any of them. They're too ridiculous. Yet here I am in the middle of a murder investigation."

"Now, Wes," Brynn said. "They aren't sure that's what happened. They're not even calling it a murder."

She stopped at a stop sign and looked over at Wes, who frowned.

"Maybe they're not calling it that yet, but I saw him. And it was definitely a murder. He couldn't have shot himself in the back like that." His voice cracked.

Brynn's heart almost jumped out of her mouth. "What? Oh, Wes. I'm so sorry you had to see that. How awful for you."

"Yeah, it was awful. I doubt I'm ever going to get it out of my head."

Brynn continued driving.

"I hope they find out who killed him soon," he said. "Whoever did it is definitely a dangerous person. We better make sure to lock up everything tonight."

Brynn shivered.

Chapter 10

Brynn was in the middle of brewing iced tea in the kitchen while Wes sat at the table talking on the phone with his father, explaining the recent events.

"I knocked on the door, and nobody answered. But I knew someone had to be home. They were expecting me. So I walked out to the barn and there he was."

A pause in the conversation.

"She'd run out to the store evidently."

Another pause.

"No, I don't need a lawyer, yet. But I promise you if I do, I'll let you know." He paused again. "No, Dad, I don't think the fact that I'm a brown man has anything to do with this. I get it. You're upset. But I found the body. They had to question me."

Brynn was glad to hear him talk so sensibly to his father, Nathaniel, who must be freaking out at the thought of his son being questioned by the police. After all, he'd agreed to allow Wes to live in Brynn's guest cottage as a cheese apprentice, after a terrible first semester at college. He didn't allow him to come here so that he'd get in trouble. The worst sort of trouble.

Romeo entered the room and jumped up on Wes's lap. Romeo, it turned out, was a girl, even though Nancy thought she was a tomcat. Romeo had a definite preference for Wes. And Wes adored her, even allowing the cat to sleep in his bed with him.

"Okay, Dad. Will do."

She poured Wes a glass of iced tea and placed a couple of sprigs of spearmint from the garden in it. She took it to the table. He glanced at her with wet eyes. "Dad is upset." He took the glass. "Thanks for the tea."

"You're welcome," Brynn said. "Of course your father is upset. He's in Massachusetts and you're here. It's tough on a parent when something happens to their kid and they can't do anything about it."

"He's afraid I need a lawyer. He thinks it's more serious than we do. He's afraid they will pin it on me because I'm a Pakistani."

Brynn paused before she said anything. These were pretty serious allegations. "I'm not going to soft-pedal this. You know that sort of thing happens every day. But you've not been charged with anything and you're in Shenandoah Springs. These people are good. Besides all that, you didn't do it. You're innocent. You're going to be fine."

He took a sip of his iced tea and set down his glass. "Innocent people go to jail every day."

Brynn didn't like the forlorn look on his face, so she tried to lighten the mood. "Not under my watch." She smiled.

Romeo sat in a curled-up ball on Wes's lap. He stroked her and it seemed to calm both the cat and Wes.

A knock at the door interrupted.

Brynn walked to the door and opened it to Willow and Schuyler.

"What the hell?" Schuyler said. "Where's Wes?"

The Shenandoah Springs grapevine was working in fine order.

"He's at the kitchen table."

"I've never heard so much bullshit in my life," Schuyler said as she marched into the kitchen, Willow trailing her.

"He's fine," Brynn said, following. "He's going to be fine."

But neither of the women was listening to her. They were already hugging Wes. They both adored him.

"We know you didn't kill anybody, Wes. Everybody knows it," Willow said, and sat down.

Brynn poured more iced tea as Wes explained to Willow and Schuyler what had happened.

"Crazy," Schuyler said, her amber eyes flashing. "What's going on around here?"

"It's like someone has it in for the summer help," Willow said.

Brynn served glasses of tea to her friends.

"It's a real scorcher out there," Schuyler said, and took a long drink of the tea. "Thank you."

Brynn nodded. "Yeah, Schuyler. You're on to something. Both of the recent deaths were of the summer helpers. It's a strong connection."

"We should brush off our sleuthing skills and figure out who did this to get Wes off," Willow said.

"Whoa! First of all, Wes hasn't been charged with anything. And he won't be. Case closed," Schuyler said.

Brynn sipped from her glass. "And besides, I'd

rather not get involved with another murder case, thank you very much."

"I hear you," Wes said. "There is one good thing about this. Josh was nowhere around. They can't accuse him of this murder. He's still in jail."

"He is?" Brynn was surprised to hear it. "Couldn't he have gotten out on bail or something?"

"I don't know what's going to happen," Willow said. "It was an accident. I don't understand why he's still in jail."

There were a few moments of silence.

"I'm still not sure what happened with the accident," Wes said. "It doesn't make any sense to me. Josh certainly didn't do it on purpose. But how did it happen?"

"I keep going over it in my mind. I was there, and it still doesn't make sense," Willow said.

"That's the nature of accidents. They don't make sense." Schuyler drank her tea.

"But Donny's death was no accident. Someone definitely killed him," Wes said.

"Which means there's a someone out there who got away with murder," Willow said.

Brynn shivered.

"For now," Schuyler said. "Hopefully not much longer."

Brynn hoped she was right.

Chapter 11

After the evening milking, Wes moseyed to the guest cottage and Brynn ambled off to the house. Most nights they had dinner together, but tonight Wes was exhausted and wanted to go to bed. Brynn was wired with worry about him—and about the murder. Who killed Donny? Whoever it was, the person was still free.

Brynn walked around the house, once again, making sure all the doors were locked and the windows were secure. She loved sleeping with the windows open, but the temperatures were so high the past few weeks that she much preferred the air conditioning.

She sat down at her computer and checked in with the online orders. There were several. She printed them off, which always made Wes chuckle. She liked to have the paper in hand to keep for her paper files—even though everything was also online. The business continued to roll along, even though her work efforts had doubled because of taking on the cheese competition at the fair. But that was okay. She expected a busy summer.

But what she hadn't expected, of course, was a murder around the corner from her—or that Wes would be the person to stumble on the body. She didn't like conflict of any kind, but here it was. But then again, the police might find the killer and wouldn't need to question Wes again.

Yes, she was sure that's what would happen—at least that's what she'd tell herself in order to get to sleep tonight.

She clicked on the cheese contest files and scanned them over, checking to make sure she'd gotten all the information she needed for the contest. The types of cheeses listed made her mouth water. Asiago. Romano. Pecorino. Parmesan. Hard cheese was a bit easier to store, so Brynn limited the contest to hard cheese and semi-hard, like Gouda.

Most of the cheese in the contest would be aged for between two and thirty-six months and, in some cases, even longer. Aging determines the intensity of the flavor. A well-aged cheese is more flavorful, less creamy, and grainier in texture. Brynn's stomach growled. She had made herself hungry.

Wasn't there a container of fresh soft cheese in the fridge?

She found her way to the kitchen, switched on a light, and opened the fridge. *Ah, yes*. There it was. She spotted a bottle of half-finished red wine on the counter and half a loaf of fresh bread and voilà, she fashioned herself a lovely light dinner.

She took her plate and a glass of wine to the living room, got comfy on the couch, and switched on the TV. She flipped the channels until she spotted the local news.

There was Sheriff Edge talking about the murder of Donny Iser.

"Do you have any suspects?" the reporter asked.

"As I said, we have several persons of interest. No suspects." His jaw twitched. "That's all I can say about an ongoing investigation."

The show snapped off to a commercial.

Several persons of interest? That meant that the police were not only looking at Wes, which was a good thing. It was such a shame that he'd run into a murder victim. Poor Wes. Such a good kid. And of all people to be involved in a tractor accident—Josh was a solid guy. Family man. Pillar of the community. And he was in jail for the accident. There must be more to that story.

Brynn finished her light dinner and continued watching the news. The big news was the upcoming fair. This year there'd be more animals, more crafts, and more rides than ever before. A special petting zoo, featuring miniature ponies, was an exciting new feature.

Miniature ponies? The camera panned over them. *How cute.* Brynn was going to make certain she visited the petting zoo.

She shut off the TV and moved to the kitchen to rinse off her plate and glass. She left them in the sink.

Brynn checked all the doors and windows again. She may be paranoid, but better safe than sorry. Everything was locked up, and she headed to bed.

She tossed and turned, contemplating Willow and what she'd witnessed, and poor Wes and what he'd stumbled on. He was too young to see such horrifying things. Brynn hoped it wouldn't affect him too much. He was so sensitive, though, she knew that it was just that measure of sensitivity that might influence him so much that he wouldn't be able to quite get over it.

Not only did he have to find a dead body, but then to be questioned about it? Wes had been chucked into a mature situation, whether he was ready for it or not.

She pulled her quilt in closer around her. But then again, how could anybody prepare for such a thing?

What would she do if it were her? She hoped and prayed it never would be.

Chapter 12

The alarm blared at five like it did every morning and Brynn rolled out of bed, slipped on her working clothes, and headed to the barn. When she opened the front door, she was smacked with a wave of humidity. Already. Her cows hated this warm weather. Particularly the new girl, with all that hair. Brynn would make sure there was more than enough water to go around.

She opened the barn door with a hard pull and Freckles greeted her, tail wagging. She crouched down to pet the dog. "How are you this morning?" The Saint Bernard–collie mix always appeared to be smiling because of the way her "freckles" were placed around her mouth. Brynn loved it. After petting Freckles and feeding her, Brynn turned to the cows. Petunia, her most vocal cow, moped a hello. She was ready to go outside, as was shy Marigold. Buttercup was currently the one in milking and Brynn reached over to the milking tubes and attached them. Where was Jewel? Brynn squinted her eyes and looked toward the corner where the Highland cow usually stood. A tuft of hair showed over the stall wall. Was she sleeping?

Brynn walked over to find her curled in the corner, almost like a cat. "Jewel?"

No response.

Brynn crouched down and petted the cow, lifting her chin, gazing into her big brown eyes. The cow blinked and didn't respond to Brynn's gentle pulling in trying to get her up.

"Are you okay, girl?"

The cow didn't move. Brynn sat down next to her, with the sound of the milking machine in the background. Petunia mooed again. She was one impatient cow. But when she mooed, Jewel stiffened and turned her head. Did she not like Petunia?

Brynn's thoughts turned. This cow had been alone for her whole life. Now she shared a barn with three cows and a dog. Perhaps she craved downtime. Quiet time. Brynn understood.

But then again, possibly Jewel was sick. You couldn't be too careful with the health of animals. She made a mental note to call Schuyler today.

The milking machine switched off. Brynn stood and walked over to the other cow and detached the tubes. She lifted the milk pan away from the cow, poured the milk into jars, and took them to the freezer. When she came back, she opened the barn door and the cows left the barn. Brynn gazed over at Jewel, who didn't even look toward the door. Brynn left it open, in case she changed her mind.

In the meantime, Brynn readied herself for a meeting of the CSA. She had thought maybe they would cancel since apparently Josh was still in jail, but they decided to have it, anyway. She showered, changed into something presentable, and was on her merry way.

Just walking from the house to the car, Brynn had started to sweat. Who knew the Shenandoah Valley would be so humid? She longed for a cool, crisp fall day. She slid into her car, cranked up the AC, giving thanks to the gods of modern cooling systems.

When she opened the door to the community center where the CSA held meetings, everybody looked up at her. They were missing their leader, and it showed. Josh was a benevolent leader and kept everybody on an even keel. This meeting was going to be interesting with him gone, especially since the official start to the fair was tonight. The opening ceremony, followed by the annual tractor pull, and pie contest were on the schedule.

"Hey," Brynn said.

Grunts and groans of greetings were exchanged.

"Who's manning our booth tonight? Josh was on the schedule."

"I can't. I'm at the craft hall," Willow said.

"Pie contest?"

"Tractor pull."

"Me too."

All eyes turned to Brynn, once again. "I can do it," she said. "Is everything over there that I'll need?"

"Yes," Willow said. "The displays have been set up, along with some of our products for sale."

"Okay. Doesn't sound too hard. I'll bring Wes with me."

The place quieted, which was unusual.

"Maybe that's not such a good idea," said Tom. "I mean, he's a suspect in a murder."

"Who told you that? He's not a suspect. He's the

person who found the body, so of course the police are looking at him," Brynn said.

"He might scare folks off; that's all I'm saying."

"Don't be ridiculous," Willow said. "Bring him along. If people have a problem with it, then too bad."

"Let's move on," Tom said. "We've got other issues to discuss. How is the renovation of the old community center coming?"

Brynn cleared her throat. This was her ongoing project. "I reported last time that I needed to take a break from it until after the fair. I'll get right on it the day after the fair is over."

"Okay, our next delivery is scheduled two days after the fair. Hope to see you all here to help."

The place quieted again. This was the quietest meeting Brynn had been to.

"When are they going to let Josh out?" someone asked.

"We don't know," Willow said. "The accident is still under investigation."

"I've never known the police to keep someone this long because of an accident," Tom said. "There must be more to this."

"They think it was on purpose," Kevin, the Christmas tree farmer, said. "They think he ran that boy over on purpose."

"That's the most ridiculous thing I've ever heard," Brynn said.

"I agree," Tom replied. "What do we do in the meantime?"

Willow cleared her throat and stood up. "We carry on as best we can. We support their family. We answer questions from the police. We support him. He's done so much for all of us. Everyone knows he didn't run him over on purpose."

"But you were there," Kevin said to Willow. "So was I." His voice cracked. "And I've gotta say it looked . . . like . . . I don't know . . . odd."

"It was an accident. Accidents look odd," Tom Andrews spoke up.

"All I know is if he was sleeping with my daughter, I'm not sure how I'd handle it," Kevin said.

"Please!" Willow's voice raised. "This needs to stop. We know him. We know that he's handled more than one prickly situation with Chelsea and he's done it with a cool head."

Brynn took it all in. She was getting acquainted with this community and didn't know much about Chelsea, but from what she gathered, the young woman had a few issues.

"That's true," Tom said. "Sitting here theorizing isn't doing him any good."

"Does anybody else consider it odd that both of the young men killed were summer helpers?" Kevin asked.

Brynn had. And had discussed that very thing with Willow.

"It's a coincidence," Tom said. "One doesn't have to do with the other. Necessarily." He looked around the table with a serious stance.

"It couldn't. Josh killed Evan, whether it was by accident or not. He was in jail when Donny was shot," Willow said.

A chill ran down Brynn's spine. Once again, the thought occurred to her that a killer lurked in Shenandoah Springs. She glanced around the table, realizing that exact concern weighed heavily on the group.

Chapter 13

When Brynn arrived at home, she was pleasantly surprised to see Tillie. She was there visiting Wes, Brynn was certain. She walked in and the two of them were sitting at the kitchen table sampling Wes's soft cheeses.

"This one is too sour." Tillie puckered her face.

"Noted," Wes said.

"Hello! How's it going?" Brynn hated interrupting what appeared to be the two of them concentrating on good stuff.

"Oh hey," Tillie said, standing and opening her arms to give Brynn a hug. Brynn and Tillie had gotten close during the investigation of the church fire.

"How was the meeting?" Wes asked.

"Okay, but you and I are going to man the booth tonight." She opened a drawer and fished out a spoon.

"What about the girls?" Wes said.

"The girls will be fine. Well, our girls will be fine. I'm not sure about Jewel. Schuyler's going to swing by. Has she left the barn?"

"No," Wes said.

"Maybe she's homesick," Tillie offered.

"Maybe. I thought she was going to fit right in, but when I walked into the barn this morning she was curled up into a little ball." Brynn dipped her spoon into the first sampling and brought it to her mouth. She plopped it in and swirled it around and swallowed. "Tillie's right. It's too sour."

Tillie beamed. "What did I tell you? World-class taste buds."

"How's everything going with you?" Brynn sat down at the table.

"Good. I've been busy helping Mom and Dad on the farm." Tillie's family owned the local apple orchard and they ran a little family store, displaying their products. "We're all a little freaked out about the two deaths."

"Yeah, we are, too." Brynn watched Wes for a reaction and there wasn't any. He seemed to have worked through his nervous fear.

"Everybody knows Wes is innocent. They have to follow protocol," Tillie said. Her amber eyes held a flicker of concern.

"Sure," Brynn said. "He has nothing to worry about."

A knock at the door, followed by it opening, interrupted their conversation. "Yoo-hoo!" It was Schuyler, there to see about Jewel.

"We're in here," Brynn said.

Schuyler popped her head in. "Hello. I'm going to go over to the barn and check Jewel out."

"I'll come with you." Brynn stood.

The two of them left through the front door.

"What a miserable day," Schuyler said, wiping her brow.

"Yeah, it's so humid. I feel like I'm swimming instead of walking."

They opened the gate to the field. Freckles ran over to greet Schuyler. "Hey, girl, how's life treating you?" Freckles' tail wagged furiously as Schuyler petted her. "Okay, now we've got to see about your new friend."

Brynn and Schuyler walked the short path to the barn, with Freckles at their feet. Brynn had left the door open, in case Jewel decided to join the other cows in the field.

"Hey, girl," Schuyler said as she crouched down next to the cow. Jewel lifted her head. Brynn watched as Schuyler worked her magic. Her touch always seemed to ease the animals—with or without her acupuncture needles. She began to hum as she petted the cow. The cow's tail flopped up and down. "Her eyes look clear."

She peered into the cow's ear. "Ears look good. Has she eaten?' "

"Not today, but yesterday she did."

"Hmmm. Let's get you up and moving," she said. She stood and gently pulled the cow. Jewel lifted herself to a standing position.

Brynn's heart raced. She was standing. That was a good thing.

"She's not eaten much or regularly for a while. She may be having some digestive issues."

"Makes sense."

"Movement should help. Their first reaction to a little stomach pain is often to curl in a ball and not move. Which is the worst thing for them." She led the cow to the barn door. Jewel followed but wasn't happy about it.

"She also doesn't like this heat. It's got to be uncomfortable for her."

"I've been making sure she gets plenty of water. I'm not sure what else I can do."

"Is the creek low?"

Brynn nodded. "When it stormed the other day, there wasn't much rain. It's not rained hard in a while. We need a huge rain. But nothing."

"She'd probably love a bath," Schuyler said as she tugged on the cow's red collar until she was out of the barn completely. "Like a nice cool hosing off."

"We can do that." Brynn's heart went out to the shaggy little cow. She had been alone with her owner for years. She wasn't used to being with other cows. She was definitely shy and having a hard time fitting in. Besides all that, Schuyler thought she had a bellyache. She must be miserable with all that hair in this heat. But she was one of the cutest cows Brynn had ever seen.

Wes and Tillie came around the corner. "Yay! She's up!"

"Hello, Jewel," Tillie said, and walked over to her. "Do you remember me?" The cow's tail flipped around.

"She needs a cool hosing off," Schuyler said.

"I'll get the hose," Wes said, and disappeared around the corner of the barn to fetch it.

"I have to get going," Schuyler said. "I'm needed over at the fairground. Some animals don't like this show business. Every year, I've got to deal with nervous animals."

As Brynn turned to walk her back to her truck, she noticed the sheriff's car coming up her driveway. Schuyler stopped in her tracks. "What does he want?"

"Probably me," Wes said, coming up behind them with the hose. "He might have more questions."

"Why don't they leave you alone? You discovered a body. End of the story." Tillie flipped her strawberry-blond hair in a huff.

"A body that was shot," Wes said. "Murdered. He's just doing his job."

Even though it was sweltering, cold swept through Brynn. Of course Wes was right. The sheriff was just doing his job. But dark doom washed over Brynn as the sheriff approached the house.

Chapter 14

Tillie took over the hosing off of Jewel as Brynn, Schuyler, and Wes walked to the driveway. Schuyler opened the door of her truck. "If you need anything, let me know." Her words felt weighty. Her tone said her concern was about more than the cow. Brynn knew that she meant it—but she hoped they wouldn't need her for anything. She turned her attention to Sheriff Edge and Wes.

"Can I help you?" Brynn said.

Sheriff Edge looked at her, then Wes. "I just have a few more questions for Wes; then I'll get out of your hair. I promise. I can see you're busy." He looked in the direction of Tillie, still hosing off Jewel, who had perked up quite a bit as the cool water washed over her.

A surge of mama bear protection tore through Brynn. She wasn't Wes's mother, but his parents had trusted her with him. He'd just turned twenty, not a boy, but certainly not an adult. She drew in a breath. "What's the problem? He answered questions before, right?"

Sheriff Edge lurched back, as if shocked that Brynn spoke.

Her face heated.

"It's okay, Brynn; I've got no problem helping the police find whoever killed Donny," Wes said with a composed voice that chilled Brynn. How could he be so calm when she herself was nervous? "You don't need to worry. I've done nothing wrong. Go ahead inside and I'll answer any questions the sheriff has."

Brynn's legs trembled. What was wrong with her? She was making too big of a deal over this. Of course, there would be more questions. It was a murder case. They had to proceed methodically.

"Are you okay?" Sheriff Edge asked.

She nodded. "I'm a little woozy. It must be the heat."

"Let me help you inside," he said.

Come on, Brynn, put on your big-girl panties. "No," she said. "I'll be okay." She willed her legs to move and they did. She glanced over at Tillie, finishing up with Jewel, and walked up to her front porch and opened the door to the cool air-conditioned air.

Sweet relief. She hadn't realized how hot she was. But she knew that wasn't her only problem. The gravity of the situation weighed on her. She tried to ensure Wes didn't see how worried she was, but she was truly nervous. A second questioning from the police? She wondered if it meant they were taking a harder look at him as a viable suspect. And how could it be? She had faith in the justice system, even though she knew it wasn't perfect. She knew Wes didn't kill anybody. How could they be considering him as a suspect? Was it only because he happened to find the victim? Or was there more to it that she didn't know? That Wes didn't know?

She walked down her hall to the kitchen and poured herself a glass of water. She sat down at the table, drinking the water and looking out over her backyard filled with her cows and dog, along with Tillie, who was gathering the hose and putting it away. Sheriff Edge and Wes had gone into the car to chat.

Brynn took another drink of water.

She'd come to rely on Wes a great deal over the past few months. She'd originally bought the farm assuming she and her fiancé would run it, but when that didn't work out she decided to do it herself—which was a lot of work. She was only too happy to accept the help that Wes gave her. Okay, she taught him how to make cheese, but he was a good and willing student.

The house phone rang. Brynn jumped. It rarely rang. They decided to get one because cell service could be sketchy in Shenandoah Springs and when there was an emergency she didn't want to deal with a squirrely cell phone.

"Hello," Brynn said.

"Hi there. This is Roy," the voice said. "Wes's friend? I've been trying to reach him. He's not answering his cell."

That's because he's sitting in a cop car being questioned by Sheriff Edge. But she decided to keep that nugget of information to herself. "He's busy right now," Brynn said. "I'll give him the message that you called."

"Thanks, yeah, please tell him to give me a call," he said, and then hung up.

That was odd. Wes had only been out of cell phone reach maybe a half an hour and Roy felt the need to call the house phone? She shrugged and took another sip of water. She glanced at the clock and realized she should get ready for the fair. She and Wes needed to be there soon to work the booth for the CSA. When she offered to do it she felt lively, but now she wanted to head to bed. Perhaps a shower would perk her up.

Someone knocked at the door and opened it. "Brynn?" It was Tillie.

"In here."

"Are you on the phone?"

Brynn realized she was still holding the receiver. "No, one of Wes's friends just called. Roy?"

"Roy? I thought he went back home to Richmond." Tillie leaned against the wall.

"Maybe he did. He didn't say where he was."

"Oh, that's cool. He was offered a gaming job, I heard."

"Gaming?"

"Yeah, you know, like computer games. He's into all that."

"Oh."

"How could they think Wes had anything to do with any of this?" she asked, her amber eyes wide with worry. "I'm kind of worried; well, I'm a nervous wreck."

Brynn hated to ask this, but given the past, she thought she was entitled to. "Do you know something I don't know?"

She laughed. "I wish. If I did, I'd go straight to the police myself. I learned my lesson. I've got to run. I need to rehearse for the gig at the fair. I hope you can swing by."

"I hope so, too, but my cheese duties might prevent me. We'll see." Brynn loved listening to Tillie sing and play guitar.

Tillie turned to leave.

"Tillie?"

"Yeah?" She turned back to face Brynn.

"Please be careful." Brynn didn't have to say more. She knew Tillie caught her drift.

Chapter 15

At some point while she was getting ready for the fair, Sheriff Edge had left the house. *Good.* She and Wes had to get moving if they were going to arrive a few minutes early to get organized for the CSA booth.

Wes was waiting for her downstairs.

"Everything okay?" she asked.

He hesitated. "For now. But I'm starting to get worried."

Brynn's stomach wavered. "Why?" She picked up her purse and keys from the hallway table and he followed her out the door.

"Why do they keep asking me the same questions over and over again?"

They walked toward the car and Brynn spotted the boxes with flyers about their farm. Wes thought of everything. She opened the door and slid in. Wes got into the passenger side.

"They keep asking you the same questions because they're investigating a murder. The timeline is important."

"But my story is still the same," he said, latching his seat belt.

"It's a technique." She turned the ignition. "They're hoping either to trip you up or that you'll remember a helpful detail while you're retelling the story."

"Okay."

"Did you know the victim?" Brynn asked.

"We'd been to a few of the same parties. We spoke, but I didn't know him well. It's odd because I thought he was seeing Chelsea. But I guess I was wrong. Evan was seeing her."

"Sounds like it might be hard to keep up with her boyfriends," Brynn said.

Wes laughed. "True."

As they drove along, they both quieted. Brynn was concerned that the police kept questioning him. She understood—and it was probably just procedure. But in such a small community, it seemed like overkill. Like they were truly suspecting him of killing that young man. Wes was one of the kindest people she knew. A good guy. She wished the police would leave him alone and find the real killer.

Maybe she could help in some way. Perhaps the police were overlooking a fact somewhere. If she could find anything at all and inform the police about it, they'd find the culprit and everything would be back to normal.

But maybe she was jumping the gun. Maybe that was the last of it. She mulled over what had happened with Nancy's death and how she tried to help the investigation. It turned out that she did help, but it didn't feel like it. She was certain she botched things up. Maybe she should leave the sleuthing to the police.

She drove along the narrow country roads, by cornfields and wildflower fields. Soon enough, they were at the fairground, pulling into the parking lot.

Brynn and Wes made their way to the building where they'd be manning the CSA booth. Brynn was pleased to see that everything had been prepared. Informative, colorful brochures were stacked on the table, along with applications for people to receive produce. There was a small shelving unit containing products from the CSA—honey, blackberry and strawberry jam, apple butter, things that had a shelf life. But Brynn had brought along cheese samples to place on the table, as well, along with the brochures Wes had created. They were just about set and the fair would open in twenty minutes.

"So tomorrow people will bring their cheese in," Brynn said more to herself than Wes. "And we taste and judge the cheese. The next day, we place the ribbons on the cheese and announce the winners."

Wes nodded. "Will it be hard to pick a winner?"

"You never know. Sometimes there's a clear winner right from the start." She straightened the stack of Buttermilk Creek Farm brochures. "Other times it's really difficult. I judged a contest once where all the cheese was so bad it was hard to choose anything!"

Wes laughed. "Bad cheese? Imagine that!"

Their booth was sandwiched between the 4-H and the Future Homemakers of America. People from each group scurried around trying to set up. Across from them, there were a few local banks with booths. The crowd of people seemed happy to be busy. The countdown had begun—five minutes until the fair officially opened.

"Hey, how are you?" Wes looked up at Roy, who'd

approached the booth. Brynn hardly recognized him. She's only seen him once before up close, but now he had a beard. What was it with all the young men growing beards?

"I'm good. Helping Brynn with the booth tonight. What are you doing here? Heard you got a gaming job?"

"Yeah, it fell through. Long story." Roy glanced at Brynn and smiled. She smiled back. "So I'm back working the fields. I don't mind. But I'd rather be gaming."

"How did you get in?" Wes asked. Brynn tried to busy herself with placing the cheese just so. She didn't want to eavesdrop on their conversation, but she was right there within listening distance.

"I walked in."

"But it's not open yet."

"I have my ways." He winked.

Winked. He actually winked. Brynn wanted him to move along.

Wes laughed nervously. "You're such a hacker."

Roy grinned.

"Would you like some cheese?" Brynn asked. She didn't like the direction of this conversation. *Hacking?*

"No, thank you," he said. "I hate cheese."

"Oh, I've never heard of anybody hating cheese," Wes said. "That's weird, dude."

"I got sick on it once. Did me in."

"Oh well, if you ever want to try again . . ." Brynn said. Didn't like cheese? She knew of people like him and had even met a few. But they were far and few between. "Looks like it's time for the fair to open."

"I better get going," he said. "Catch you later, Wes."

The air brimmed with an excitement suddenly. A bell rang announcing the official start of the fair. Brynn's childhood memories lightened her heart—the thought of attending the fair with clunky rides, smelly animals, and so much good food—and filled her with joy. She hoped it would last.

Chapter 16

About an hour later, after answering questions about the CSA, handing out brochures, and even making a few sales, Brynn heard a woman's screeching voice: "What is he? Where does he come from?"

Brynn looked around to see who or what she was talking about. It was a small, elderly, but spry lady, white hair pulled into a bun, hands balled in a fist, heading for the booth.

"I'm sorry. Is everything okay?" Brynn said.

"What's he doing here?" She pointed at Wes, who was helping a customer purchase honey.

Confused, Brynn's mouth dropped open; then she gathered herself. "He's helping with the booth. Why? What's the problem?"

"What is he? Some kind of terrorist?"

"I have no idea what you're talking about." Brynn's face heated. "You should move along."

The woman stood with her hands on her hip. "Shenandoah Springs ain't no place for a man like him."

Enraged and embarrassed by the scene the woman was creating, Brynn tamped down the impulse to shove her away before Wes caught on. "I think you should go," Brynn said with her teeth clenched.

"No, honey, he should go. Far away!"

Who was this woman? Brynn had never seen her before.

"The courts will deal with him. I hope they put him away for good. What he did to that poor man . . ."

Mike Rafferty came along about then. He was Schuyler's brother and the fire marshal. "What's going on here, Helen?"

The woman looked like a deer caught in headlights. Her face fell. "I'm sorry. I have to say what's on my mind. On everybody's mind. That terrorist needs to go back to where he came from."

"Boston?" Brynn said. "He's American. And even if he weren't, it's none of your concern."

"Thanks, Brynn," she heard Wes from behind her. She hoped he didn't hear any of that. First he's accused of murder, then of being a terrorist.

"He's from Boston," Mike said, reiterating. "You need to move along. I'm going to take you into custody in about five seconds if you don't."

"Never thought I'd see the day Mike Rafferty would be all PC," she muttered, and left the table.

Mike stood with his hands on his hips. "Sorry about that."

"Who is she?" Brynn asked, her heart breaking and racing at the same time.

"Helen Donnelley."

"Should I know her?"

"Nah, you're better off not knowing her." Mike laughed.

Brynn tried to smile, but it went nowhere. "I've

never seen her before and she came marching over here accusing Wes of all sorts of things."

"Unfortunately, he's been in the news. It will blow over."

"I hope so," Wes said as he sat down. "If my dad gets wind of this, he's going to make me come home. I don't want that." He paused. "I don't care what people like Helen think of me. I've been dealing with that my whole life."

"I do care, Wes," Brynn said after a minute. "It's ignorant and inexcusable."

"I agree," Mike said. "Other than Helen causing trouble, how's it going?"

Brynn had no idea what to say. Flummoxed and trying to remember what she was doing here, she shrugged. "Okay, I guess."

She straightened the brochures again. The CSA, yes, she was here to promote the CSA. "Would you like one?" She held one up for Mike.

"Nah, I'm already a member. Love it."

"Oh good," Brynn said, smiling. "How about some cheese?"

His face lit up. "Okay. I'll take a sample. I hear you're having a contest."

"Yep." She handed him a napkin with a few crackers with cheese on it. "I'm excited about it. It's tomorrow. You should come by the cheese shed."

He nodded and popped a cracker with cheese in his mouth. "My God, this is good cheese," he said after swallowing.

"Excuse me," said a voice on the other side of him. "How do I join the CSA?"

Wes stood and handed her an application.

"I better get going," Mike said. "Good seeing you, Brynn."

"Hey, thanks for helping with Helen."

"You're welcome."

As he walked away, Brynn recalled how he had investigated the fire that took Nancy's life. That's when she first met him. He struck her as capable and he was. But he didn't solve that case—she did. Once again, she found herself wondering how to help the police. After all, they were understaffed. Maybe they'd welcome the help.

She had no idea where to start. But as she considered all the events, she felt a sense of urgency. Rumors were spreading. Not only was her heart breaking for Wes, but she was concerned about her new enterprise. She had yet to make a profit. If Buttermilk Farms was connected with a murder—no matter how ridiculous it was—it might put them under.

First, she needed to research the victim. What sort of person was he? Who were his associates? Why would someone kill him?

If she could answer those questions, perhaps she could help the police and nip this business in the bud.

After Wes took a break and walked around the fairground, Brynn followed suit. The night air was steamy, but the atmosphere was festive. The merry-go-round music in the background, lights strung, a few well-lit game booths. She heard the roar of the crowd and followed it to the far end of the fairground, passing the kiddie rides, booths, the trained animals going around in circles, carrying little ones waving to their parents and grandparents.

Brynn made her way to the crowd and spotted a

tractor pulling a load of people—creeping along. The crowd cheered them on. Another two people stepped on the back—and it stopped in a puff of smoke and steam. The crowd jeered.

When the crowd calmed down, the tractor driver exited the vehicle and waved to everybody. Brynn knew the tractor pull was a longtime tradition. It seemed like good fun for the farm community. It was an oddly charming tradition. She recalled the conversation she'd had about tractors being so powerful now.

Her thoughts were interrupted by a gnawing in her stomach. She'd told Wes that she would pick them up a couple of orders of French fries. The scent wafted into the building and had been tempting them all evening.

She turned to find the French fries and bumped into David Reese, the tractor salesman. "Oh, I'm sorry," she said.

"No worries," he said, and grinned at her. "Checking out the tractor pull, are you?"

She nodded. "Why are they using old tractors?"

"For two reasons," he said. "One is most small farmers buy a tractor for life. Or they inherit. And the other reason is the old tractors are more fun." He winked at her, which made Brynn want to heave.

"Do you have something in your eye?" she said without thinking.

His face blanked. "I don't think so. I better get going."

Yes, you better. What was it with some of these older men? If you actually talked to them they thought you were interested in them? What the heck? Brynn wasn't interested in anybody. Period. She was glad she let him know.

She found the French fry stand and took her place in the long line.

"What are you doing here?" she heard a voice say.

She turned to find Willow.

"You're supposed to be at the booth."

"I left Wes at the booth. I want some fries."

Willow grinned. "Best fries ever. Great sweet potato fries over there."

"Not tonight," Brynn said. "We've been smelling these fries all evening."

"I hear ya."

"So what's the scoop on this Helen character?" Brynn asked as the line moved forward.

"Helen? Little old woman?" Willow gestured. "About this high?"

Brynn nodded. "She made a scene tonight. Called Wes a terrorist and a murderer."

"Good God. She's crazy," Willow said. "I'm sorry about that. She doesn't come out of the hills often. But she does come for the fair every year."

"What's her problem?" Brynn said. Now two people stood between her and the French fry counter. Was she drooling?

"I don't know. She's lived up in the hills forever. And some of those old folks are still suspicious of outsiders."

"Still? What do you mean?"

"Back in the day, the government came here and took our land, for a start. Outsiders have been coming into Appalachia for years and trying to tell us how to eat, pray, and live. The people who live in the mountains had it harder than the rest of us." She paused. "But still it's not 1950. She has no excuse for that ignorant behavior. She needs to get over it. Wes has done nothing to her and wants nothing from her."

"Right," Brynn said.

"Next!" the man in the trailer yelled.

"Two large fries," Brynn said, handing him exact change.

He took her money and slid two cardboard containers across the counter full of crispy hot fries. Brynn's mouth watered.

"Hey, are you the lady harboring a killer?"

Brynn looked behind her. Who was he talking to?

Willow stepped up. "Mind your own business, Zach, and get me some fries."

Brynn reached for her fries. "Was he talking to me?" Her face heated.

Willow nodded. "Yes, now don't worry about it. Take your fries and go back to the booth. I'll handle this." Brynn's stomach roiled. "Okay," she said.

She made her way through the crowd. The lights, the games, the people, who all had an air of festivity two minutes ago, seemed meaningless to Brynn now. Were they all looking at her? She kept her chin up and walked to the building where Wes waited. She felt like they were all looking at her. But that couldn't be. Could people entertain the notion that Wes was a murderer?

She drew in a breath. She needed to put a stop to all this nonsense.

Chapter 17

Brynn was happy to see Wes engaged in a conversation about the CSA. Intent, she sat down with the fries and tucked into hers, listening to their conversation.

"For now, we make deliveries, but we're hoping by the fall we'll have a farm stand open and people can come and get their produce, too," Wes said.

"What a great idea," the man said. "You'll be getting my application soon. I'm so sick of the produce I'm getting from the local grocery stores. The tomatoes have no flavor."

Wes grinned. "We hear that a lot."

"Thank you," the man said, and he walked away with an application in his hand.

Wes turned his attention to Brynn and the fries. "Oh my God, those fries smell great!"

Brynn nodded as she shoved another one in her mouth. Should she tell Wes about the conversation with Zach, the French fry man? She ate another fry and mulled it over. What purpose would it serve? Wes was already nervous enough about all this, especially from Helen causing a scene. It wasn't like she was keeping a secret. It was that, well, it might hurt him unnecessarily.

The crowd was thinning. Almost quitting time. Brynn looked forward to closing up shop here so she could go home, tend to the cows, and prepare for tomorrow's contest. She didn't know if she'd find time to begin to look into the backgrounds of the murder victims. But she hoped she did. Anything she could find that would help the police focus their attention on someone other than Wes would be a good start. She, of course, had no idea what she was looking for—and when she tried to find answers concerning her neighbor's death, she was led on a few wild-goose chases. But if she approached this more methodically, she might succeed. She had to do something. For Wes—and for the farm.

"What's wrong?" Wes said as they packed up the booth, tucking boxes under the table for tomorrow's crew to find.

"I'm tired, I guess," Brynn said. But she was wired. Not one, but two incidents happened at the fair, where the locals let it be known that they suspected Wes of murder. "We've got a lot of work left at home tonight."

"No worries. I'll take care of the girls while you get ready for the contest. How's that sound?"

Brynn warmed. How could anybody think anything but the best thoughts about Wes? "That sounds good."

As they walked through the crowd-less fairground with the lights still on and people closing up, the night winding down, Brynn had a conversation with herself. It was two people. That didn't mean everybody believed the nonsense about Wes. Willow stood up for Wes with the French fry man and Mike stood up for him with Helen. Brynn held on to the thought that most of the local community was like Willow and Mike. She chose to believe that. She'd not dwell on the others—but she planned to arm herself with more knowledge about the victim.

As they walked around the corner toward the parking lot, a young girl came out of one of the trailers, with a young man; she kissed him good night and looked up at Wes. "Hey, Wes," she said.

Brynn was startled. The young woman was unusually beautiful, striking green eyes and long dark hair. There was something familiar about her.

"Hey, Chelsea," Wes said, but kept moving. Brynn followed his lead. Was that who she thought it was?

After they were safely inside the car, Brynn turned the ignition and asked Wes her burning question— even though she wasn't sure she wanted to know.

Brynn pulled out of the parking lot. "Was that Chelsea, Josh's daughter?"

"Yes."

"What is she doing here when her dad is still in jail?"

"I wondered the same thing."

"On a date?" Brynn asked.

Wes didn't respond.

"When her family is in crisis? What kind of a person is she?" Brynn's heart sped in her chest as she thought about Josh and the whole family.

"Chelsea has issues."

That was the second time someone had mentioned that to Brynn. "How well do you know her?"

"I've been to a few parties with her. We've talked a few times. But I don't know her well."

"Yet you know her well enough to know she has issues," Brynn pointed out as she stopped at a stop sign and looked both ways.

"Everybody knows she has issues. Mostly, she sleeps around. I've steered clear of her."

Brynn was not into slut shaming. What grown women did or didn't do in terms of their sex lives was no concern of anybody's—let alone hers, unless they were hurting other people. But Chelsea was a sixteen-year-old girl. Brynn knew things had changed since she was a girl. Sex was much more casual. But had they changed that much?

"Wasn't she dating the young man who was killed?"

"Yes, she was," Wes said. "But it looks like she's dating someone else already. You see what I mean? Issues. Like how could you even consider dating immediately after your boyfriend was killed in an accident where your dad was driving the tractor?"

"I'm glad to hear you say that because that's what I was wondering. I mean, I hate judging others, but sometimes you've gotta wonder about people."

They rode the rest of the way in silence. When Brynn pulled into her driveway and glanced toward her field, she noticed that her cows were not there— but the next thing she noticed was Tillie coming out of the barn. She'd taken care of the cows for the evening. Brynn wanted to run over to her and kiss her. Instead, she parked the car, and she and Wes exited the vehicle and walked over to Tillie.

"Thank you, Tillie," Brynn said. "We're a little later than we thought we'd be."

"No problem," she said. "You know I love your girls. I'm a little worried about Jewel, your new cow."

"She's not mine. We're fostering her until we can find someone else to take care of her. I'm worried about her, too."

"We need to give her time," Wes said, walking up to them. "She's shy and she's different from the other cows. They're not too sure about her, either. She looks different, smells different, you know. Once they get used to her, they will be fine."

Brynn hoped he was right. Jewel tugged at her heart, as any animal in her condition would. She reminded herself not to get too attached. After all, she was fostering the cow until Schuyler found a home for her.

After the evening chores, Brynn sat down and opened her laptop. She wanted to look up Highland cattle, hoping she'd get an insight into Jewel's behavior. She also wanted to do a quick search on Donny Iser, the young man who Wes found.

From everything that Brynn read, whatever Jewel's problem was, it probably had nothing to do with the breed. They were known for their good nature. But something she read did catch her eye. Cows raised in isolation never learned how to socialize. That was probably the issue. And Schuyler and Wes were probably right—that it was going to take time.

Then she keyed in "Donny Iser." Internet research wasn't going to give her everything she needed on the young man, but it was a good place to start. Who was he? Where was he from? And who were his enemies?

She pressed enter and saw his Facebook account, Instagram, and Twitter. She also had those accounts, so she should check his out. His Facebook settings were private. Strike one.

She checked out Instagram next. A ton of pictures splayed on his page—mostly of the Shenandoah Valley. Sunsets. Cows. Barns. She scrolled down farther. Okay. Finally photos of people. A group of young people who Brynn assumed were other workers on the farm. They were sitting around a fire. Her heart sank. This poor young man. He appreciated the beauty of the area and had friends. She scrolled down even farther. Photos of a young woman, a beautiful young woman. Wasn't that Chelsea? She enlarged the photo. Yes, yes, it was.

This one young woman seemed to be the common denominator for all the trouble. So why weren't the police focused on her, instead of Wes?

Perhaps they were and Brynn didn't know. After all, why would she? But it seemed as if the young woman didn't have a care in the world. She was happily on a date at the fair tonight. Brynn's eyes burned. She yawned. Tomorrow was a big day. She should get some sleep.

But sleep didn't come easy. She didn't want to acknowledge it, but she had a deep sense of foreboding. She wanted to ignore Helen and the way she frightened her. Brynn understood people like her existed, but she tried to steer clear of them. And she always felt like if she could sit down with them and talk, they'd change their minds about their views. But after being so close to Helen and seeing the fear and hatred in her eyes, Brynn wasn't so sure of that anymore. She'd always chosen to seek the good in people. But she was struggling with finding it in Helen.

"Some folks are just born bad," Granny Rose used to say. "Ain't nothing you can do about it, Brynn, except stay away from them."

Helen was old enough to know better and was probably beyond help. But Chelsea was another matter altogether. She had a good family, as far as Brynn knew. What prompted her to be so man crazy? People were complex and there were no easy answers, but usually young women who slept around had daddy issues. And Josh was decent.

A weird tingle swept through her. You never knew what happened behind closed doors. Maybe he wasn't as good of a father as Brynn assumed. She didn't want to follow that trail in her mind. No. She'd keep believing in him and knowing he'd never hurt anybody.

The next morning, she and Wes worked together like a well-oiled machine. Got the cows milked, fed, and out, ate breakfast, and headed to the fairground. The carnival rides and such didn't open until the late afternoon. But the rest of the fair opened at nine. Brynn and Wes got to their cheese shed at seven thirty in order to prepare and to greet the contestants.

Everything appeared to be in order. The temperature of the building was correct and all the lined shelves and tables were the way Brynn had imagined them. She loved the look of that brown linen fabric lining the shelves.

She and Wes swept the floor and dusted and tidied up—when it comes to cheese, you can't be too clean.

Brynn heard laughter and chattering at the door, then a knock. When she opened it, there stood two people carrying bags and platters.

"Hello," Brynn said. "I'm Brynn MacAlister and this is Wes Scors."

"Wes!" The white-haired woman ran to him. "I knew your grandmother! I miss her so much!" She grabbed him and hugged him. He looked over her shoulder with a quizzical glance at Brynn. "She was involved with the local blood donation center. I'm a nurse, was, I mean. I've retired, but I volunteer at the bloodmobile."

"How nice of you," Wes said, recovering his composure. "What do you have there?"

"Cheese," she said, laughing, holding up her bag. Wes took over and led her to the tables. Brynn turned to the other person standing there. A young man with dreadlocks swept off his head by a bandanna.

"Hi, I'm Rad," he said. "Here for the cheese contest." He was soft-spoken and had a respectful air about him.

"Nice to meet you, Rad," Brynn said. "What do you have there?"

"I've been experimenting with an Asiago," he said. "I don't expect to win the contest, but I'm looking for feedback."

Brynn smiled. She loved that attitude. "You'll get plenty of that. We'll make sure of it." She and Rad placed his cheese on the shelf and looked around. "Cool building."

"Yeah, we thought it was a good option." Brynn handed him a form to fill out, a questionnaire about his cheese, and ingredients, as she spotted a new group of cheesemakers entering.

She was thrilled to see such an interest in cheesemaking, hoping this contest might be a yearly draw for the fair. As more and more people entered, a wave a gratitude moved through her—maybe this whole thing with Wes wasn't as big a deal as she figured. People trickled in for the contest—maybe they hadn't even heard about the problems he was having, or the murder. Who knew? She felt a deep sigh of relief and focused on the task at hand.

Chapter 18

Cheese competitions at fairs were never as popular as the pie contest. Brynn knew that, and the crowd wasn't nearly as big as she would have liked. But still, there was a crowd, and it was the first year of what she hoped to be the start of a long tradition.

She took in the group, a mix of ages and genders. Cheese touched everybody, as Grandma Rose used to say. Didn't matter who you were, there was a cheese for you. When Brynn met someone who didn't like cheese, she was immediately suspicious. Not being able to eat cheese for health reasons—or ethical reasons—was one thing. But not *liking* it? She'd never understand.

Brynn eyed the cheddar. Uniform, with no irregular finishes, no waves or lumps. Good body and sound-looking texture. Perfect creamy orange color. She bored a hole into it. She sliced a piece and brought it to her nose. She loved the tangy scent of a good cheddar. She bit into it.

The smooth cheese crumbled nicely in her mouth and the flavor popped. *Cheddar finish with a distinct note of butterscotch or butter caramel on upper back of palate.*

This was a beautifully crafted cheddar. She glanced at the tag: "Mary Rogers, Waynesboro, Va." She scanned the crowd in an attempt to figure out who Mary was. Was she the short, birdlike woman, dressed in a track-suit? Or was she the tall, curvy woman with long gray hair, wearing jeans and a Lynyrd Skynyrd T-shirt? Or perhaps she was the woman with a pageboy wearing a long denim skirt?

Whoever she was, Brynn was enamored.

The cheddar was the third cheese she'd tasted, and while the others were fine, this was extraordinary. She bit an apple slice to cleanse her palate and took a drink of water. She wanted more, of course—but she had fifteen other cheeses to sample. She filled out her judging form and moved on to the next, passed a cowboy-hat-wearing man who seemed to be watching her intently. He nodded at her as she walked by. She smiled politely.

She glanced at Wes, happily tasting cheese, and eyed her next tasting—Parmigiano-Reggiano—brought by Sophia D'Amico.

Brynn fancied any sort of Parmigiano cheese. Crowned the king of cheeses, it's an Italian pure-blood cheese—sharp, intense, and full-bodied in taste. She eyed it as a block of cheese. Firm but a bit granular and crystallized as it should be—because that happened when this cheese aged a bit. And it should age at least twelve months because the secret to its iconic flavor lies in its maturation. The cheese flavor lingered in her mouth—delicious, but not as extraordinary as the cheddar.

Brynn was mulling over the medley of flavors in

her mouth, took a bite of an apple, and a scream interrupted her. She whipped around toward the noise. A small group of people gathered around something on the floor. She rushed over, elbowing her way in.

Wes! Why was he lying on the floor?

"Oh my God!" someone said. "He's been shot!"

What? That couldn't be? Was this some sick joke? *Shot?* Fear tore through Brynn. What was going on?

"I'll call 9-1-1!" another voice said.

Brynn's heart raced as she kneeled on the floor next to him. "Wes! Wes." His eyes rolled around, as if he was trying to stay awake. "Get him," he said, barely coherent.

"What? Who?" Brynn's focus zoomed in on him. She brushed hair off his forehead. "Wes? What happened?"

"Dreadlocks," Wes said before he passed out.

"Did he say 'dreadlocks'?" the cowboy-hat man asked over Brynn's shoulder.

Numb, Brynn nodded.

"I know that little jerk," the man said. "I'm going to get his ass."

The next thing Brynn knew, the man was gone and the medic arrived on the scene, shooing everybody away. Time was moving in drips and waves. The building swayed as a man's arm lifted her to her feet. She was covered in a sticky substance. Dark. *Blood!* Everywhere. The floor was covered as well.

As the paramedics lifted Wes onto the stretcher, Brynn wobbled, with a man behind her holding her up. "Brynn," he said. She turned to see Mike Rafferty trying to catch her before her head thwacked the floor and all went black.

* * *

When she awakened, she was on a stretcher, being wheeled into the hospital. She tried to sit up, but straps prevented it. Why was she on a stretcher? She'd just passed out, for God's sake. Flashes of Wes's face in agony sprang to her mind.

"Wes," she said to the paramedic next to her. "Is Wes okay?"

"Who?"

"The young man who was shot?"

The paramedic didn't answer as they wheeled her into the room, unstrapped her, and transferred her to a bed. The room spun. Pain shot through her head.

"Do you know? How is Wes Scors?" Her stomach roiled from the movement.

"I'm sorry. I don't know. All I know is you have a nasty concussion, thirteen stitches in your head. You're going to need to take it easy for a while."

She must have hit her head on the ground when she fainted. Brynn's stomach soured. "Think I'm going to be sick," she said right before he handed her a pan.

Brynn heard faraway voices, reminding her of a game she played as a kid with tin cans. Pretending they were phones. She suddenly wanted her mother.

"Will she be okay?" A woman's voice.

"She has a concussion. It's going to take some time. But she'll be okay." A man's voice.

Pain thudded in Brynn's temples.

"Did they get the guy?" Another man's voice.

She tried to lift her eyelids. But they were too heavy. Voices kept sounding.

"I believe so." A woman's voice.

Something in Brynn's mind eased, gave way, and she drifted off.

Light shone in her eyes, which prompted her to awaken. She batted her eyes. The light was coming from outside. Sunlight streamed into the room. She turned her face away from it and saw Schuyler curled up on a chair in the corner. "Schuyler?"

She shot up out of the chair.

"Brynn. How are you feeling?"

"The light . . . hurts."

Schuyler walked over to the window and pulled the curtains shut.

"What happened?"

Schuyler smiled and leaned over the bed. "You passed out and conked your head."

Memories slowly waved into her brain. The cheese contest. Wes.

"Wes?"

"He's going to be fine. Superficial wound, but he did bleed a lot. I had no idea you are so skittish about blood."

All the blood. Everywhere. "Me either," Brynn said, grimacing as a shot of pain moved through her head. "Who shot Wes?"

"It was Rad."

The nurse walked in. "Hello, I'm Sherry, your nurse. I need to take your vitals. I won't be but a moment." She slipped a blood pressure cuff on Brynn.

"Should I know him?" Brynn asked Schuyler.

Schuyler shook her head. "No. Not unless you've wanted to score some crack or something."

The blood pressure cuff tightened and then loosened as the nurse read the dial. Then she slipped it off.

"How does someone like that know Wes?"

"I don't think he did. He heard Wes killed Donny and was stoned out of his mind and went off on a tangent, thought he was a vigilante." Schuyler crossed her arms.

The nurse slipped her fingers onto Brynn's wrist and watched her pulse.

Brynn and Schuyler quieted. After the nurse was done and walked out of the room, Schuyler sat down on the edge of Brynn's bed. "This has been crazy."

"What? What's happening?"

"They have a guard posted at Wes's room for his protection. Do you believe it's come to that?"

Brynn's heart raced. He was such a great kid and had wanted to find a place and people he could belong with. He thought he found it with Brynn and in Shenandoah Springs. Who knew about a racist element here?

"It's bizarre."

"His dad is coming to visit," Schuyler said. "He's fit to be tied."

Would he make Wes go home? Brynn didn't want to consider it. She'd come to rely on Wes. Even though she was his teacher, there were things he'd helped her with that she'd still be struggling with if it weren't for him.

But was she being selfish? If it was dangerous here for him, her little cheese business and micro-dairy farm didn't matter. His life was more important than any of that.

"I imagine," Brynn said, "I am, too. I don't understand what's going on." Right now, she struggled to put a single thought together in her mind. "Schuyler. Help me out. What's happening?"

"What do you mean?" She leaned forward and looked down into Brynn's face.

"Why is everybody against Wes?"

"That's not true," she said with a soft tone in her voice, making Brynn suspicious. She may have been conked on her head, but she knew Schuyler didn't do soft, unless it was with an animal.

Brynn crossed her arms. "If you're not going to be honest with me, then who will be?"

Schuyler drew back and frowned. "I don't know what you want me to say. I'm not against him. Nobody I know is against him. But the police . . . seem to be suspecting him. So, yes, people are leery of him. Plus there are some racist asses around. But you know all that."

Brynn wished her brain would work quicker. She almost remembered something. "Something . . . I remember . . . thinking . . . there's one common denominator."

"You're right about that," Schuyler said. "It's Chelsea."

"Chelsea. Yes. We saw her on a date. I thought it was suspicious. Her dad is still in jail. She was dating the man who he ran over. Why would she be on a date?"

"She was also dating the man that Wes found in the barn, Donny?"

"Sounds like a lover spurned out there who may be behind all this."

"And? You mean like setting Wes up? Man, you did take a blow to the head." Schuyler grinned.

Perhaps she wasn't making any sense. It sounded crazy, admittedly.

"Well, something's wrong if the police are looking seriously at Wes. He just discovered a body. He didn't kill anybody."

Schuyler hesitated. "Brynn, try not to worry about any of this. Try to relax and concentrate on getting better. We've got the farm covered. Wes is being well taken care of. His dad will be here soon." She paused. "Concussions can be serious, especially if you push yourself. So please try to relax."

Brynn appreciated her friend's concern, but she should have known better. Brynn wasn't going to relax until she knew Wes was completely off the hook and was okay—concussion or not.

Chapter 19

Brynn wished for sleep. It seemed as if every time she fell asleep, some nurse or doctor was waking her up to take her vitals or give her medicine. No wonder people got sicker in hospitals.

She glanced at the clock on her bedside table. It was 8:00 AM. Funny, she had no sense of time. Where were her bag and cell phone? She needed to call her sister and parents. She gazed around the room and sat up, but she slammed back into her pillow, too dizzy to even sit up.

She beeped for the nurse. But as she lay back onto her pillow, she drifted off before the nurse came.

Later, a nurse entered the room and awakened her. "Good morning," he said. "Time for medicine."

She struggled to open her eyes. "Good morning," she muttered. It hurt to talk. Her head felt like it had been hit by a cement block.

She sat up to take the medicine, hoping it would help. Just then, the aide came in with breakfast. A wave of nausea rolled through her as she placed the meal on her bedside tray, "Are you going to be able to eat this morning?" the nurse asked.

"I'm not sure."

"Well, try. You don't have to eat the whole thing." His voice soothed and Brynn's tension gave way just a bit.

"Okay," she said.

"Is there anything I can get you?" he asked.

Brynn looked into his dark brown eyes. He was in the exact right job, she decided. Comfort oozed from him. "I don't know if anybody brought my purse and I'd like it because it has my cell phone. I need to make a few calls."

"Of course," he said. "I think your purse is in this drawer." He walked over, opened the drawer, and brought it to her. "Now, you know, you're not supposed to have any screen time. As in none."

"I want to make some calls. I'm not going to play games on my phone," she said.

"Good," he said. "Is there anything else?"

"No," Brynn said as she dug through her bag to find her phone, pulled it out, and was relieved to find the battery hadn't died. "Thank you."

With that, the nurse with the soothing voice and calming eyes left the room.

She held her phone in her hand and wondered how she was going to make this call. What she would say to her sister, Becky, without prompting her to freak out.

She set the phone down on the table, next to her plate of scrambled eggs. She wondered how Wes was doing. Were there still guards at his door? Or was he safely home?

She took a bite of her egg. Her stomach didn't like

it. But then she took a bite of dry toast and it was exactly what she needed. She took another.

A rapping noise came from her door. Willow stepped through the doorway and into her room.

"Hey," she said, cheerier than she should be.

"Hey, Willow," Brynn said.

She eyed the food. "You're eating. That's great."

Brynn held up the toast. "Toast," she said. "Can't quite do eggs yet."

"How are you feeling?" She put a bunch of bags on the chair next to Brynn's bed.

"My head hurts and I'm tired. They don't let you sleep around here."

Willow smiled. "So I hear. I've been to see Wes. He's going to be sprung later today. He's doing well. The gunshot wound is superficial."

"Oh good," Brynn said. "But will he be safe?"

"The police seemed to think so. They've already gotten the guy who shot him."

"That's a relief!" Brynn took another bite of toast. "Did he say why he shot him? It doesn't make sense."

"He's a druggy. Nothing he does makes sense. He had in his warped mind that Wes was seeing Chelsea and killed Donny so he could have her to himself. But he also thought Wes had been sent here by Al-Qaeda, that he's a spy for them. He's been spreading that rumor around, evidently."

"Oh dear."

"I don't know one person who knows him who thinks any of that's plausible," Willow said, and grinned. "That's the good news."

Brynn swallowed her toast. "What's the bad news?"

Willow took a breath and sighed. "Wes's father is here, and he's not happy. He wants to take Wes home with him. It's adding stress to an already stressful situation, unfortunately."

Brynn thought about Nathaniel Scors, Wes's father, and knew he was a good person and parent. He was a great son to Brynn's friend Nancy. What would she do if her son appeared to be in danger? "I can't blame him for wanting to take him home."

"I know, right? But Wes can't leave until the investigation is over, and his dad is furious. Plus, Wes doesn't want to leave."

That made Brynn happy. She didn't want him to leave, either. But she certainly didn't want to put him in danger.

Brynn needed to find out who was behind all of this. It would get Wes off the hook for everything, rebuilding his reputation.

"I'm certain all of this has something to do with Chelsea," Brynn said. "My brain isn't working as quickly as it should, but I think that's right. This all has something to do with her."

Willow leaned toward her. "You may be right. I've been thinking the same thing. But then I catch myself and remember she's only sixteen. She's troubled, yes. But she's not a killer. At least I don't think so."

"What if it's some kind of weird love triangle?" Brynn said. "Seems like she has a lot of boyfriends."

Willow's eyebrows shot up. "You may be on to something. As in the person who killed Donny? Maybe he was a spurned lover?"

"Yes."

Willow folded her arms. "Trouble is we'd have a hard time choosing one. There are so many. And I don't even think we know all of them."

Brynn shivered. "Let's figure out what we know.

There's a small notebook in my bag. Time to make a list."

After they made their list, Brynn realized she didn't know most of the young men around Shenandoah Springs. But why would she?

"There's one man missing. The carnival guy."

"I don't know him," Willow said. "You said she came out of his trailer? Which one was it?"

Brynn's brain hurt as she tried to think. She shrugged. "I don't recall. I'll need to mull this over."

"You look tired," Willow said. "You should get some sleep. I need to get a move on, anyway."

"I am tired," Brynn said. "And my head hurts. Constantly." She sank back into her pillow and closed her eyes. The last thing she remembered before falling asleep was Willow looking down at her and smiling sweetly.

She woke up to the sound of her phone ringing. Damn, she should have shut that off.

It was Becky. *Uh-oh.*

"Hello," Brynn said, trying to sound like she hadn't just been awakened.

"Hey, what's up? How did the cheese contest go? I've been waiting on news from you. I know you're busy, but geez."

Brynn took a deep breath. She hadn't called and told her sister yet about the concussion. "The cheese contest was interrupted. Someone shot Wes. He's fine. It was a superficial wound." "Superficial wound." It felt odd coming out of her mouth.

"What? How awful!"

"I passed out and conked my head pretty good. In fact, I'm in Augusta Medical with a concussion."

Silence on the other end of the phone.

"Becky?"

"Why didn't you call?"

"I planned to call today. But I've been so tired and my head hurts."

"We'll be right up."

"Wait. There's no need for you to come. I know you're busy. My friends have the farm covered. There's nothing left to do with the cheese competition. There's no reason for you to come and look at me lying in this bed." Brynn's sister cut and styled hair for a living, and if she left even for a day or two it took money out of her hands.

"I don't care about any of that. I want to see you. I can shuffle a few appointments around. Don't worry."

"Are you certain?" Brynn wanted to cry, overwhelmed her sister would make a trip from Richmond to see her. She blinked away a tear.

"Thank you."

"Did you say Wes was shot?"

"Yes, but they caught the young man. He was convinced that Wes is a member of Al-Qaeda."

"That's pretty specific," Becky said.

"He's on drugs, evidently. He saw that Wes is a person of interest in a local murder case and went crazy."

"Did he know the victim?" Becky asked.

"Yes, they were friends evidently."

"So possibly the victim was a druggy, too."

Brynn hadn't thought of that. When she first moved to Shenandoah Springs earlier in the year, she was shocked to find out about the drug problem

here. "That's a good point. But Willow was here earlier today. It seems like all the accidents and deaths
have one person in common. A young woman named
Chelsea."

"What do you mean?"

Brynn pulled the covers closer. She was suddenly
cold and shivery. "The first accident victim was seeing her. He was way too old for her." She struggled to
put words together. "The murder victim was also seeing her."

"Love triangles and drugs. So the plot thickens.
Hmmm. Lily, get down off of there!" Lily was Becky's
daughter. "I've got to go. My child is driving me nuts.
But I hope to see you tomorrow."

She clicked off the phone.

The fact that Becky was coming to see Brynn
warmed her. Just as she sank back into another sleep,
the doctor awakened her.

"Hello, Brynn," he said. "How are you? Head still
hurt?"

"Yes," she said. "And I'm so sleepy."

"Part of that is the pain medicine. But it's also the
concussion. You took a hard hit to the head." He
pulled out a small pen-like instrument. It was a flash-
light. He shone it into her eyes.

"I realize this is going to be a bit tough, but no TV
or computer screens at all for the next two weeks.
Phone screens only when necessary. Even when you
go home. Studies have shown that it's detrimental to
healing from a concussion."

"I don't watch much TV. But I do have a business
to run."

"Is the computer important to it?"

"We get orders from the computer and then there's
the website maintenance."

"Have any help with that?"

Did she? *Wait. Yes, of course.* "Wes can take care of all of that, I guess. As long as he's up to it. He was shot, you know."

The doctor nodded. "What year is this?"

"Twenty-seventeen. No, wait. Twenty-nineteen." Brynn was shocked "Twenty-seventeen" came out of her mouth.

"We're going to have to keep you a few more days," the doctor said.

"I have a farm to take care of. I need to get out of here," she replied.

"Sorry. You have a concussion and won't be going anywhere for a while," he said, and left the room.

Brynn wanted to cry. Except it'd make her head hurt worse than it already did. She was worried about Wes, worried about her girls, and worried about the new cow. All that worry was not good for her own healing. It seemed to her as if she'd do much better at home. She'd mention that to the doctor the next time he came in. In the meantime, she lay back into her bed, pulled the covers up over her shoulders, and curled onto her side.

Chapter 20

Brynn wasn't supposed to be looking at the computer screen or her phone, but she would be quick. She needed to research this young woman to see what was so special about her. She keyed in "Chelsea O'Connor" and a whole slew of things came up.

She was the captain of the cheerleaders. Of course.

On the homecoming court last year.

Honor roll student.

This girl's life read like it was straight out of a book. All-American girl, who dated older men, a lot of boys, and was the captain of the cheerleading squad? How did she have time for all of it?

A picture of her with the boy who had dreadlocks popped onto the screen. The one who shot Wes. A tingle traveled up Brynn's spine. The young woman actually did date the young man with the dreads. The young man who was on drugs and who shot Wes.

Could they be trying to set Wes up? If so, were the police following false leads about Wes? Was their questioning of him more than just because he'd discovered the body?

How would Brynn find out?

A knock sounded at her door. "Yoo-hoo, visitors!"

"Wes!" Brynn sat up in bed a little too quickly and became dizzy.

He rushed to her bedside. "Take it easy, Brynn!"

His dad, Nathaniel, came up beside him. "Hey, Brynn." He looked serious, tired, and forlorn. "How are you feeling?"

"Better. I want to go home. I'd do much better there."

"When are they going to spring you?" Wes asked.

"I have no idea," she said, trying to will away the wave of weariness washing over her.

"Get better," Wes said. "We've got everything under control. The farm. The cheese. Everything. I'm lucky the bullet only grazed me and I've a superficial wound. Doesn't even bother me at this point."

"Well, everything is not quite under control," Nathaniel said. He had the same droopy puppy-dog eyes as his mother, Nancy. "Wes still appears to be under suspicion. I've hired a lawyer to deal with it."

"Dad! Let's not worry Brynn with all this. It's going to be okay. I didn't do it."

"I'm glad your dad brought it up. I wondered how things were going. I've been trying to figure it all out from my bed. So frustrating."

"You shouldn't be doing that. Concussions are tricky. Try not to think too hard," Nathaniel said.

"Don't waste your breath, Dad," Wes said in a joking tone. "Once Brynn latches on to something, she doesn't let it go."

A smile cracked onto Nathaniel's face. "That's right. I remember."

An awkward pause continued as they were each into their own thoughts. Brynn wasn't sure, but she thought they all might be remembering Nancy, Nathaniel's mom and Wes's grandmother. At the time, Brynn didn't rest until she figured out that mess.

"How well do you know Chelsea?" Brynn asked Wes.

"I think I told you . . . maybe you don't remember? I don't know her well."

"Who's Chelsea?" Nathaniel asked.

"I'm certain this case revolves around her. She's the one common denominator. She's sixteen. The daughter of Josh. She was dating the man killed in the accident, and the man who was murdered."

"I'm sure the police are looking into it," Wes said with a note of discomfort in his voice.

"Are they? It seems to me they are focused on you," his father said. "I'd like to know why it's gotten to be more than the fact that you found a body, right?"

Wes shrugged, frustrated.

A nurse walked in the room with Brynn's medication. The two men stepped aside while the nurse gave her the pills.

"When can I go home?" Brynn missed her girls, her cat, and her dog. She missed the view from her window. She missed her own bed. She missed the new cow. All of it.

"That's up to the doctor," the nurse replied. "He should be in shortly. You can ask him then. Do you need anything?"

My own bed.

"I guess not," Brynn said.

"I'd like to know more about Chelsea," Nathaniel said after the nurse left.

"She's just a girl who's a bit confused," Wes said. "She's not a killer."

"Yes, but we suspect she dated the man who shot you," Brynn said, pulling the photos up on her phone.

Wes reached for it. "Let me see that. Yes, yes, that's him all right. He can rot in jail for the rest of his life, for all I care." His jaw clenched. "I didn't know they knew each other. But then again, in a place like this, everybody seems to know one another—or at least know someone in their family or a friend." Wes tucked his thumbs into his jean pockets. "I've got to admit, now, that connection between Chelsea, everybody else, and me getting shot is intriguing. But I still don't see her killing someone."

Brynn tried to think, but her head hurt. She paused. "I don't know her. But I do know that people surprise you. Young women have killed people."

"Also, maybe some nutjob with a crush on her has something to do with it," Nathaniel said, frowning,

Wes's eyebrows shot up. "I know at least three guys who have a crush on her and she wants nothing to do with any of them."

"Who are they, Wes?"

"I think the only one you know is Roy, the guy who stopped by the booth that night at the fair. The other two are guys who work at Mrs. Rowe's. We've been trying to sell them cheese. They're both high school seniors and wash dishes over there."

"You get around," Nathaniel said, lifting one eyebrow.

"It's part of my job."

Wes took his work seriously and Brynn was grateful for it. She was prepared to do it all herself. But she counted her blessings more than once when it came to Wes coming along and helping her out.

She reflected on Roy. Tall, skinny, bad complexion. She wished she'd paid more attention to him. But she didn't remember picking up any bad vibes or any-thing. "Isn't he the computer geek?"

"That's right. A gamer. His new job in Richmond didn't work out, so he came back here to finish work-ing for the summer," Wes said.

"How long was he gone?"

"I'm not sure. A week?"

"Doesn't seem like enough time for him to judge if a job is going to work out," Nathaniel said.

"I don't know. He said it wasn't anything like they'd advertised."

Brynn mulled that over. Even though her brain was still fuzzy and thoughts weren't forming as quickly as she'd have liked, her guts said Chelsea was involved in all this—and maybe one of these young men. As soon as she was out of this place, she'd start making more inquiries.

"Do you mind writing down the names of those young men for me?" She pulled over the tablet she and Schuyler had listed names on.

"Sure," Wes said, glancing over the list. "Uh, Brynn. These guys are already on your list. Except for Roy."

Brynn's heart skipped a few beats. She was on to something here. Something that might help Wes out.

Chapter 21

Brynn's mind raced as she lay in bed. It was 2:00 AM, and the nurse had awakened her to give her medicine. Now she found getting back to sleep difficult. Her mind was clearing and disappointment swam through her. Her first cheese contest had been ruined by someone shooting Wes. Wes was being investigated. The awful woman stopping by their booth. Mike's face flashed in her mind. He'd helped. He was a lawman, even though he wasn't a police officer. He was a fire marshal. Could he find out why they were looking so closely at Wes?

She reached for her tablet and jotted down his name so she'd not forget to call him in the morning. She smiled remembering the first time she met his sister, Schuyler, and the way those two picked on each other. Brynn had been lucky to meet the best of the best in Shenandoah Springs. Evidently there was a bad element here that she had only an inkling about from her investigating the fire that took Nancy's life.

She supposed she and her ex-fiancé may have had unrealistic notions about the bucolic Shenandoah

Valley when they had first visited. There were problems and crime here, like everywhere.

Her eyelids felt heavy as the medicine started to take effect. The next thing she knew, she was being awakened again by another nurse with more medicines. An uneasy pattern that had become Brynn's life.

The doctor was examining Brynn when Becky entered the room.

"Hey," she said to Brynn, then to the doctor. "I'm her sister, Becky."

"Good to meet you," he said. "Are you local?"

"I live in Richmond. Just got in to check on her."

He frowned. "I'd like to release her. But she needs to be watched for a little while longer. She's still getting dizzy and we don't want her falling on the way to the bathroom or something."

"I'm going to be here a few days," Becky said. "My daughter is at camp. We can get some of Brynn's friends to stay with her. Plus there's Wes."

"I'm sure I'll be fine," Brynn said. "There will be a lot of folks checking on me." And it dawned on her that she had made a life for herself, despite what her ex-fiancé had predicted. She had friends, a pretty decent farm and business, and much to be grateful for. She didn't want to stay in this hospital room any longer than necessary.

"Okay," the doctor said. "Let's give it a go. I want to see you back next week."

It wasn't as easy as Brynn had thought. The car ride home made her sick and she got dizzy walking into her house. But when she sat down on her couch, a wave of relief came over her. It was as if each muscle unraveled. She lay back and kicked her feet up.

"Let me get you a pillow," Becky said. She came back a minute later and Brynn was almost asleep.

"She doesn't need to be bothered with this," Becky said.

"I think she'd want to know," another voice said. "I mean, she asked me to check into this."

"Well, she's sleeping right now," Becky said.

Brynn lifted her heavy eyelids. "I'm awake."

"Hey there," Willow said.

Becky crossed her arms. "I told her you weren't to be bothered."

"It's okay," Brynn said. "What did you find out?"

"I found out the name of the carnival guy. And get this, he's got a record a mile long. His name is Ian Fellows."

Becky sat down. "How do you know about his record?"

"Well, Mike looked him up for us."

"I meant to call Mike, and I forgot . . ." Brynn said.

"Ian Fellows is an ex-con, in prison for attempted murder."

Brynn's heart nearly leaped out of her chest. She sat forward.

"How long has he been in the area?" Becky asked.

"Well, we don't know that. But what we do know is he's been here at least a few days before the fair opened because he was helping set up the rides, right?"

Brynn's head spun as she tried to remember the day Wes found the body of Donny Iser.

"That puts him here when the murder happened," Willow said, her brown eyes as wide as saucers.

"Do the police know about this?" Becky asked.

"They do now," Willow said. "I talked to Mike, like I said, and he's going to tell them all this. Maybe it will get them off Wes's back."

"This is the best news I've heard in days," Brynn said.

"How are you today?" Willow said.

"I'm glad to be home. But I'm still not so hot. I need to get out to the barn and check on the girls. I'm worried about the new cow. We need to fatten her up."

"Are you hungry?" Becky asked. "I made some chicken soup."

The words "chicken soup" conjured images of steaming soup with chunks of vegetables and noodles, prompting her stomach to growl. "Sounds so good," Brynn said.

"Would you like to join us?" Becky asked Willow.

"I'd love to, but I can't. I told Wes I'd help with the cheese shed today. The owners are coming to get it and we need to make sure it's clean."

Brynn's heart sank. That was her job. She should be helping.

Just then, Willow's phone rang. "Sorry, I need to get this." She answered the phone. "What? Are you serious? That's the most ridiculous—"

She hung up the phone and took a deep breath. "Wes isn't going to need me. It's been taken care of. And he's now in police custody."

"What do you mean?" Becky said. "Has he been arrested?"

"Yes, for the murder of Donny Iser."

Chapter 22

Brynn's heart raced as she attempted to stand, got dizzy, and fell back onto the couch.

"Whoa," Becky said, racing up to her, along with Willow.

"I need to get over there," Brynn said.

"Where? The station? I don't think so," Becky said. "You're going to sit on the couch."

"Don't tell me what to do!"

"I'll go," Willow said. "I'll go and report back to you."

Tears stung Brynn's eyes. *They arrested Wes! He didn't do it!* She couldn't even help him because she couldn't move around without getting dizzy!

"Brynn, don't cry," Becky said, sitting down next to her with her arm wrapped around her. "If you cry, your head's going to hurt worse. Take some deep breaths."

Willow crouched down in front of her. "Look, I'm going to head over there and I'll let you know something as soon as I can. His dad is there and his lawyer. There's nothing you can do but stay here and take care of yourself." Willow's deep brown eyes were serious. She patted Brynn's shoulder.

Brynn swallowed back a sob. She couldn't picture sweet, kind, hardworking Wes in jail! *What a mess!* She nodded. "Please. Yes. Please let me know something as soon as you do. This . . . is a nightmare."

"They can't hold him without evidence," Becky said. "I'm sure they'll be letting him go soon."

Brynn's worry lessened—a bit. "That's true. But innocent people go to jail every day."

"You've been watching too much true-crime TV," Willow said, standing. "Don't think about that stuff. This is Shenandoah Springs. We don't keep innocent people in jail."

Brynn wanted to believe that.

Becky didn't say a word, though Brynn knew she wanted to. So far, Becky wasn't thrilled with the place Brynn had chosen to live and farm. She was concerned about odd events after the church fire, and now this. Brynn was touched by her concern, but she loved it here.

"Okay," Brynn said to Willow. "Please keep me in the loop."

"I will. Believe me," Willow said, and left.

Brynn and Becky sat on the couch for a few moments in silence. Becky's eyes were as wide as the moon. Brynn's temples pounded. She lay back on the couch and closed her eyes.

"I can't believe it," she said. "He's one of the nicest people."

"Thank goodness he has a lawyer. I don't care what Willow says. This place ain't all that great. Look at what happened with Nancy. And they were targeting you next."

What her sister said was all true, but the police helped, and they did have to go by the book—even in Shenandoah Springs.

"That's all over," Brynn said. "I'd rather not think about it. I've got enough on my plate right now."

"Yeah," Becky said. "Perhaps too much. Why don't you sell the place and come back to Richmond? I miss you so much and Lily would love to have you closer. And then there's Mom and Dad."

Why didn't Becky understand? This life was her dream. Her micro-dairy farm and cheesemaking company. She'd worked hard for this.

"I'm not leaving," Brynn said. "Any place has good things and bad things about it. I love the CSA. I've made good friends. I love my cows. I'm not going anywhere."

Becky sighed. "From my standpoint there's been nothing for you but trouble."

Brynn could see that. "Yes, but my business is growing. I'm making more sales. All of this other stuff? Happenstance. A blip."

"I'd not call your assistant in jail for murder a blip, Brynn. I'm sorry. That's serious."

Brynn's heart sank. It was. She knew that, but she wanted to remain hopeful. "I know," she snapped. "But I know he didn't kill anybody and I'm going to help prove it."

"How? You're recovering from a concussion."

"I already have a list of suspects. I'm not allowed to look at the screen, but you are. Let's do some research."

"Brynn—"

"Come on. It will be fun—and useful. We won't be able to find out everything from the internet, but it will be a start. I've done a little research already and found out the man who shot Wes also had been seeing Chelsea. It all revolves around her, it seems."

"Who? The sixteen-year-old girl? Come on, Brynn.

You've really taken a hit to the head." She paused. "Let me get your soup." She stood.

"I'm not eating it," Brynn said. "Not hungry."

"You've got to eat, whether you're hungry or not."

"No, I don't."

"Okay, I'll research for you after you eat. Eat first and rest. Give me your list and I'll take care of it."

Brynn smiled. "We've got a deal."

As Brynn ate her chicken noodle soup and watched her sister at her laptop, she decided she had the better end of the deal. The soup was incredibly delicious, salty enough with small chunks of veggies, noodles, and chicken. Her sister was sighing and moaning and groaning over the computer.

Her cell phone interrupted Brynn's eating. It was Willow.

"Yes?" Brynn said.

"Okay, here's what I've been able to find out from Mike. They are not telling anybody anything. But Mike said the gun that was used was registered to Wes."

Brynn's stomach clenched. Wes bought a gun? If she'd known that, she wasn't sure how she'd like him living on her property. But then again, several people had told her she should own one living in the country. Perhaps that's why he'd purchased it.

"I didn't know he has a gun."

"He doesn't. Wes claims he never bought it, but all the evidence says he did."

Brynn shifted from shock to anger in a split second. "Someone is setting him up."

Becky looked up from her screen.

"My thoughts exactly," Willow said.

"I agree that's what it looks like," Becky said, looking up from her laptop. "There may be a lot going on that we don't know about. We're not privy to all the information that the police have gathered on the case."

"True," Brynn said. "But Wes isn't a liar. If he'd purchased the gun, he'd say so." She tried to will away the headache creeping into her temples.

"Wes is twenty years old. There may be a lot we don't know about him, but one thing I know is that when I was twenty I was keeping a lot of secrets from everybody. I didn't consider it lying. I considered it my private life. It was nobody's business."

Brynn pondered all of that. She pulled the blankets in closer around her as a wave of weariness came over her. She closed her eyes. Was Wes keeping secrets? Did he purchase a gun, knowing how Brynn felt about guns? They discussed it several times when Brynn was being harassed. The sheriff suggested she buy a gun. She couldn't do it.

Things were a bit different in the country, she knew, and most people had guns, especially farmers with animals. You never knew when you'd have problems with wild animals. Brynn shuddered to imagine it. This was one reason she didn't keep chickens, even though she'd love fresh eggs in the morning.

"Did you find out anything?" Brynn asked.

"Not much more than we already know. Rad, the young man who is now in jail for shooting Wes, has a record. Mostly drugs. Could he be behind this?"

"Why not? Someone is."

"In that case, he's already in jail."

"But what if it's not him? What about the other guy—the guy who's already been to prison? Ian Fellows?"

"I've not found anything online about him, except his Facebook page, and it seems like he's been working hard to stay out of prison. He's posted about trying to find better work, about his kids from a previous wife, and so on. I know this stuff can be fabricated, but it looks as if he's trying to stay clean," Becky said.

Brynn hated to make assumptions. People could change—but it was hard for people who'd gotten out of jail to start again, sometimes through no fault of their own.

"I don't know. Is it a coincidence he's seeing Chelsea? A guy who was in prison for attempted murder? And one of her boyfriends is killed?"

"I'm certain the police are looking into him. Don't you think?"

"I hope so. I'll mention it to Nathaniel. He can check with Wes's lawyer," Brynn said. Her headache was getting worse. "It must be time for more medicine."

"It is," Becky said. "Do you need some water?"

"No, I have plenty." Brynn eyed the coffee table, full of medicine, water, spent plates, and bowls. It looked as though she'd been sick for weeks. She knew Becky would clean up as soon as she was done researching.

Brynn popped a few pills in and swallowed. "Did you find anything else?"

"Let me ask you a few questions. Was she dating the guy who was killed in the tractor accident?" Becky asked.

"Yes."

"And she was dating the guy who was shot?"

"Yes."

"And at one point she dated Rad?"

"Yes."

"And now she's dating the carnie?"

"Yes, I think so. I mean, I don't really know her. Even Wes doesn't know her. Perhaps the carnie was a onetime date." Brynn shrugged. Woozy, she lay back into her pillow.

"Do you know anybody who might know her better?"

Brynn's brain fogged. Was it the medicine? Had she been trying too hard? "I need to think about that."

"You look tired."

"Yeah, all of a sudden. I think I'm going to take a nap."

Becky smiled. "I think you are, too."

When Brynn awakened, the clutter had been cleared away and Becky was nowhere to be found. She stood up because she wanted to use the bathroom and prepared herself for the onslaught of dizziness. But it didn't happen. Not this time.

When she came out of the bathroom, Becky was standing there with her hands on her hips. "What are you doing up?"

"I needed to use the bathroom. It's okay. I didn't get dizzy at all."

"Well, good. Do you need help to get back to the couch?"

"I'm good."

"How about more soup?"

"That would be good," Brynn said as she made her way back to the couch.

Becky brought her soup to her. "You look better. Not as pale."

"I feel better," Brynn said. "In fact, I'd like to go and see my girls."

"Tillie's coming over to take care of the night milking. Maybe it would be best for you to wait one more day."

Brynn missed them, even Jewel, who she'd barely gotten to know. People said all sorts of bad things about cows, but Brynn knew they were as attached to her as she was to them.

"This soup is perfect," Brynn said, taking another spoonful.

Becky smiled. "Well, I do make a mean chicken noodle soup."

"Did you say Tillie was coming over?" Brynn took another bite.

"Yep."

"Good. I want to talk to her. She goes to school with Chelsea. She must know more about her than anybody."

"Good idea!" Becky said. "I'll try to nab her before she leaves. Oh look. I forgot to tell you. Mike Rafferty sent you get-well flowers."

"What? Oh, how sweet of him," Brynn said as Becky brought the flowers to her. It was a simple arrangement of daisies and petunias. *So sweet.* "He's such a nice guy."

"Come on, Brynn. It's more than that. Men don't send flowers unless they like you."

"Nah," Brynn said. "I don't think so. He's Schuyler's brother. She probably put him up to it. Besides, he was there right after Wes got shot. Plus he happened to be at the fair when that woman caused a scene. He's probably concerned since he was a witness to most of it."

Becky rolled her eyes. "Okay. Whatever you say."

Chapter 23

Brynn's eyes grew heavy, but she was also trying to stay awake so that she could talk with Tillie. With the fair in full force, Brynn knew she didn't have a lot of time. Nobody did.

The door creaked open and Tillie walked into the room.

"How are you feeling?"

"I've been better. How are the girls?"

"I'm sure they miss you. Especially Jewel. She's still not acclimated."

Brynn felt a surge of longing for the little Highland cow. *Poor thing. She's lost the only person she'd ever known and, until that point, had been living a secluded life in the mountains, having no cow friends.* Brynn thought she might try to sneak out and see Jewel and her other cows tomorrow.

"Do you have a moment?" Brynn asked.

"Not a long one, unfortunately," Tillie said. "What's up?" She plopped onto a chair.

Becky walked into the room. "Can I get you anything, Tillie?"

"Nah, I'm good, thanks," she said. "What's up, Brynn?"

"I wonder how well you know Chelsea?"

"She's a couple of years younger than me, but I do know her."

"This is going to sound strange, but . . . I think she may have something to do with all of this madness . . . the murder . . . Wes being accused."

"What do you mean? Like her setting him up? That kind of thing?" Tillie asked.

"I'm not sure. But something." Brynn watched as Tillie looked away, then she checked her phone.

"I don't like talking bad about people—"

"I know she's got a lot of boyfriends," Brynn said.

"That's not what I mean."

"What do you mean?"

"She's not smart enough. I can't see her planning anything at all. She was held back twice. She's got a learning disability or something. I don't know what. She's beautiful and all the boys like her, but not because she's smart. Do you know what I mean?"

Chelsea's character became a little more sympathetic to Brynn. Not smart. Learning disability. And so troubled like that at the age of sixteen, she slept around. Frequently.

"I had no idea," Brynn said.

"Yeah. Why would you?" Tillie said. "I only know because we go to the same school." She paused. "But if you can think of anything to help Wes out, I'm here. Just let me know."

Brynn explained her theory about Chelsea and her boyfriends.

"As I said, I don't see Chelsea doing that, but possibly one of her boyfriends," Tillie said. "I'm sorry. I've got to go. I need to help out at the fair tonight.

Mom and Dad signed me up to help at the CSA booth."

"Have fun," Brynn said, and smiled.

"Right," Tillie said, and laughed.

The next day, Brynn awakened at her usual time, 5:00 AM. The room was still dark with a hint of light, and she took a moment and felt a wave of gratitude. She was going to be okay. Wes could have been killed, and he wasn't. They had survived an attack at the cheese shed. Much to be grateful for.

But he was in jail for a murder he didn't commit. Something needed to be done.

She mulled over what she learned from Tillie and almost ruled Chelsea out. But just because a person isn't bright in school didn't mean they couldn't be a brilliant, devious thief or murderer.

She untangled herself from her covers as the sound of a car in the driveway prompted her—it was Schuyler or Willow to see to the cows. She wasn't sure which one of them had the duty today. She felt like such a slug.

She slowly stood and walked to her bedroom door, opened it to the scent of coffee. Becky must be messing about in the kitchen. Brynn descended the stairs and was happy that she didn't get dizzy. Not once.

Maybe she could visit her cows.

She breathed in the scent of coffee. It sent pings through her—just the scent alerted her senses.

"Brynn, you're awake," Becky said as Brynn entered the kitchen. "You should have let me help you downstairs,"

"I did okay," Brynn said. "I didn't get dizzy once. I think I'm all better."

Becky shot Brynn a look of incredulity. "Just because you are able to get downstairs doesn't mean you're all better."

Brynn knew that. "Let me celebrate my small success with a huge mug of coffee, please!"

Becky smiled. "Sit down. I'll get it for you."

"So what did you find out from Tillie last night?" Becky asked as she poured coffee.

"Not much, really. Just that Chelsea may have a learning disability or something. She's been held back twice in school."

Becky put the cup of steaming coffee in front of Brynn. "So she's not the criminal mastermind you thought she could be."

"No, but that doesn't mean none of her boyfriends are." Brynn held the coffee in her hands and let the warmth of it travel through her.

"I've been thinking," Becky said.

"Uh-oh."

She waved her sister off. "What if this has nothing to do with her at all, but everything to do with Wes?"

Brynn set her cup on the table. "What do you mean?"

"Of course I don't mean that he actually killed someone. But perhaps someone has it in for him and is setting him up."

"But why?"

"Brynn, I know it's difficult to believe there're racists in the world. But there are. What I'm saying is someone wants to get rid of Wes."

"By killing someone else? That doesn't make sense."

"No," Becky said. "That's not exactly what I mean. They may not have killed the person to set Wes up, but since they already did it . . ."

"They tried to frame him." Brynn had already thought of that. But didn't give it too much weight. Seemed like a lot of trouble for someone to go to. But then again, you couldn't get in more trouble than killing a person in cold blood. Brynn tried to clear her mind.

"I'm going to take a walk outside to visit with the girls," Brynn said.

"I'll come with you," Becky said.

"Fine, but I swear I'm better."

"You don't want my company?"

"Stop. Of course I do."

"Let's go, then."

The two sisters walked out into the morning air—it was already hot and humid at 6:00 AM. Willow walked around the corner and saw them. "Good morning," she said. "You're looking great." She cocked an eyebrow. Both women were still in their pajamas.

"Nothing but cows out here this morning, right?" Becky said.

"Everything is done," Willow said. "You don't need to worry about anything."

"I miss the girls," Brynn said, walking toward the field. "I thought the fresh air might do me good. I had no idea it was so hot already this morning."

"Yes, temperatures have been setting records. Attendance at the fair has sucked because of the heat. I'd say we need a good storm to cool things off, but so many times it makes it worse."

"We could use the rain," Brynn said. The grass was brown and crunchy. She wouldn't water the lawn, considering it a waste of good water.

They walked through the gate and into the field.

Petunia, Marigold, and Buttercup sauntered over to her. Jewel started to come but spotted the other cows and stopped. The dog circled Brynn's legs. She oohed and ahhed over her girls—scratching them in their preferred spots: Petunia, behind the ears, Buttercup, under the chin, and Marigold, on the nose.

"My sweet girls," she said.

The little Highland cow lifted her head and looked toward the party. Brynn walked over to her and her tail swayed. "Hello, girl. How are you doing?"

The cow blinked her big cow eyes, mooed, and nuzzled Brynn. Her heart nearly broke from the gesture. Jewel had missed her, too.

It had only been a few days, but it was clear she'd been missed by her animals. She petted the furry cow and drew in a breath. The heat was obnoxious.

"How are you?" Becky said. "We should go back inside."

"Yeah, you should. It's too hot out here for anybody, let alone a person with a concussion," Willow said. "I've got to get going. The craft hall had problems last night, and I told them I'd help with repairs this morning."

"Thanks for helping out," Brynn said. "I can't tell you how much I appreciate it." The three of them walked toward the gate and opened it, then walked through it toward the car and the house.

"Is Wes still in jail?" Willow asked.

"I think so. The last thing I heard was from you yesterday. I've not even seen Nathaniel." They glanced in the direction of the guest house where Was lived and Nathaniel was staying. His car was there. Brynn didn't recall hearing it last night, so she had no idea when he'd gotten in. "He must be livid with the local police and investigation."

"And scared," Becky said. "I know if it was Lily, I'd be so afraid for her."

"Me too," Brynn said. "Surely they will let Wes out on bail or something."

"I don't know how any of that world works," Willow said as she opened her car door. She stopped, turned around, and hugged Brynn. "Take care of yourself today. Try not to overdo it."

"Have you met my sister, Becky? She's the queen of concussion care." Brynn smiled and Becky laughed.

"Whatever," Becky said.

Becky and Brynn stopped and waved as Willow drove off.

"Let's go back inside," Becky said. "Where it's nice and cool."

"Good idea." Brynn hadn't quite gotten her fill of the cows, but it was better than nothing and she had to admit to a sense of weakness—but only to herself. It was strange how one conk on the head set you back. With memory. With energy. With thinking.

Becky and Brynn headed for the house and into the kitchen.

"I made a little something light for breakfast this morning," Becky said. "It won't be too much on your stomach." She opened the fridge and pulled out two bowls. Brynn peered inside as she placed them on the table.

A big, plump deep purple blackberry sat on the top of creamy yogurt. "Looks delicious," Brynn said, and took a bite, with the berry bobbling around in her mouth before she bit into it, releasing the sweet juice. "Gosh, that's good," she said after she chewed and swallowed. "Did you add vanilla or something in there, too?"

"Yes. Glad you like it. There's some dry oatmeal

and nuts sort of down toward the bottom, too. Not much. I worried about your stomach."

Brynn tucked back into her yogurt. "You're so good to me."

"You're the only sister I got." Becky smiled. "I talked with our brother last night. He said he hopes you feel better soon."

"Is he still talking about giving us a cruise on his ship?"

"Yes. Maybe next Christmas. All of us."

Brynn's spirits lifted imagining their whole family on a cruise for Christmas. It would be odd without snow, but that was never a guarantee, especially in Virginia. Last Christmas was her first Christmas alone—after her breakup with her fiancé. Becky surprised her by coming for a visit.

Her brain started to fog up again. She supposed it would be this way for a few days—a few moments of clarity, and then fogginess.

She sighed a heavy sigh of frustration.

"What's wrong?"

"I'm getting a bit frustrated with my head," Brynn replied, and smiled.

"Oh, that. I've been frustrated with your head for years," Becky said, and laughed.

Sisters, ya gotta love them.

Chapter 24

After her active morning, Brynn took a nap in her room. She was awakened by voices downstairs and rose from her bed to see who was with Becky.

As she entered the living room, she was surprised to find Nathaniel and Max, Wes's brother.

"Max?"

He stood and came over to her, hugged her. "How are you, Brynn?" She'd gotten close to the whole family when they were here because of Nancy's death.

"I'm getting there," she said. "Thought you were working as an intern in New York?"

"Yes, but with all that's happening here, I took a few days off." There was an awkward pause.

"Well, let's sit down," Brynn said, noting that her sister had already gotten them drinks and snacks. "Have you seen Wes?"

"No. But Dad has."

All eyes shifted to Nathaniel.

"Yeah, he's doing well, considering he's in jail."

"We're working on bail," Max said.

Nathaniel cleared his throat. His eyes were

rimmed in red and the surrounding lines were pronounced. "They'll let him out on bail, according to his lawyer," Nathaniel said. "I'm waiting to hear from my bank."

"Well, at least he can come home," Brynn said. She suddenly remembered the business about the gun. "I've heard that they say he owns the gun used to kill Donny."

"My brother has never bought a gun," Max said.

"Yes, that's ludicrous," Nathaniel said. "Evidently someone used his name. The gun was purchased at one of those gun fairs. They have lax security."

He took a drink of his iced tea. "The question is who used his name and identification."

"Well, if they know where the gun was purchased that's a good start. Don't they have security tape they can look over?" Becky asked. "Please have more." She slid a plate of cheese and crackers toward Max.

"I don't think those gun shows do that. I mean, they travel around the country from town to town, holding shop in huge convention centers. I don't know how feasible it would be to have security cameras," Nathaniel said.

"But it's definitely something we need to check into," Max said.

Nathaniel's jaw tightened. "We will. But you'd think the cops would be looking into all of this."

"Maybe they are," Brynn said.

Max shoved more cheese into his mouth.

"Do you like the cheese? It's something your brother has been working on. I think he found his thing."

"I love it," Max said.

The doorbell interrupted Brynn's next thought.

"I'll get it," Becky said.

When she came back into the room, a few more people were with her, with bags of food in their hands. Tom Andrews and his wife, Elsie, along with Miriam O'Reilly, entered the room. "We brought you food to help get you through the week," she said.

"Sorry we've not gotten here sooner, but the fair has been taking up a lot of our time," Elsie said.

"Oh my goodness!" Brynn stood. "Thank you so much."

Becky stood and helped carry the food into the kitchen.

"How are you, dear?" Elsie asked.

"I'm getting a little stronger every day."

"What an awful thing to happen," Miriam said. "I'm so sorry." Miriam was Tillie's mother.

"Yeah, I'm disappointed about the cheese contest and I'm worried about Wes. He's still in jail for a crime he didn't commit."

"Of course he didn't," Miriam said, opening the fridge and sliding in several casseroles. "I'm not sure how much of an appetite you have, but if you want to eat, we've got you covered."

"Thank you so much."

The members of the CSA had her back. She warmed at the thought of her group.

"If he didn't then who did?" Tom asked as he stepped into the kitchen. "It seems to me that's the question."

"I've got some theories," Brynn said.

"What kind of theories?"

Brynn wasn't sure she should mention Chelsea. "I'd like to mull it over a bit more before I share, Tom. Let's say there's a common denominator in all of this. But I know enough about life to realize things aren't always as they seem. I don't want to get into details."

"I hear you," he said. "But we're all pretty much imagining the same thing, I bet."

"Maybe," she said. "Then why do the police have Wes?"

"They're doing their jobs," Miriam said. "He'll be home before you know it."

Once again, even though Brynn's head hurt and she was concerned about Wes, a warm contentment spread through her. She was building a life for herself. She had friends and community. She'd get through anything with them.

"You've got some pretty amazing friends," Becky said to Brynn later.

"Yes, the CSA and my neighbors have all been wonderful." Brynn was lying on the couch again. She was getting so bored she wanted to scream. No screen? At all. No reading. Nothing.

"Can you do me a favor and log on to our website and see if we have any orders?"

"Yeah, I can do that." She reached for the laptop.

"It would be easier from my computer. Wes has it set up, so it's a few clicks and I don't have to remember passwords."

"Oh, okay."

She followed Brynn to the area of the house she and Wes were now calling their office. "Wow, this has come a long way."

"Yeah," Brynn said, and flipped on the computer.

Becky sat down in front of it and Brynn instructed her. When she clicked on the link for the website, the computer screen froze and a message warning of a virus came across the screen.

"What?" Brynn said.

"We need to shut this down until Wes gets home to look at it," Becky said. "Do you know anything about computer viruses?"

"No! But I have a business to run. I may not be able to wait." Brynn tried to think of someone to help. But the gears of her brain were still moving slowly. "Perhaps Willow would know someone." But Willow was at the fair tonight. It wouldn't hurt to text her.

"I'll text her and see if she knows anyone who can help."

The crunch of tires on gravel prompted Brynn to look out the window. "It's the sheriff," Brynn said.

"What?" Becky said, voice lifting.

"Maybe he has Wes with him?" Brynn and Becky nearly flew to the front door and opened it.

Sheriff Edge was standing there and smiled. "Well, that's the nicest greeting I've gotten all day."

When Brynn realized he was alone, she frowned. "I thought you might have Wes with you."

"I'm sorry. He's still being held at the jail." He paused. "But he's the reason I'm here. Can I come in?"

"Certainly," Brynn said as she opened the door and led him to the kitchen. "Can we get you anything? Coffee?"

He nodded. "That would be great."

Brynn moved to the coffeemaker and Becky stopped her. "Sit down. I'll take care of it."

Brynn sat down at the table.

"How are you feeling?" the sheriff asked.

"Weird," she replied after considering it for a few moments.

He cracked a smile. "Concussions are definitely like that. I had one a few years ago and when I thought I was okay I'd have a setback. It was frustrating."

"Exactly!"

Becky set a cup of coffee in front of the sheriff. "How do you take it?"

"Black is fine," he said. "Thank you."

She sat down at the other end of the table.

"What can I do for you, Sheriff?" Brynn asked.

"I have a few questions for you," the sheriff said.

"Okay. I'm always happy to help. You know that."

"You know Wes well, correct?"

She nodded. "Of course. I can't say enough good things about him and his family."

"His dad has a bit of a temper."

She was surprised to hear that. "Well, I'd be upset if my kid were in jail for a murder he didn't commit. I guess he can be forgiven that."

He motioned as if he were going to speak but didn't. He sipped his coffee. "Why do you think he purchased a gun?"

"I can't imagine him purchasing a gun, unless it was because of the strange incidents after his grandmother died. Remember, you suggested we get a gun. And I said no. But possibly he overheard that. I simply don't know."

"Did he mention a gun to you at all?"

"No," she said. "His dad and I talked about this. He doesn't think Wes would buy a gun. And I have to say it's hard to imagine."

"He did. He purchased a pistol, and it was the same one that killed Donny."

A wave of panic tore through her, followed by anger. "Someone else must have taken it and used it." Her voice quivered.

Becky reached out and touched Brynn's hand, a calming gesture. "Is there any other evidence to support his arrest?"

Thank goodness for Becky. Brynn's foggy brain worsened by the minute.

"No, but that's strong enough, along with finding the body. This happens a lot, I'm sorry to say. People who kill often stage it so they call the police and get attention; they try to say they didn't do it."

Brynn dizzied. "Sheriff, Wes and his family are some of the best people I know. Wes is a gentle soul and wouldn't hurt anybody, let alone kill them."

"For the record, Brynn, I agree with you. But I have a job to do and that job is collecting evidence. It's methodical. It's painful, sometimes. But I have to follow the evidence. Do you understand?"

"Of course," she said. "But something's not right here. The evidence is all wrong."

He drank his coffee. "Until we can find facts to support that, then I'm sorry, I have to go with the evidence."

What was he saying? Wasn't he going to let Wes out of jail on bail?

"Of course," Becky said. "But let's work a little harder to dig beneath. Just a quick scan on my computer told me a lot about the victim. He had been dating Chelsea. And so was the young man who shot Wes. There was even a blog post written by the shooter about foreigners."

"You didn't tell me that," Brynn said.

"What are you suggesting, that a sixteen-year-old girl is setting Wes up?" His eyes flared with incredulity.

"Look," Becky said. "I don't know her. I couldn't care less about her reputation. She dates a lot. She dates older guys, younger guys, whatever. But all I'm saying is don't discount it. Sixteen-year-old girls are often smarter than old guys give them credit for."

His eyebrows shot up.

"Not that you're old. But you know what I mean."

There was an awkward pause.

"Not only that," Becky continued, "but you've got young men involved with all those hormones and all that ego. One man is an ex-con. I'm sure you know that. Attempted murder. And you're looking at a young cheesemaker?"

Brynn was astonished by her sister's rant. But she was inwardly jumping for joy.

"Ex-con? Who are you talking about?" He pulled out his notebook and started flipping through pages.

"Ian Fellows. He works at the carnival."

He wrote the name down. "I don't know anything about him. But it doesn't change the evidence. Does it?"

Brynn recalled her conversation with Nathaniel. "Were there any security tapes at the gun show?"

"None."

"Of course not," Becky said with a wry note.

A knock at Brynn's front door interrupted the conversation.

Becky stood, leaving Brynn and Sheriff Edge at the table. Brynn was getting tired and her head was aching. She wanted the sheriff to leave. It seemed as if they had come to an impasse.

Brynn didn't know what he was still doing sitting at her table, other than he wanted to finish his coffee.

Becky brought Max and Nathaniel into the kitchen. Every muscle in Brynn's neck tightened. Nathaniel stepped forward, with something in his hand. "Sheriff," he said.

"Mr. Scors."

"I've been trying to get a handle on some of Wes's bills. I don't want him to fall behind while he's in jail. I found this online statement." He placed it on the table. "It looks like Wes purchased the gun with this credit card."

The room chilled and silenced.

"What?" Brynn finally said. "I can't imagine!"

"Wait for it," Max said.

"But this card was also used yesterday while he was already in jail." Nathaniel pointed to another entry. "Because it's online, it's up-to-date minute by minute."

The sheriff's mouth dropped.

"We need to find out who has Wes's card," Becky said.

"He probably doesn't even know it's gone," Nathaniel said. "He doesn't use it often."

Brynn's heart raced. "Please sit down."

"Thank you, but I'm headed to the jail to see if I can visit with him and find out more about this credit card. I also need to call the company and cancel it. Whoever this person is, they are having a great time charging more guns, beer, well, you get the picture."

"Hang on," Sheriff Edge said. "I'll put out a bulletin about the card. So the next time he or she uses it, the police will be alerted. Don't cancel it yet."

"Can you let him out of jail now?" Brynn asked.

"Maybe," the sheriff said. "Let's keep working on it. Given some of the local incidents, he may be safer in jail, sorry to say."

Brynn's heart sank. She didn't want Nathaniel to know about those things, but now he was leaning forward and the sheriff was telling him everything. She listened as he described the shooting, Helen's display of ignorance, and the French fry guy.

Nathaniel's face reddened with anger. "I'll be

here," he said. "Don't worry about the safety of my boy. I'd like to take him home to Boston." He shot Brynn a look of concern. "He loves it here, I know. But I'm beginning to wonder if it's safe for him."

Brynn opened her mouth to protest, then thought better of it. Nathaniel was Wes's dad. She had no say in this decision. But she hoped he'd change his mind.

"Well, I best be going," the sheriff said. "Would you like a ride to the courthouse?"

"No, I have my rental. We'll be there soon," Nathaniel said.

Max sat down at the table, with a shell-shocked expression, as the sheriff left.

"I can't believe they didn't check into the credit card and things like that," Becky said after a few minutes.

"Right?" Max said.

"The level of ineptitude is dangerous," Nathaniel said.

"They don't have a lot of resources," Brynn replied. "It's not like a big-city police department."

"No excuses," Nathaniel snapped. "My son is in jail. It took one quick look at his credit card for me to see someone else is using it."

Max looked away in embarrassment.

"They're not trying to prove his innocence," Brynn said. "They are trying to prove his guilt. It's up to his lawyer to put a case together in his defense. That said, whatever you need, I'm here. We've done a little research earlier. We've yet to talk about it all. But Becky found out some stuff, too. The sheriff didn't know this, but he does now. There is an ex-con working at the fair and dating Chelsea. So he's going to look into it."

"Another thing the sheriff didn't know?" Nathaniel's arms flailed out. "What the hell?"

Brynn wondered the same thing.

She was trying to keep calm, but it did appear as if the police hadn't done a great job. Law enforcement were up against a lot in this rural area, with a lot of ground to cover and not a huge staff. But still.

"I wish I could help more," she said.

"You need to get better," Becky said.

"Yes, of course," Nathaniel said, and sat down. Sometimes an expression came over his face that reminded Brynn of Nancy. A winsome guise. "I'm sorry. I'm so worried." He paused. "How are you feeling?"

"I'm not sure. Sometimes I feel strong, but the next minute I don't." Like right now. She wanted to climb into her bed and sleep for days, wake up to a painless head and a solid stomach. "Good work on the credit card bill. Nobody who knows Wes would imagine he bought a gun, let alone that he'd hurt someone with it."

He nodded. "I was shocked and disappointed, until I saw the charge yesterday."

"Where was it from?" Becky asked.

"The fair. The person purchased a meal, then a quilt."

"A quilt?"

"I know, right?" Max said. "I guess killers need to stay warm, too?"

Brynn's mind spun. Was Willow working in the craft building yesterday? She couldn't remember. She must have been. Tillie tended the cows last night. Willow must have been working at the fair.

She reached for her phone and texted Willow: "Were you working in crafts yesterday?"

A text message came back: "No. I was working at the CSA booth, remember? Why?"

"We think the killer purchased a quilt."

"WHAT?"

"Sorry. Long story. Will fill you in later."

"Okay. Will you be able to make it to the show?"

"Is it tonight?"

"Yes."

Brynn needed a nap if she was going to try to get to Tillie's concert. How could she miss it?

"I'll try."

"Who are you texting?" Becky asked.

"I thought Willow was working in the craft building yesterday. She wasn't. But she reminded me about Tillie's concert tonight. I want to go."

"That's not a good idea. It's going to be loud, with a lot of people," Becky said.

"Your sister is right. That's no place for someone with a concussion," Nathaniel said.

"I'm going to take a nap," Brynn said, and stood. "I want to go to the concert. I'd appreciate some help when I go. If not, I'll go myself."

Becky, Nathaniel, and Max watched as Brynn walked upstairs to her room. She'd had absolutely enough of staying in this house. She knew she had to take it slow. But, for God's sake, what could happen to her at a concert?

Chapter 25

Brynn awakened from her nap with no headache. She was getting better and excited about Tillie's concert.

"I still don't think this is a good idea," Becky said as she drove Brynn, Nathaniel, and Max to the fairground.

"Me either," Max said. "But you know Brynn. Once she gets an idea, there's no stopping her."

Brynn smiled to herself. True. But she felt better, and she wanted to support Tillie. And she had to admit, she hated the frustration of having to stay at home. She didn't want to miss Tillie's concert because she was a wonderful singer. That's all there was to it. But a pang of guilt swam through her because Wes couldn't be there. Tillie and Wes were good friends.

But Brynn was certain with the latest turn of events he'd be released tomorrow, if not tonight. Surely the person using his credit card would be caught soon— and arrested for the murder. Things were looking up.

As they pulled into the parking lot, the view of the

fair caught Brynn by surprise. In the twilight, the rides were lit and the strung lights sparkled on. The sky was a dusty blue, and the mountains loomed over it all.

As they walked to the fairground, Brynn realized they had parked near the animals. The scent of manure was pungent, so they moved along quickly toward the concert area.

The tiny stage sat at the edge of the fairground. Facing it, you were facing away from the fair. They'd gotten to the fair a bit early, so they had their choice of seats, and by the time they made their way to the concert arena Brynn was only too happy to take a seat. She was a little tired.

"Can I get you some water or something?" Becky asked.

"Yes, please."

"Wait," Max said. "I'll get us all water. You two sit still." He turned to leave and Roy came up to him and looked a bit startled.

"Max? Man, I thought you were Wes. I thought they'd let him out of jail." He looked around. "But I guess not."

"Not yet. But probably tomorrow," Max said.

They stood in silence for a few moments. "I'm off to fetch water."

"Oh. Okay. I'll tag along," he said, and as they walked away, he gave a little wave to Brynn and the others sitting there.

"Who was that?" Nathaniel asked.

"Roy. He's a friend of Wes's. Kind of. I'm not sure how good of a friend he is," Brynn replied.

Nathaniel's jaw tightened. "I think he's the young man who's the hacker. Wes told me about him."

"Hacker?" Becky said. "What do you mean, like he hacks people's computer accounts or something?"

"Yes. He'd gotten a good job in Richmond, but he was fired because they caught him doing something unethical. Wes says he's brilliant and can hack into anybody's computer. Think about that. Bank records. Credit cards. Identity. These computer guys . . . if they don't have good solid ethics, they could be ripping us off left and right."

Brynn didn't want to think about it. She was not a complete technophobe, but she didn't like the fact that most of her business was now online. It concerned her. They changed passwords all the time, at least once a week, and took several other security measures—making sure the system was up-to-date. But that was Wes's job.

"Thank goodness for Wes or I'd be lost."

"Well, I can't wait for this concert." Becky changed the subject. She was trying to keep Brynn's mind on pleasant things—she knew what her sister was up to. But Brynn was worried about Wes spending another night in jail. She was certain it was not a horrible jail to be in—it was clean and probably safe—this was Shenandoah Springs, after all. But if he was imprisoned, Brynn shuddered to imagine it.

But he wouldn't be. He was innocent. And now that they had that credit card bill to prove it, the police would have to let him go. She closed her eyes and said a little prayer to the universe.

"Water boy is here!" Max said as he arrived back at their seats, handing out water.

The cold bottle felt good in Brynn's hands. It was a hot night, the sort of evening when you felt like you were walking through a steam bath instead of night air.

The crowd was picking up, and as she looked

around she recognized several familiar faces, mostly
CSA members, including Tom and his wife, Elsie. They
smiled, nodded, or waved to her.

Brynn's gaze fell on a young woman. Smiling and
beautiful. It was Chelsea, standing at the edge of the
concert area. Behind her was Roy, whose arm slipped
casually across her shoulder.

Roy and Chelsea? That was quite a pair—the
young woman who was dating every available man in
the county and the young man who was a hacker.
Lovely.

Brynn watched as they walked away, behind the
stage area.

She stood. "I'd like to go and see Tillie for a minute."

"Now wait," Becky said, standing. "Why? What's
the point?"

"I want to wish her luck," Brynn replied. "Or to break
a leg or whatever."

Becky followed Brynn, snaking through the crowd.
When they reached backstage, Tillie was nowhere to
be found.

Neither were Roy and Chelsea.

"Tillie likes to take a walk before performances.
I'm sorry you missed her," Miriam, Tillie's mom,
said. "I'll let her know you stopped."

"Thanks," Brynn said, but seeing Tillie was just
one reason she'd come backstage. She was curious
about what Roy and Chelsea were up to. And it
looked like they were already gone. Long gone.

Soon enough, the concert started and Brynn's
mind was on nothing but the music. Tillie's voice
had a soothing effect on her. By the end of the show,
Brynn was ready for bed.

"What are you doing here?" Tillie said as Brynn approached her to tell her what a great job she'd done.

"I couldn't miss it. You were . . . amazing," Brynn said.

"Completely," Becky agreed.

"Thank you. But your head. How are you?"

"Tired. We need to go, but it was so worth it," Brynn said, and hugged her.

As Becky, Brynn, Max, and Nathaniel walked through the crowd, finding their way to the edge of it, she took in the sights of the fair as it was closing for the night. An almost empty promenade. The ride lights were off, with strings of lights and lamps from food vendors brightening their way. The scent of cotton candy filled the air.

Brynn's head pounded. Her thoughts had become muddled again. But the thought of Roy and Chelsea was lodged in her mind. She'd need to talk with Wes about them. She hoped he'd get out of jail tomorrow and the worst part of all this would be over. *Poor Wes! Shot at the cheese contest, then carted off to jail for a murder he didn't commit.*

"I can see why you didn't want to miss the concert. She's an amazing singer," Nathaniel said on the ride home.

Everybody agreed.

"I'm sure you're exhausted," Becky said. "We'll get you home and to bed. You can rest all day tomorrow."

Brynn was too tired to even speak. She watched the silhouetted trees go by as they rode along on the darkened country roads, the farmhouses lit in the distance. The mountain behind them. The sky with its bright half-moon and twinkling stars. She closed her eyes.

* * *

Brynn awakened the next day in her own bed with the sun streaming in. It took her a moment to remember getting there in her sleepy haze from the car. Her headache subsided, though it was on the edge of being a full-blown one. She supposed she need more medicine. She untangled herself from her quilt and made her way downstairs. Becky was in the kitchen, making coffee. "Good morning," she said. "Your medicine is right there."

"I need it," Brynn said. "Along with the other medicine. Coffee."

"It'll be ready soon."

Brynn looked at the calendar, realizing it was Friday. The days had blurred together. Her friends were taking care of her life and she hated that. She missed the daily visits with her cows, making cheese, and well, the rhythm of her normal life. She could at least check out the online orders for cheese today.

"What smells so good?" Brynn asked.

"Blackberry breakfast bread. I needed to use these berries before they went bad. I noticed there's more to be picked over on the far edge of your property, toward the church."

"Blackberry bread? Oh my God, it smells heavenly." But Brynn's stomach was queasy. She hoped it settled by the time the bread was ready.

Brynn sat down at the table and swallowed her pills. She looked out the window at her cows grazing. Jewel was still off by herself. Would the sweet Highland cow ever fit in with her cows? *Wait.* It really didn't matter because she was fostering her. Schuyler was looking for a home for her, wasn't she?

Becky set a cup of coffee in front of her.

"Thanks," Brynn said. "I've been watching my girls."

"It's a great window," Becky said. "I talked with Lily this morning. She sends her love."

"Is she having fun at camp?" Brynn imagined her sweet niece loving horse camp, bonding with new friends, learning new things.

"She's a bit homesick, but she'll be fine." Becky opened the oven door and checked the bread. "I think this is done." The smell filled the room. Hot blackberries, sweet bread. Cinnamon. *Heavenly.* She pulled it out and placed it on the counter. "We need to let it cool a bit."

Brynn's stomach growled. Cinnamon was good for a sick stomach, right? "I'm not sure how long I can wait."

Becky grinned.

"Is Wes home yet?"

"It's still early, Brynn. I doubt the courts have been open long."

"Right." Her brain still wasn't firing 100 percent. "It's Friday. I need to check the online orders." She started to stand.

"Sit down. I'll bring you the laptop."

"Okay." Brynn did not usually like being catered to, but she loved having her sister around—and she knew there was no arguing with her.

Becky brought the laptop over and put it on the table. Brynn opened it and booted it up.

"Hmmm. Maybe it's safe to cut the bread," Becky said more to herself than Brynn.

"Perhaps," Brynn said, and watched her laptop screen come on. "Do you mind helping me with the computer? I'm not supposed to be looking at it." She clicked on the website order program and a pop-up came on: "Pay $100,000 to enter this website."

She tried getting it off the screen. "Jesus! What's this?"

Becky rushed over and looked. "I have no idea. Just restart it. That's what they always say to do, right?"

"Yes, but this is strange."

"It is. I've never seen anything like it." Becky fussed over the bread while Brynn restarted the computer.

The same thing happened. She had no idea what to do. Wes was her IT guy. Who else could she call?

She dialed Willow.

"Hey, Brynn. How are you feeling?"

"Not so good. Something's going on with my computer." She explained what was happening.

"I can't help you. I'm sorry. If it was an art program, like an Adobe thing, I could help. But that sounds like ransom ware."

"Ransom ware? What's that?"

"It's a hacking thing. Someone might have hacked into your computer and won't let you have access until you pay the money."

Panic tore through Brynn. "Why would someone imagine I have that kind of money?"

"I have no idea. But a lot of businesses end up paying it. And now they've made it illegal to pay them. I recently read an article about that."

"So what do I do? I have orders to access and to fill."

"There's a guy in Staunton who works on computers. I'll text you his name and number."

"Thanks."

After they clicked off from the call, Becky set a

plate of sliced blackberry bread on the table, along with fresh cream cheese and butter.

"What's going on? You're as white as a ghost," Becky said.

"Someone hacked my computer and they are trying to get money from me," Brynn said. "I need to call this guy to service it."

"I've heard of that! But I've never known anybody it's happened to!" She looked over Brynn's shoulders. "One hundred thousand dollars?" Becky laughed. "That's too much. Why would they think you've got that sort of money?"

"I have no idea." She shut the computer off, closed it. Dread came over her. "I need to call this IT guy in Staunton."

"Why don't you eat first? Who wants to talk computers on an empty stomach?"

Brynn mulled it over, and between the scent of the bread, her sister's caring words, and her stomach growling she decided Becky was right. She'd eat first and then call the IT guy.

Chapter 26

Charlie, the IT expert, said he'd stop by in the afternoon. Brynn shut off the computer, took a shower, and set off to visit her girls, under the watchful eye of Becky.

Petunia and her best friend, Freckles, greeted Brynn as usual. She rubbed Petunia behind the ears and stooped down to pet the dog. "Oh, Petunia, we've been hacked."

The cow's eyes squinted pleasure as Brynn rubbed her. "Who would do such a thing?"

"She doesn't appear to be answering," Becky said.

"Right, but remember Granny Rose always told us you had to keep your cows informed." Brynn wiped away sweat from her brow.

"It's a scorcher," Becky said.

Brynn made her way through her cows and then to Jewel, who was standing all alone and grazing.

"Hello, girl," she said. The cow's ears flicked. "How are you?" Brynn theorized if her other cows saw her with Jewel enough, they'd come to accept her. Even though she wasn't keeping her, she wanted to make her as comfortable as possible.

Jewel stopped eating and looked at Brynn and Becky. She took a step toward them. Brynn moved closer to her and reached out to pet her. The cow's hair was wiry and thick.

"Your other cows are watching you," Becky said.

Brynn sidled up closer to the cow and wrapped an arm around her neck. The gesture seemed to calm Jewel, as she laid her head on Brynn's shoulder.

"Oh my goodness," Becky said. "She's so sweet. I've never seen anything like it."

Brynn's heart broke for the sweetness of the cow snuggling up to her. Jewel's previous owner must have done this very thing. Jewel probably missed her with all of her little cow heart. Brynn started to move away and the cow snuggled even more. She was not ready for Brynn to leave.

"I'm going to have to go sometime, sweetie. But I'll be back." She pulled away and held Jewel's face in her hand, looked her in the eye. "I'll be back." The cow blinked and mooed.

"So sweet," Becky said.

Brynn turned to see a car coming up the driveway. "Looks like our computer guy is here."

"Finally," Becky said. "How are you feeling?"

"I'm ready for a nap, but I need to deal with this first." One minute Brynn felt strong, as if she was capable of doing her chores, but the next minute she wanted to fall into bed. It was the concussion, but it was hard to be patient with herself. She had so much to do. She loved her work, tending the cows, making cheese, but it was all physical and she knew she'd have to take it easy if she was to get back to top speed.

* * *

After she got Charlie settled in front of her laptop, Brynn sat down at the kitchen table. Becky brought them both a glass of iced tea.

"Thank you," Charlie said, and took a sip. "Great tea."

"Thanks," Becky said.

His fingers clicked quickly over the keyboard. "What is your password?"

"Petunia123," Brynn said.

"Okay, let's see what's going on." *Click. Click. Click.* His long fingers seemed to be made for the keyboard—or maybe the piano.

The message came up again.

"Ah-ha," he said. "Ransom ware."

"What can we do about it?"

"Depends on how good this hacker is." He took another drink of tea. "I'm assuming you don't want to pay."

"Absolutely not."

"Good, the FBI is saying you should never pay." His fingers clicked away again. "Well, this is good. Your files haven't been encrypted. I can clean this. But you're going to need some security measures put in place. I can do that today. If you want. But first, you're going to need to call your credit card companies. Looks like those files have been stolen."

Brynn's heart raced. "Which credit cards?"

"There are two here—one under the name of Buttermilk Creek Farms and the other to Wes Scors. Both have been used within the past twenty-four hours."

Brynn drew in air. They knew about Wes's card being stolen, but hers?

"Let me be clear," he said. "This doesn't mean your

actual card has been taken. Thieves don't even need to do that anymore. They can set it up to use through their phones."

"What! You mean like Apple Pay?" Becky asked.

"Yes, something like that." He refocused on the computer. "I'm going to run this software to clean your computer. It's going to take a few minutes. In the meantime, I suggest you call your credit card company."

"One is mine," Brynn said, standing to get her purse, which was on the kitchen counter. "But the other one belongs to my assistant and the police have been watching the card."

"The other one?"

"Yeah." Brynn waved him off. "Long story." She dug in her purse and found her card. He was right. It hadn't been stolen. The thief had taken everything off of the computer.

"It's getting pretty scary. Everything is on the computer these days," Becky said.

"True, and that's why I'm so busy. I can't keep up. Suddenly this virus is ramped in the valley. Someone seems to be targeting people in this community."

Brynn leaned closer to him. "How can you tell?"

"It's the same code. The hacker has been using the same code everywhere. It's almost like his signature. A couple of people have even tried to pay."

"How did it happen?" Brynn asked.

"It's hard to say, really. But usually it comes through e-mail. You click on the wrong link and, um, you've got a virus. These guys are getting really good at posing as a legit business," he said.

Brynn's mind was reeling. Technology was supposed to make your life easier, not make you more vulnerable. Recalling the credit cards, Brynn wondered where Wes was. Surely he was home from jail by now. And if he was home, he'd have finally stopped by here. Where was he? She needed to tell him it didn't have to be a stolen card. His numbers could have been lifted from the computer.

As soon as Charlie left, she'd call Wes and see what was going on. He needed to be aware of all this—he was the man in charge of the computers.

"You're not the first local to have this same exact virus. I wonder what's going on."

"Is someone trying to get money out of other people the same exact way?" Becky asked.

He nodded. "Yes. I'd say there's a sophisticated hacker among us. But he or she doesn't have to be anywhere nearby. Could be in India or China. But since this is so specific . . . I've got a few ideas. I'm going to work on this, try to find the root of this virus. But I don't have much time, running from person to person who already has the darn thing."

The more Brynn knew about how all records now were online—medical, financial, and so on—the more it made her want to crawl into bed and pull the covers over her head.

Chapter 27

Brynn wasn't alone in her ransom ware attack, but it didn't make her feel any better. What was happening in this community? First Josh was still in jail for manslaughter, Wes was still in jail for murder, after being shot, and now this. Some hacker had been trying to get money from Brynn and her friends and neighbors.

She hadn't been in Shenandoah Springs a year yet. Shortly after she moved here, her friend Nancy died and odd things started happening to her. Now this. Becky had urged her to move then, and Brynn was certain she'd want her to move now. But she couldn't imagine another place to go where land was as cheap. She wouldn't leave her girls—or her dream. Her ex-fiancé would love to hear of her failure and she was bound and determined to succeed.

This was supposed to be their place, but he'd cheated on her and she told him to pack his bags. She'd never forget the sneer on his face: "You think you can do it alone? Well, you can't."

"That remains to be seen," she said out loud in her

bedroom. She was lying in her bed, there from the exhaustion of the morning. Just lying down helped. Her eyelids felt heavy, and she drifted off to sleep.

She awakened to voices downstairs. She untangled herself from her quilts and sat up, rubbing her eyes, yawning. Who was here?

She marched downstairs and saw Schuyler and Willow sitting with her sister drinking tea and eating the last of the blackberry breakfast bread.

"There she is!" Becky said.

"Still alive, I see," Schuyler said.

"Yeah," Brynn muttered, sitting down at the table.

"Good news," Willow said. "Josh is home!"

Brynn grinned. "This is good news. What happened?"

"Well, they found a problem with the tractor. He really did lose control of it, but it wasn't his fault. There's going to be a huge lawsuit."

"I can imagine. What on earth could happen to a tractor like that? It's so sophisticated. The sales guy was telling me how slick and techie tractors are now."

"That's the problem," Willow said. "The computer inside of it. Something to do with the Wi-Fi signal—"

"It was sonar signals," Schuyler said.

"Okay. But he lost control and was able to prove it."

Brynn's brain felt a bit cottony, but she now considered technology the big bad wolf. She wanted to change the subject. "How is the fair?"

"Rained out today."

"What?" Brynn said.

"You slept through the storm, but it was a doozie. It's still raining."

"Yeah, there's no electricity in half the county. The

fair is down. I'm kind of glad. It's not been a good year," Willow said.

"No," Brynn said. "I suppose next year there will have to be more security."

"That would be a good thing, but I doubt it will happen."

"After Wes getting shot, you'd think they would tighten it," Becky said.

They all agreed.

"Speaking of Wes . . . has he gotten out of jail while I was asleep?"

"I've not seen him or his family," Becky replied.

"Well, let's hope it means they are off celebrating his freedom," Willow said.

"Yes," Brynn said. But she thought it odd that he wouldn't have at least stopped by. After all, she was his employer—and friend.

"How's your head?" Schuyler asked.

"Getting better. It's not aching now and that's a good thing. But my brain isn't working one hundred percent yet. You know? Sometimes it takes a while. . . . Unfortunately, I've a lot of figuring out to do. It's frustrating."

"Figuring out?" Schuyler sad. "What are you talking about? We've got everything covered."

"I'm trying to figure out who killed Donny."

Silence engulfed the room.

"Why?" Schuyler finally said. "The police are on it, right?"

"I'm not so sure." She relayed the information about Wes and his credit card. "I don't think they're really investigating this. It's like they want justice but are willing to pin the blame on an innocent man because on the surface it looks like he did it. They should have checked his credit card and everything.

But no. His dad investigated and found it all. It's troubling."

"I agree they should have investigated more thoroughly," Schuyler said. "But they don't really have a lot of resources. That's no excuse, though." She paused. "So what ideas do you have in that aching head of yours?"

"Nothing makes much sense, unfortunately. There's Chelsea. Everything keeps coming back to her."

"A sixteen-year-old girl?" Willow said.

"She's the common denominator—Rad dated her, Donny dated her, and Evan dated her. Could it be a coincidence?" Brynn answered. "Also, she was dating a carnie guy with a record for attempted murder."

"Would you like some tea?" Becky asked her as everybody sat mulling all of it over.

"Yes, but I'd also like some justice," Brynn said.

"Tea and justice!" Willow said, and held up her cup.

"To tea and justice," Schuyler said.

They were on their second cup of tea when the front door opened. Becky stood. "What?"

Wes, Max, and their father walked into the room and the women all rushed Wes.

"Whoa! I've only been gone two days!" He laughed.

"How are you doing?" Brynn asked.

"What was it like?" Schuyler asked,

"Are you still under suspicion?" Willow asked.

"What was the food like?" Becky asked.

"Give me a break! All in due time," he said.

His dad put his arm around him. "He needs some rest. We're taking him back to the guest house. But he wanted to stop here first."

"He didn't sleep much in jail," Max said.

"Guys, I'm standing right here and can speak for myself." He turned to the women. "Yes, I'm tired and am going home to rest. But I plan to be back to work tomorrow, Brynn."

"If you need to take another day, it would be fine."

"No, I think it's best I keep busy. But thank you."

He looked like he'd aged ten years. Brynn was certain it was weariness. The jail in Shenandoah Springs was not like a maximum-security prison.

But it wasn't simply the weakness from not sleeping, but probably the weight of being accused of murder. Brynn's frustration burned. She needed to help him out more. This concussion needed to go away.

She moved in and hugged him. "Go and get rested up. But if you need another day, it's fine, too."

"Go ahead over, boys. I want to talk with Brynn," Nathaniel said.

Wes and Max took their leave.

"Please have a seat," Brynn said. "Would you like some tea?"

"I want my boy to come home," Nathaniel said.

Willow started clearing the dishes. Schuyler leaned forward. And Becky sat, stunned.

Brynn's heart dropped. "I totally get that. I never wanted any problems for him. You know that."

He nodded. "I do. But there's no guarantee of his safety here."

"Is there a guarantee in Boston?" Schuyler said.

"Of course not, but he's not so singled out there, if you know what I mean."

"We're not all racist," she said.

"Of course not," Brynn replied.

"Not you-all, certainly." Nathaniel took a deep

breath. "But he's being threatened, arrested, accused of murder. This is serious stuff. You can't deny there's a strong racist element in this valley."

"He's right," Willow said as she walked back into the room. If any of them understood racism, it would be her. "It's not something I talk about often, but my family and I have had problems, too, through the years."

"I'm sorry to hear that," Nathaniel said.

Brynn was shocked. She had no idea.

"Every person who's not white has had some kind of experience." Willow sat down. "It's not just this area. But there's fewer brown-skinned people here, so it seems like it's this area. There are racists everywhere."

Brynn set her teacup down. "We'd considered that Wes is being framed. Do you think it's racism?"

"I have no idea. It could be. I thought he was being framed, too. Whoever is using his credit card."

"Why didn't they cancel the card?" Becky asked.

"They're trying to track him down with it. The last I heard, the police are on to something. But the crook is messing with them, almost like he realizes he's being watched. There was a charge in Staunton and then fifteen minutes later in Culpeper. That can't be. He's wily."

Brynn, once again, was disturbed by the online stuff. All of her personal information was online. Between this and the attack on her computer, she was beginning to consider deleting everything and doing things the old-fashioned way. Her head hurt when she thought about it. It seems like it would take a lot of work to disengage herself and her business.

"So his card is being charged?" Schuyler said.

"Yes, but the police will take care of the expenses."

"That's something anyway," Becky said.

Schuyler leaned forward. "They know someone had his card. The card that paid for the gun. So why don't they absolve him of all this?"

"It's not easy. They have to follow the law. If the evidence says one thing they have to follow up on it. That's all. And of course, they don't know if Wes is a partner with this person," Nathaniel explained.

"I hadn't thought of that," Brynn said. "But what we need to do is take the matter into our own hands. We've led the police in the right directions so far. We can continue. You discovered his credit card was being used. I told them about the ex-con carnie."

"He had an alibi," Nathaniel said. "But I'm not sure there's anything much else to be done here. I agree there's not much in the way of police resources and any help we could give them would benefit my son. But where to start?"

"I think we start with Chelsea," Brynn said. "I'd like to talk with her. But I can't imagine how to approach her without her being suspicious."

"The sixteen-year-old?" Schuyler waved her off.

"Yes, I agree," Nathaniel said. "She's too young to be brought into this."

"Everything leads back to her, though," Becky said.

There was an awkward pause.

"I think you're right," Willow said. "Chelsea has something to do with this."

"She is sixteen. A beauty queen . . . likes boys. How can we lure her here and question her?" Brynn said.

"I don't think you should do this." Nathaniel stood. "She's a child."

"She's sixteen, but she's no child," Willow said. "Believe me."

"Okay then," Schuyler said. "Let's ask her to tea to discuss something. . . . Brynn, you need a spokesperson? A pretty young woman to represent your brand?"

"That's a great idea!"

As Brynn thought it over, this was definitely something she could do. She didn't have to hire her. She could question her and then decide against it. It would help to get a sense of her personality. Why would such a young woman be involved with all these men—two of whom had been killed? One by her father, albeit accidentally.

Chapter 28

Later that evening, Brynn sat down at her computer and drafted a note to all the people who were in the cheese contest. What a failure it was. But it wasn't in her control, unfortunately. What should she do next year? Have armed guards standing outside of her cheese shed? If that's what she needed to do in order to have a successful cheese competition, then that's what she'd do. What an utter and complete disaster. Pangs of disappointment zoomed through her.

Then she wrote an e-mail to Chelsea. A part of her felt bad for luring a sixteen-year-old to her farm on false pretenses. But she had to remind herself this was no normal sixteen-year-old.

But as she wrote the e-mail, she stopped. She'd planned a visit with Chelsea's father, Josh, to offer her support. Perhaps that would be a better way to bring up the subject. Yes, she'd take the cheese Danish out of the freezer.

"What are you up to?" Becky said, walking into the room. "You're not supposed to be at the computer."

"I'm done. I wanted to send e-mails to the cheese contestants."

"I could've done that for you."

"I know. But here's something you can do for me. I want to go out to the O'Connor farm. I'm going to offer my support for the family and take them some cheese Danish. You in?"

"Of course," she said.

"Good. I've got cheese Danish in the freezer I want to take along."

"That'll cheer them up. As Granny Rose used to say, a little something sweet will turn a sour disposition. Have the charges been dropped?"

"I have no idea."

As the two readied for their journey, Brynn found herself wondering about Wes and hoping he was getting rest. She imagined he was more upset than he let on. She needed to touch base with him tomorrow. His dad and brother were here seeing to him. But she still was obliged to make sure he was okay. After all, he was more than an employee; he was a friend, and the grandson of one of her dearest friends. A wave of weariness came over her. The concussion, again. When was she going to get better?

One thing at a time, she told herself as she placed the Danish in a plastic container. Really, she was taking care of three things while visiting Josh and his family. Support, Chelsea, and Wes. After all, she was trying to prove his innocence.

Becky came into the kitchen. "Time for your medicine." She handed her the pills.

Brynn finished what she was doing and downed the pills. "Ready to roll!"

The drive to the O'Connor farm was a feast for the eyes. Because of all the rain, the field held a plump, full bright green color, along with the trees Farmhouses were edged in colorful flowers and the mountains loomed over it all.

The O'Connors were known for their honey, but they also farmed other things. When the sisters pulled up to the O'Connors' driveway, Brynn was taken with the gorgeous, detailed bee house at the edge of it. She wondered if Samantha Hildebrand had made it.

"Isn't that sweet?" Becky said, and she turned into the long driveway.

"I love it."

The house was simple but large: a white clapboard house. Brynn adored the simple designs of the local farmhouses. A red barn sat in the distance.

Becky parked the car and the two sisters exited the vehicle and made their way down the daylily-lined sidewalk to the front porch. Brynn rang the doorbell.

After a few moments, the door creaked open. "Brynn?" As the door swung open farther, Josh stood there looking almost like another person. He'd lost weight and gained some gray hair. His wrinkles were pronounced and dark circles surrounded his eyes.

Brynn forced a smile. "Hey, Josh. Brought you some Danish."

He grinned. "Well, well. Come on in. Hannah? Brynn's here."

His wife, Hannah, showed up and led them into the well-kept living room, with photos of their children on the walls, along with religious paintings.

"Please sit down," Josh said.

Brynn handed Hannah the container of Danish.

"Thank you," she said. "I'll put this in the kitchen."

"How are you doing, Brynn? I heard about the concussion, about Wes getting shot."

Brynn was touched he'd ask about her when his own troubles were looming. "I'll be okay. This is Becky, my sister. She's been taking good care of me."

"Nice to meet you, Becky. Can we get you-all something to drink?" he asked.

"No, thank you. I wanted to stop by and see how you're doing, offer my support. If there's anything I can do . . ."

He frowned. "Thank you, Brynn. I think things are going to work out with the lawsuit and everything." He turned to look at Hannah as she walked in. "But I still can't make sense of it . . . and I killed that boy." His voice cracked.

"But you didn't mean to," Hannah said, sitting down next to him on the couch. "Accidents happen."

"I know, but I swear it was as if the tractor was being controlled by someone else."

For some reason, Brynn remembered the remote cars she and Becky had as girls. "You mean it might have been controlled remotely?"

"Yes, precisely. I know it doesn't make any sense. But I had it in drive and the damned thing kept reversing and turning." His face grew pink. "I know it sounds crazy."

"No, it doesn't," Hannah said. "All of these new tractors are sophisticated computers. So when they break, or something's wrong with them, things go wacky. They'll figure it out."

"I'm sure they will," Brynn said. "These days, I'm almost afraid to use the computer. We were hacked with something called ransom ware."

"Us too!" Josh said. "We were talking about that. We had to get Charlie out here to fix our computer."

Brynn nodded. "That's one busy guy."

Hannah sat forward. "Isn't it strange? Technology

is supposed to help us, to make our lives easier. I swear sometimes it would be better to go completely off the grid."

Just then Chelsea came into the room. "I'm heading out," she said.

"Wait," Josh said. "Have you met Brynn? And this is her sister Becky."

She smiled. "Hey good to meet you." She gave a little wave.

"Actually, you're part of the reason we're here," Brynn said.

Chelsea suddenly looked like a doe caught in headlights.

"Me?"

"Yes, and I'm glad your parents are right here because what I have to say is something you should consider together."

"I really have to run," she said. "Just talk to them. I'm sure whatever it is—"

"Sit down, Chelsea," her dad said, and she complied.

Brynn cleared her throat. "It's an idea we've been kicking around at Buttermilk Creek. We're considering hiring a spokesmodel. And Chelsea was homecoming queen and has won some other contests. She really does have that . . . fresh appeal we want to give off, to have associated with our products."

Silence permeated the room.

"Well, please think about it. And Chelsea, I'd love it if you came out to the farm. I could show you around and get to know you. It's not a done deal yet, simply something we're thinking about."

"Well, thank you for all your kind words and thanks for considering me." She seemed genuine and maybe embarrassed. Brynn felt a pang of guilt for every bad thing she'd thought about the young woman. And for manipulating the situation. It wasn't like her at all, which spoke of her desperation.

"I don't know," Josh said. "She's busy with school."

"It's true," Hannah chimed in.

"Okay, well, it's something to consider. The invitation stands."

As Brynn and Becky took their leave, Brynn sensed she'd stepped into something she hadn't quite counted on.

Chapter 29

Brynn hated to admit defeat, but her body wouldn't allow anything else. The trip to see Josh and his family was more than she bargained for. Becky insisted on her eating, but she went to bed. As she lay in her bed, she listened to the sound of thunder in the distance and wondered if the fair would get canceled again tonight.

The next morning when she awakened, she heard voices downstairs. She rolled over. She was so tired, her head felt heavy and it ached. She continued to sleep. She woke up later feeling a bit better, but glancing at the clock, she was surprised to realize she'd slept until 9:00 AM.

She sat up and glanced out the window at her cows grazing in the startlingly green field, dotted with newly sprouted dandelions.

She stood and reached for her robe, padded down the stairs to face the day.

"Well, you're alive." Becky sat at the kitchen table with her laptop.

"Aunt Brynn!" came a voice from the computer.

"Lily?" Brynn walked over to see her niece's sweet face.

"It's called face time!" she said. "We can see each other!"

As she and her five-year-old niece talked with each other, Becky poured Brynn coffee. "Thank you."

After she and Lily caught up, they rang off until tomorrow. Brynn felt a pang of guilt. "Are you missing her?"

"Of course," Becky answered. "But I'm needed here. And she's having a blast at her friend's house, now that camp is over. Her mother is one of those stay-at-home moms who come up with countless activities for the kids. She's being kept busy."

As she drank her coffee, Brynn slowly awakened even more.

"You must have been exhausted," Becky said. "The trip was too much for you."

Brynn nodded. "I feel like an old lady."

"You have a concussion. It's nothing to mess around with."

"I hear ya. And so does my body." She slumped over the table and stared into her coffee as if it held answers to all the questions in the universe.

"Can I get you something? Eggs? Toast?" Becky asked.

"Toast only. I don't think I could eat anything else this morning."

Becky walked over to the counter and sliced bread. "Wes and his dad were here earlier."

"Good news?" Brynn's heart jumped at the thought of it.

"No news." She slid the bread into the toaster and pushed down. "None."

"Where is Wes?"

"He's cleaning the barn and milking parlor with Max and Nathaniel. Isn't that nice? I promised them a good lunch."

"I'm sure you can manage. I'll help."

"No, you won't," she said with a scolding tone. "I've already got soup on and I'm going to make cheese sandwiches. It will be easy and fine."

Brynn's thoughts turned to Chelsea. "Do you think Chelsea will stop by or e-mail or anything?"

"I've been considering that." The toast popped up, and she spread thick salted butter on each slice. "I think you appealed to her ego. For a sixteen-year-old, I think it's heady stuff. But I got this weird vibe from her parents."

"I did, too. There's more going on there than what we know, of course." The smell of hot buttered toast filled the room.

"I agree. I've been trying to imagine how I'd deal with this as a parent. I mean, thank goodness Lily isn't into the beauty pageants and stuff. I don't think I could handle it. I'd always be suspicious of the surrounding people." She shrugged. "I already am, I suppose. But that seems like you're really tempting the hand of fate by putting your kid in the spotlight." She put a plate of toast in front of Brynn.

"I totally get that. But Chelsea is sixteen. Her personality is such that . . . well . . . homecoming queen, lots of boyfriends. Maybe her parents are trying different tactics with her now. But of course they'd be concerned. I'm talking about using their daughter's face on my products."

"I don't think I'd go for it. Even at the age of sixteen, I wouldn't like it. If Lily is a clear-thinking, level-headed kid, I'd probably leave it up to her."

That surprised Brynn. "Really?"

"Sure. I'm hoping we'd discuss it together of course, go over the pros and cons, and then she'd decide."

Brynn bit into her toast and her mouth exploded with butter flavor.

"I've been watching Wes with his dad. It seems like they have a good relationship, though Wes hasn't exactly done what Nathaniel expected of him. He's given him a lot of leeway."

"I'm afraid he's going to want Wes to go home with him and I can't blame him."

What would she do without Wes? He'd inserted himself into the running of Buttermilk Creek Farms. He managed the computers and ran the website and the website orders, along with crafting excellent cheese. Besides all that, he was excellent company for her.

But she realized someday he would leave. He had to. He was young and would take everything he learned from her and move on to the next step in his life. She was mentally prepared for it to happen. Someday. Just not so soon.

Several hours later, Brynn's doorbell rang. She was sitting in the living room, trying not to nod off. No screen time. No TV. No reading. How did people live like this?

Becky's voice rang from the kitchen. "I'll get it."

Brynn listened to the commotion at the door, figuring it was the mail- or UPS man. When Becky brought Chelsea into the room, Brynn perked right up. "Chelsea! Thanks for coming."

"I'm really eager to hear about your plans," she said with a sweet smile.

Plans? Oh boy, Brynn hadn't thought this through.

She shot Becky a look of panic and then recovered herself.

"Can I get you something to drink?" Becky said. "I made lemonade."

"Sounds great," Chelsea said.

"Have a seat," Brynn said. "I'm not normally this lazy, but I'm recovering from a concussion."

Chelsea sat down on the chair next to the couch. "I heard something about it. I hope you feel better real soon."

"Thank you."

They sat in awkward silence for a few minutes.

Becky entered the room with the lemonade and put the cool glasses down on the table. Brynn reached for hers and took a long drink. Her taste buds popped from the flavor. Becky had added lime to the drink, and the result was delicious. "So, to tell you the truth, Chelsea, this is an evolving concept."

"I see," she said, disappointment playing over her face.

"But I was thinking about things like our cheese contest that we held at the fair—or tried to hold—"

"Yeah, heard about that."

"So what you'd do is stand there and welcome people."

"By that point they'd know who you are, of course," Becky chimed in, and sat down next to Brynn. "Because we'd use your face on packaging and the website."

Thank goodness for Becky.

Chelsea sat forward. "I'm comfortable in front of crowds. I've been in a lot of plays. Last year I had the lead in *Annie Get Your Gun.*" Suddenly she looked like nothing more than a girl with dreams. A look flashed in her eyes. She was the sort of pretty that conjured up images of fresh country air and innocence, of mountain streams and wildflowers and fresh, wholesome dairy products.

Brynn felt a pang of guilt for lying to her and leading her on. But she had told her they were simply considering it. Nothing was in writing yet.

"Good to know." Brynn took another sip of her drink.

Chelsea lifted the glass to her lips and drank. Even her hands were beautiful. Long fingers, nicely painted nails. A diamond tennis bracelet and sparkly rings. *Sapphires?*

Brynn had no idea Chelsea's family had the money to afford these things for their sixteen-year-old.

"We have so many plans for the business. We want to expand our cheese line, of course, but Wes is doing other exciting things with our dairy products."

She perked up at the mention of Wes. "I thought he was in jail." Her hand played with a gold necklace with a diamond angel charm.

Brynn's heart skipped a few beats. This was a great opportunity to gauge her reaction about Wes and the murder. She didn't want to blow it. "No. He's out on bail."

Her perfect eyebrows lifted, and she set her glass down with a bit of a thud. "I'm not sure how I feel about that."

"What do you mean?"

"I mean, if he killed Donny he should be in jail." She shrugged. "He seems real nice, but so did Ted Bundy, you know."

How did we get to Ted Bundy?

"Wes didn't kill Donny. I can assure you."

She bit her lip. "Perhaps you should find someone

else for this job. I don't know . . . I'd love to help you out, but now I'm uncomfortable."

"Why? Because of Wes?"

She nodded. She really looked confused and frightened.

"I'm sorry to hear that, Chelsea. Do you know something we don't know? Wes is a good guy. He comes from a good family and he's been nothing but kind and helpful since he moved here."

"Then why did the police put him in jail? They had to have evidence, right?" Chelsea asked.

"They thought they did, but the evidence was wrong." Brynn wanted to be careful here. She didn't want to tell Chelsea too much. But she was certain Chelsea knew more than what she was saying.

Silence filled the room.

"Someone said they found his prints on the gun and it was his gun."

"Wrong on both counts. Who told you that?"

She looked away. "I don't know. Everybody's talking about it."

She was lying. One glance at Becky told Brynn she thought so, as well. Who was Chelsea protecting?

"Would you like to meet my girls?" Brynn asked, hoping to escape this tense moment.

"Your girls?"

"My cows." Brynn grinned.

"Sure!" Her expression lost the tension it was holding. "I love cows."

That did it. The girl couldn't be so bad. She loved cows.

Maybe Brynn wouldn't get all the information she needed from Chelsea this first meeting, but she'd keep working on her. Right now, she'd let her cows charm her a bit.

They finished their lemonade and walked together out of the house into the field. It felt as if they walked into a wall of heat. The temperatures were nearing one hundred today. The cows slowly walked toward the three of them.

Chelsea looked beyond them. "Jewel?"

The still too skinny Highland cow looked up when Chelsea said her name.

"Is that Jewel?" she asked, excited. The beautiful young woman lost a few years in that moment. Her face turned into a five-year-old face full of sweetness, awe, and enthusiasm.

"It is," Brynn answered.

"I used to help Mrs. Rhodes with her sometimes."

The cow came walking over to Chelsea, making her way around the others, who were curious but more wanting to see Brynn.

Chelsea's arms opened and Jewel laid her head on her shoulder. Chelsea hugged her. The cow's eyes closed in pleasure and relief. It was as if she was thinking, *Here's a familiar face.*

Chapter 30

"You can come and see Jewel anytime you want. Well, as long as I'm fostering her," Brynn said as Chelsea slipped into her car.

"Thank you, Brynn. I'll think over everything else, too," she said, and started her car. Becky and Brynn waved as she pulled away.

Becky sighed. "I'm not sure how I feel about her, but we better get inside." The skies were growing dark and the wind was whipping the trees around.

As they turned toward the house, Wes and Max were walking over from the guest house.

"What was she doing here?" Wes asked, not even bothering to say hello.

"Come inside and we'll talk," Brynn answered.

He hesitated. "I'm not sure she should be anywhere around me."

They went toward the house.

Becky opened the door. "We've got a plan."

They entered through the door and into the house, spilling out into the living room.

Brynn recapped their plans with Chelsea.

"Clever," said Max.

"Wait a minute," Wes said. "It's too dangerous. Some sophisticated hacker is out there trying to frame me for murder. I figure Chelsea has something to do with it. I don't know what. But in any case, I'm uncomfortable with her being here."

Brynn's heart dropped. She should have thought about that. "Okay, I'm sorry. But it was a ruse. We're not planning on doing any of this. We're just digging for information."

"Brynn, I realize you're trying to help, but this is serious. I could go to prison for this murder."

"A murder you didn't commit," Max chimed in. "And law enforcement is moving too slowly, if you ask me. Brynn's trying to help. It's a brilliant idea. I'm in. What can I do?"

"You are not in," Wes said. "You're going back to New York and finishing your internship. Dad is going back home and my lawyer will deal with this, without any help from Brynn."

Duly scolded, Brynn sat with her hands in her lap.

Wes softened as he looked at Brynn. "You almost got yourself killed when you were investigating Gram's murder. I won't have it."

He was right. What did she think she was doing?

"I'm sorry."

"You need to focus on healing," Wes said.

"Hear, hear," Becky said. "Speaking of which, it's pill time. I'll go and get your next dose."

Brynn didn't want to take any more pills. She didn't want her sister and others fussing over her. She wanted her life back—which included the happy Wes working around her kitchen, experimenting with cheese, or hunched over the computer intent on some project.

Or him hanging out and watching *Downton Abbey* with her.

"Wes, like Dad said, the cops wouldn't have even known about the credit card without him finding it," Max said. "Don't be foolish. They have very little staff and resources. They're overlooking a lot, I'm sure. It won't hurt if we help you." He paused. "Brynn's plan with Chelsea was brilliant. I think she should continue to reel her in. If she's completely innocent, what harm would it do? If not, maybe she'll slip up and reveal a nugget that'll turn the case."

"I don't like the girl. She makes me nervous," Wes said.

"But you don't have to be around her. Brynn, did you get any information?"

Brynn took a few minutes to consider it. Her head was unclear. "Well, I think she's afraid of Wes."

"What?" he exclaimed.

"She seems to believe you killed Donny, and she was leery of working for me because of it."

Silence filled the room.

"That means nothing," Wes said. "She's a good actress. Don't believe a word she said. She's been stringing Roy along for months. I've caught her in some whoppers and called her on it. She doesn't like me, but is she afraid of me? No. She's not afraid of anybody."

"She sounds diabolical," Becky said as she entered the room with Brynn's medication.

"Good word for her," Wes said.

"Did you say she's been stringing Roy along?" Brynn remembered the pimply-faced young man from the first night of the fair—and then later at the concert. He was with Chelsea that night—or at least it appeared so.

"Yes," Wes answered.

Brynn leaned forward. "Well, they were pretty snug during the concert."

"What? That can't be. I don't believe it," Wes said, jaw tight. "Why would Chelsea go out with him? As I said, she's been stringing him along. I've no idea why. But the guy is a waste of space. I mean, he's good at hacking and gaming. But that's it. He's not nice, and he's completely unattractive."

True. And Chelsea didn't seem like the sort of person to discount looks.

"I'm telling you what I saw," Brynn said. "I remembered it because I thought it was strange."

"Stranger than you think," Wes said.

A cold shiver passed through Brynn.

Chapter 31

That evening, the Scors men and the MacAlister women gathered for dinner made by Wes and Becky. Fresh pesto crafted from basil they grew themselves, cheese they made, and pine nuts they bought at the local grocery store. Wes and Becky made pasta from scratch and they had fresh bread from Hoff's Bakery.

After Wes poured wine for everybody, he sat down but held his glass up. "A toast to the best friends and family a guy could ask for."

Brynn swallowed a lump of emotion creeping up her throat.

"I'm not certain what's going to happen, but I'm innocent and I appreciate you all standing by me and supporting me. Now, let's dig in." He rubbed his hands together.

The dinner was quiet and filled with small talk. Nobody wanted to speak about the elephant in the room—or the cow, as it were.

"This pesto is the best I ever had," Nathaniel said.

"Fresh makes all the difference," Wes replied. "Just

picked the basil and made the cheese last week before all the madness."

His phone rang. "Speaking of the madness. This is my lawyer. I need to take it." He stood and moved into the kitchen.

"He seems to be doing well," Becky said. "I'd be a nervous wreck if I were him."

"He's not quite himself," Nathaniel said. "Believe me."

"I agree," Brynn said, but she couldn't put her finger on what was off about him.

Wes walked back into the room. "The police have another suspect. But he's lawyered up. They're not getting much information from him."

"Who is it?"

"Some guy who worked at the carnival." He sat back down to his plate of pasta.

"Ian?" Brynn asked.

"How did you know?"

"I did a little research," Becky said. "He's an ex-con. Attempted murder." The words sounded odd coming from Becky's mouth. "Ex-con." "Murder."

Wes shot Brynn a glare. "Getting your sister to do your dirty work?"

Brynn's face heated. "I've got to be careful with screen time. That guy has a record a mile long, and I saw him on a date with you know who."

"I thought I told you to stop."

"We were doing it while you were in jail. It was before you told me to back off."

"What's the harm?" Max said after drinking a sip of wine. "She helped. The cops wouldn't have been aware of this connection without Brynn's help."

"It could be dangerous for her. Remember when Gram died?" Wes said.

The room silenced.

"Yeah, but this is different. If Gram were still alive, she'd be doing even more trying to prove your innocence. You need to get a grip."

"Well, there's also the fact we don't want to mess up his case. Whatever case the lawyer is building. We need to be careful," Becky said. "I get that. But so far we've done nothing but help."

"I have mixed feelings about this amateur sleuthing," Nathaniel said as he twirled the pasta around on his plate. "The local police seem to have their hands full with the fair and maybe aren't able to fully investigate."

"Fair?" Brynn asked.

Nathaniel crossed his arms. "Every night a different incident. Drug bust one night. The next night, the computer systems are screwed up and the rides won't work. It's like a microcosm for all of society's ills over there."

Brynn had been so focused on her own problems she knew nothing about what else was happening in her community. Everything Nathaniel said was right. So much was going on in their small town the police resources were being pulled thin. And yet Wes was adamant they not help him. A wave of weariness came over her. She'd felt so good having everybody gathered here together at her table.

"Brynn? Are you okay?" Becky asked, standing.

"I'm sorry." She tried to smile. "I need to go to bed."

Brynn took her leave and didn't even bother changing her clothes. She just lay down on top of her quilt. Alone with her thoughts, she did the other thing she knew to do, which was pray. Wes was young, he was innocent, and surely things would turn out okay—with or without her help.

She rolled over to her side and the image of Chelsea's jewelry sprang to her mind. Brynn knew she was the common denominator and Wes didn't like her, but she didn't judge her as badly as everybody else. Something was going on with her, for sure, but it wasn't covering up a murder case. What was it?

She tried to take comfort in the fact that the police had Ian in custody, but she wondered what his motive was in killing Donny. Did they even know each other? Did he randomly kill Donny or was there a reason? What would that reason be?

She should have felt better now that the police had another suspect. But she didn't. She wanted to be certain Wes was cleared. She wouldn't rest until she knew he was safe. She vowed to continue her efforts, with or without Wes's blessing. What he didn't know wouldn't hurt him. Not this time, anyway.

Brynn woke up the next morning fully clothed with Romeo on her chest, purring and looking at her as if she was studying her. She reached up and stroked the cat, who usually chose to spend her nights with Wes. "Good morning, Romeo."

Brynn wondered how much the cat thought of Nancy, if she missed her, dreamed of her, and so on. They had been quite close.

Brynn took a few minutes to pet the cat. Then she sat up and glanced out the window at the gray, dreary weather. Another rainy, muggy day. The cat hopped down off of her bed and meowed.

Warmth spread through her as she remembered Wes was home. She had to assume he wouldn't be found guilty. But she had her work cut out for her.

First, she'd research more about the other suspect. Was he really viable? Or were they just looking at him because of his record?

"Brynn?" Becky rapped on her door and opened it. Her eyes swept up and down taking Brynn in. "You're still in yesterday's outfit?"

"I fell asleep in it." Brynn grinned as her sister shook her head, smiling. "I'll get showered and come downstairs in a minute."

"What are you doing sitting here in yesterday's clothes?"

"I just woke up. Trying to get it together. Man, I really slept. Like I don't remember anything. Such a deep sleep."

"That's probably just what you needed."

"I've been thinking about Ian and wondering what his motive would be to kill Donny."

"Did he need one? Sounds like he's just troubled." Becky sat down on the edge of the bed.

"I wonder did he even know Donny?"

"Who knows? But he is acquainted with Chelsea."

"About Chelsea . . . what do you think of her?"

Becky shrugged. "I think she's a confused young woman. Wouldn't be the first one. But I don't sense she's violent or dangerous in any way."

"I keep seeing her with Jewel. I may be cow crazy, but that cow loves her."

"Granny Rose used to say animals were better judges of people than people."

"It's so true."

Becky stood. "You better get that shower. I'll put a fresh pot of coffee on and get some breakfast together. How about a cheese omelet?"

"Don't go to all that trouble. I'll make a bowl of oatmeal."

"Whatever floats your boat." Becky left the room

and Brynn readied for her shower and her day. She was losing track of the time and felt the need to get back into the swing of things. She'd go and check on her cheese in the basement today and give it a good washing. That surely wouldn't be too much for her.

Later, at the breakfast table, Brynn downed her coffee and looked out her picture window to her field at her cows. It looked as if Jewel might be gaining a little weight. She was eating and that was a good thing.

Brynn finished her e-mail and checked her phone to see if there were any text messages. One from Schuyler, checking on her. One from Willow, doing the same. A note from the CSA about needing help tonight at the fair.

Another, a strange note with no return number. She opened it, and it read: "Back off, lady. Mind your own business and leave Chelsea alone. Or you're next." A shock of fear tore through her as she dropped her phone and gasped.

"What is it?" Becky said, running to her.

"The phone! Look at the message!" Brynn slid the phone to her sister, whose face reddened and mouth dropped as she read it.

"We need to get the police over here," Becky said.

Brynn hesitated. How would they explain why Chelsea had been here yesterday? Would they need to lie to the police? Granny Rose was right. When you tell one lie, you'll have to tell another to cover it up.

"What's wrong?"

"How are we going to explain why Chelsea was here?"

Becky thought a moment. "We'll tell them the same thing we told her."

"You mean lie again."

"Precisely." She paused. "Do you have a better plan?"

Her words hung in the air. They'd have to lie to Sheriff Edge. Brynn didn't like that at all.

"I have no plan." Brynn put her face in her hands, elbows on the table.

"I'll call the sheriff."

An hour later, Sheriff Edge was sitting at Brynn's kitchen table as Becky fixed him a cup of coffee.

"So you're saying Chelsea was here yesterday to discuss this opportunity and then today you received this text message?" he asked.

"Yes," Brynn answered.

Becky set the cup of coffee in front of him.

"Who knew she was here?" he asked.

"Well, all of us. Becky, me; Wes found out later as she was leaving. I think her parents probably knew she was here as well."

Sheriff Edge cocked an eyebrow. "One would hope."

Becky sat down at the table. "Indeed."

"I'm going to have to take your phone with me. We have a guy at the station who specializes in technology. That would not be me." He smiled. "Good coffee."

"Thanks," Becky said.

"What can they tell? I mean, there's not a return number or anything," Brynn asked.

"Look, that stuff is beyond me. I'm a boots-on-the-ground cop. I prefer old school. But most of the crimes these days are cyber oriented. It's a strange world we live in. So now the guys at the academy are learning more about computers than interviewing techniques," he grumbled.

"How serious is this?" Becky asked.

But Brynn knew the answer. Whoever sent the text was completely serious. It was a threat. Plain and simple. A threat because she'd gotten involved with Chelsea. A threat on her life. This person probably killed Donny Iser.

"Brynn, I can see those wheels in your head turning. It's best if you stay home and take care of yourself and leave this to us." He turned to Becky. "I think she should take this seriously. Especially given there's been a murder and a strange accidental death recently. She should take all of it seriously."

It was as she suspected. A stone-cold chill traveled up and down her spine.

Chapter 32

After the sheriff left with her phone, Brynn sat at the kitchen table with her thoughts spinning. Wes a suspect for murder. Two dead summer helpers. The carnie ex-con. Chelsea. Now her creepy phone message. Okay, perhaps Sheriff Edge was right: She had no business being involved in this. Maybe the police were investigating more than what she thought. More than what everybody thought. Nathaniel wasn't pleased with the investigation at all. But Wes was his son, and he definitely wasn't seeing things clearly.

She needed to get some air, to get outside and gain some perspective.

"Do you want to go for a walk?' she asked Becky.

Becky groaned. "Okay. I'll go with you."

"I'd like to see the girls; I really am going stir-crazy."

"You have a concussion. What do you want? To go out dancing?"

"Not quite. Just get some fresh air."

Becky grinned. "Okay, let's go."

* * *

First things first: a visit with her girls.

Freckles met them at the gate.

Brynn rubbed the dog's head. "I swear she's grown another two inches!" The dog's thick pink tongue hung out of her mouth. The day was mosquito filled, muggy, and hot. Freckles raised her nose for more attention, allowing a better view of the markings over her nose and mouth, tiny red spots resembling freckles. Hence the name Freckles.

"I think you're right. Oh look, your girls are jealous." The cows ambled to Brynn as she paid attention to the dog.

"Uh-oh." Brynn grinned.

"I have to say if I'd gotten a death threat, I'd be in bed with the covers over my head." Becky stooped over and petted Freckles as Brynn moved on to Petunia.

"Well, I needed to clear my head. Coming outside and visiting with my girls always puts things into perspective for me. This is what's important. My cows, my business. I need to step away from the whole murder thing."

Becky was silent as she scratched Buttercup behind her ears.

"It's been a disappointing summer. I mean, I was so excited about the fair, about the cheese contest, and then not only was it a disaster, but it's been a downward spiral ever since." Brynn watched as Jewel came closer, though still behind the other cows, tentative.

Brynn moved in closer to Jewel, and Jewel stood, allowing her to rub her nose. She let out a jubilant moo. Brynn's heart bloomed.

"It's been a disaster, except for one thing," Becky said. "You've got a new friend."

"Let's hope so." Brynn tried to look at the cow's eyes, but they were covered by long swaths of hair. The other cows were watching as Brynn fussed over Jewel. She had gained some weight and looked healthy.

"Such a sweet girl," Becky said.

"Right?"

The two of them took their leave from the cows and walked up over the hilly field.

"Is that the church Nancy lived in?"

Brynn nodded. "Yeah, they've done a great job with it. I hear it will be open for the first service in a month or so. Beyond the church, through that patch of woods, is the O'Reilly Apple Orchard. Tillie's family."

The two of them took in the view. The skies were gray and clouds were rolling in. It was going to rain.

"I'm proud of you for starting your life again here," Becky said.

"Thanks, but believe me, sometimes I wonder if this is the right thing. Given everything that's happened."

"I hear you. I wanted you to come home. You know that. But I can see why you like it here."

Brynn loved it in the Shenandoah Valley. Even with all the trouble she'd had, she didn't suppose she'd live anywhere else. And the community of Shenandoah Springs was what she'd always wanted. A group of farmers and craftspeople, committed to healthy farming practices. It would be perfect if it weren't for all the recent tragedies. Deaths. Murders. She shivered.

"I thought the idea with Chelsea was brilliant. I'm sorry. I should have thought that through more," Becky said.

"What? It wasn't your fault, Becky."

"I didn't realize it was going to be so dangerous."

"And it happened right away, so we understand whoever sent it knows her. Knows she came out here to talk with us."

Brynn wiped the sweat from her brow with her sleeve. "I'm certain she's got something to do with all of this. But what?"

"Remember that boy who was obsessed with you? What was his name?" Becky asked.

"Randy. Yes, I remember. He followed me everywhere. Always called the house. Sent me flowers."

"And Dad had a word with him. It didn't do any good."

"Not until he spoke with his parents." Brynn remembered. He scared her, but at the same time it made her feel a little special because she was not a boy magnet. At first, she kind of liked the attention. But then it started to scare her. "I wonder if Chelsea's gotten herself involved with someone like that?"

"Or worse. These days, there's cyberstalking. They stalk your social media. Send you e-mails, read all your posts . . ." Becky and Brynn looked at each other.

Brynn drew in a breath. "I said I was going to leave this alone."

"It won't hurt to look," Becky replied.

They turned from the view and headed for the house.

* * *

The sisters settled in at the kitchen table, chairs together, and Becky looked at the screen, counting Chelsea's Facebook likes, Twitter likes and retweets, and Instagram likes. Brynn kept a tally.

"Okay, so this is interesting," Brynn said, scanning the numbers and names. "Donny Iser had more likes than anybody, even Evan."

Becky sat back in her chair. "Are they the top two?"

"Yes, but that doesn't tell us much, right? We knew those two were interested in her. We're looking for someone who could be kind of . . . I don't know . . . stalking her."

"Nothing surprising there, I guess," Becky said.

Brynn heard the front door open. "Yoo-hoo, Brynn!" It was Wes.

"We're in here," Brynn called.

Wes and Max walked into the kitchen. Greetings were exchanged.

"Our milk stores are really piling up. So I'm making a big batch of crème fraîche. I called Hoff's and he's wanting to—" His eyes widened as he caught a glimpse of the computer screen. "What are you doing with Chelsea's Instagram feed on the screen?"

"Well, I—"

"Brynn, we talked about this."

"This morning, I received a threat on my phone. The police came and took my phone."

"What's Chelsea got to do with it?" Wes asked.

"The message told me to stay away from her." Brynn felt her jaw tighten.

Wes sat down. Max leaned on the table. "That's messed up."

"So, we're trying to look at her social media to see if, I don't know, anything jumped out at us," Becky chimed in.

"It's almost as if every move Chelsea makes is being watched," Brynn said.

"So you two are investigating by looking over her social?" Wes asked, shaking his head.

"Someone threatened her," Becky said with a hard note in her voice. "We're trying to figure all of this out. It's not hurting anyone."

The room quieted.

"No, I don't suppose it is. Maybe I'm being paranoid. I just don't want anything to go wrong with my case."

"Okay," Brynn said, and took a deep breath. "We don't know if this has anything to do with your case. They used Donny's name, but that means nothing. It doesn't mean it has to be the person who killed him. Everybody in the community is aware of it."

"I'm betting it does," Max said. "It's too coincidental."

A knock came at the front door. Wes stood. "I'll get it."

He exited the room, leaving the three people there in a state of confusion. But now that Brynn's life had been threatened, she wasn't going to sit back and do nothing. Concussion be damned. She'd do what she could. It seemed to be taking Wes a while at the door. Brynn wondered who it could be and what the heck was taking him so long. Finally, he came back into the room.

"Look what the cow dragged in," Wes said, with Willow and Schuyler standing there.

"We've been trying to call," Willow said.

"There's a good explanation why I've not been answering my phone. Sit down, ladies. I'll get you some coffee or tea." Brynn started to stand.

"I'll do it," Becky said, leaving Brynn to explain the situation with her phone.

Willow's mouth dropped. Schuyler's brows knit. "What the hell?"

"She should stay away from Chelsea," Wes said. "She's no good."

"Come on, Wes, she's a sixteen-year-old girl who is struggling with someone. She's confused," Schuyler said.

Brynn remembered what Willow told her about Schuyler, who'd been attacked when she was a young woman and had a rough time coming back.

"I agree there has to be more to her story," Willow said. "But on the face of it, I also agree with Wes. You've been warned. So you should stay away from her."

Brynn hadn't considered continuing a relationship with her—since the whole spokesperson thing was a ruse. But now she wondered.

Becky set Schuyler's peppermint tea in front of her and Willow's coffee on the table.

"The phone and situation are in the hands of the cops," Becky said. "So it doesn't really matter what we think. I don't like the idea of anybody threatening my sister. I want to know what the hell is going on around here."

Uh-oh, Becky was wound up. Nothing to do but let her finish.

"A young man was killed by a freak accident. Another young man shot in a barn. Wes found him and is suddenly a suspect. Now Brynn's life is threatened. In the meantime, someone is going around town trying to get ransom through your computers. What the hell? Brynn, I realize you love it here. You've got great friends, and it's beautiful. But really?"

Once again, the room silenced.

"I'm not going anywhere," Brynn said. "Calm down, please."

Willow took a deep breath. "There's a few more days of the fair. Perhaps things will get back to semi-normal after it. There's been a lot of trouble this year." She looked at Becky. "I can see why you're concerned about Brynn. But Shenandoah Springs is a nice, safe, place. It's just this past year has been crazy. Things'll calm down soon."

"Even with all of the crap going on, I'd say we have less of it than most communities our size," Schuyler said.

"The cops here, man . . ." Max said.

"I agree. We need more police. We're growing and the force hasn't grown. I think the fair has definitely shown them they need more help. Let's hope they get some."

Brynn's low-grade headache was starting to get worse. She'd pushed herself a little too far. "I'm sorry, guys. I need some medicine and to get a little rest."

"Okay," Willow said. "Yes. Get some rest. We'll see you later."

Brynn stood and left the room, weary and confused. And frightened.

Chapter 33

Brynn awakened to the sound of thunder. She sat up in her bed and saw the skies light with a veiny crack of lightning. She glanced at the clock—2:00 AM. Rain pelted her windows, and as the skies lit up she glimpsed trees swaying in the wind. Wow, what a horrible week for the fair—rained out almost every night.

Pangs of disappointment zoomed through her. She had such high hopes for the fair and cheese contest. And man, the cheddar was extraordinary. She wanted to speak to the person who made it. Cheddars were not easy to make. It used to be it could only be made in the village of Cheddar in England for it to be considered real cheddar. A few snobby cheese heads still felt the same way. Brynn thought that was ridiculous. *Cheddar cheese for everybody!*

A silver thread of lightning cracked against the sky and a loud boom shook the house. Romeo jumped up onto her bed and mewed, then curled up next to Brynn as she lay back down beneath the covers.

Brynn closed her eyes. The storm would be over

soon. For now, there was warmth, a soft bed, and a cat purring next to her.

The next morning, Brynn was awakened by her sister knocking at the bedroom door. "Are you awake?"

"I am now."

"Ha," she said as she opened the door. "How are you feeling? You slept a long time."

"Okay. No headache this morning," Brynn said, sitting up in bed.

"There's a couple of trees down. They weren't struck by lightning, but Wes stopped by earlier and said he'd called someone to clear them."

Brynn untangled herself from her covers. "Oh no! Which trees were they? Here I've been sleeping, leaving Wes to deal with all of this!"

"You're recovering from a concussion. Need I remind you?"

Brynn's heart sank. She felt useless. She'd like to strangle the man with the dreadlocks. Why did he shoot Wes? And why did she have to pass out and crack her head on the floor? She swayed as she stood.

"Whoa, where are you going?" Becky was by her side.

"I was going to the bathroom. Do you want to come with me?" Brynn grinned.

"I'll pass on that. But are you dizzy?"

"I was. I'm fine now."

"Okay, I'll see you downstairs. Wes made breakfast. It smells heavenly."

Brynn's stomach growled at the mention of breakfast. She was hungry, and that was a good sign.

The scents in the kitchen pulled her in, ignited her curiosity. What had he made? The table was already set, and the food was waiting for them. *How wonderful of Wes.* Brynn nearly cried.

"Good morning," he said. "I'm trying out a new recipe. I hope you like it. Coffee's on the table."

"How wonderful!" Becky said.

Brynn sat down. "Where's your dad and Max?" She reached for her cup of coffee, drank from the cup. *Perfect.*

"They ate earlier."

Stacks of whole wheat tortillas, sliced apples, honey, and jars of white cheese were on the table.

He sat down and spread the cheese on his tortillas, sliced apples, and then drizzled honey onto it. Brynn and Becky followed suit.

The tortillas were still warm from the oven and the cheese so fresh you could also taste the cow in it, as Granny Rose used to say.

"It's delicious!" Becky said with her mouth still full.

A smile cracked onto Wes's face. "Glad to hear it. Is there anything you'd add?"

Brynn thought about it a moment. "Some nuts?"

"Walnuts? Yes! I think you're right!"

"I don't like walnuts," Becky said. "So if you serve them again I'd place the nuts on the side and people could choose whether they want them."

"I've never heard of anybody not liking walnuts." Brynn shoved another bite of the fresh delight in her mouth, relishing the melding of the flavors.

"Well, you have now," Becky said.

Brynn sat and enjoyed her breakfast, looking out at her field and cows. Jewel was hanging out with the other cows. That was a blessing. In fact, this whole situation was a blessing. Brynn had a roof over her head, good food, good friends. And for this moment, she wasn't reflecting on the murder case. No, she was thinking about how happy she was. This tableau reminded her of a less complicated time before all of this craziness.

She felt a sliver of hope. Maybe the police would solve the murder case. Maybe they already had, which meant they'd leave Wes alone. She could heal without any worries about him, Chelsea, or whatever fool had sent her the text message. It would be done. Maybe. She could hope for that. It seemed possible right this moment.

She ached for her daily routine. Cows. Cheese. Business. The CSA. She wanted her sister to feel free to go home to Lily. She didn't want people fussing over her. She wanted her life back.

Chapter 34

After breakfast, Brynn opened her laptop while still sitting at the kitchen table. "I'm allowed an hour of screen time every day, so I can check on orders and see what else can be done in an hour."

"Good luck with that," Becky said.

Brynn clicked on the computer and the screen froze. Restarted. "We may need a new computer, Wes."

"I'm not even sure how old it is." He walked over to watch as the screen flicked back on. After the restart, the screen froze again. "Let me see." He pulled up a chair next to Brynn. His fingers clicked over the keyboard. He finally urged the screen to unlock. Clicked on the e-mail messages. He and Brynn both scanned the list of messages. Sure enough, another ransom ware notice popped onto the screen.

"I don't get it. Didn't you say you called Charlie and he fixed it?"

"Yes, but he said a lot of people received these messages and some have even paid the ransom." Once again, Brynn marveled at the power technology had in her life. What was going on?

"I suppose we'll have to call him again, and he's one busy guy."

"If he can't fix it, I'll get Roy. He's pretty good with this stuff," Wes said.

Brynn thought of Roy and shivered as she remembered him and Chelsea together at the fair. A completely unsuitable couple. "I hope it doesn't come to that."

"Me too," Wes said. "I'll call Charlie and try to get him out here today."

"Thanks, Wes," Brynn said. She had planned to sit there this morning and print off orders for cheese. Now she was at sea.

Wes closed the laptop. "Why don't you go and see your girls? Schuyler said she thinks they're missing you."

"Great idea," Becky said. "I'll come with you. Everything is done here. The kitchen is spotless and Wes is calling the computer guy. Let's get some cow loving in."

The sisters left the room and made for the door. A cool breeze met Brynn on opening the door. The grass was greener, the flowers had perked up, and the air had low humidity. *What a glorious morning.*

Brynn swung open the field gate and Freckles, along with all four cows, greeted her. Becky and Brynn rubbed, scratched, and petted all of them. Jewel waited until all the others greeted Brynn and received their rubs. Then she cautiously walked up to her, eyes blinking beneath hair and looking at Brynn with warmth.

Oh my. Brynn's heart bloomed. She reached for

Jewel and the cow gave off a noise much like a sigh. She was lonely, sad, missing her previous owner, perhaps. This cow needed a home where she'd be loved and appreciated.

"What a sweetie," Becky said. "You've got a great group of cows."

"Shh. Don't let them hear you say that." Brynn grinned. "They already think they're people."

Becky laughed. "Then maybe they can fix your computer."

"I wish they could! What an odd thing. A lot of people have been infected with this ransom ware. And now we've gotten it twice. I'd like to understand how to prevent this."

"I'm not sure you can. It seems to be one of those modern annoyances."

Jewel seemed as if she couldn't get enough attention. Brynn hated to leave her. She followed Brynn to the gate. "I'll be back later." The cow blinked.

Jewel had to be happier with the brief respite of cooler weather—the shaggy little cow was made for the cold.

"Where are you going?" Becky asked, following Brynn.

"To check out the make and see what needs to be done. I mean, it's where we make the cheese, so it needs a good cleaning. And I'm sure there's enough milk for a ton of cheese by now."

"Let's not go in there today," Becky said.

Brynn stopped. "What? Why?"

"I think you've done enough for one day," Becky stammered.

"That's ridiculous. What have I done? Tried to work. And visited with my cows. I want to peek in."

"No, you don't. If I let you peek in, you'll find something to do, Brynn MacAlister. I know you better than that." Her voice was stern.

"I promise I won't."

"Let's go back inside," she said, almost pleading.

What was going on here?

Brynn smelled a rat. But she knew better than to argue with Becky. Was she hiding something in the make? Had something happened in the make? Was her milk okay? Her products?

She'd sneak away later and check on it herself. "Whatever you say."

"Okay. Never thought I'd hear those words coming from you. But I'll take it," she said, and opened the front door.

Brynn didn't want to admit it to herself, but Becky was probably right. She was certain the make needed a good cleaning, and if she saw it she'd have to do something about it. The fact that milk stores were piling up was also driving her crazy. She was losing money every day milk was sitting in the stores untouched. Wes was doing his best to use it. But he was only one person, who did have other responsibilities, as well as a murder suspicion weighing on him.

Chapter 35

Brynn had almost forgotten about her checkup today. She still didn't have her phone or computer, which were what she'd been using for calendar reminders. So efficient, right? Except when your computer was taken over by ransom ware and your phone was confiscated by the police.

After her checkup, Brynn talked Becky into stopping by the sheriff's office to check on her phone.

"The doctor said to go home and rest," Becky pointed out.

"I will. I want to see if they have any news about my phone."

"I'm sure they'd have informed you by now."

"Not necessarily. I guess the fair has really stressed them. They don't have enough people. I'd not be surprised if they've done nothing with it yet."

Becky pulled the car into the parking lot of the sheriff's station. "Okay. Have it your way."

When the sisters walked into the office, they were surprised by the activity all around them. This was not a sleepy sheriff's department. Most of it focused on one guy at the computer. A few people were gathered around and others were making phone calls. There didn't seem to be anybody who was free to help them. A woman rounded the corner and almost ran into Brynn. "Oh, sorry!" she said. "Can I help you?"

"I'm Brynn MacAlister. The sheriff has my phone. I wondered if I can have it back."

"Phone?" She looked surprised. "Hmm. I'm not sure. Let me check on that." She disappeared into the back.

Brynn eyed the scene. Who were all these people? They weren't locals, she didn't think. What were they doing here? What was going on? She glanced at Becky, who lifted her eyebrows.

"This perp is good! Damn! I can't get a bead on this credit card. He's messing with us!"

Credit card? Were they talking about Wes's case?

"I'm sorry. I think it's a woman. Look, there's jewelry and a ton of cosmetics."

"Yeah, but it doesn't mean a woman is buying them."

Brynn stood and soaked all of it in. She was certain they were talking about Wes's credit card. Jewelry. Cosmetics. Considering those two things, her mind shifted to Chelsea. Was she conniving enough to pull this off?

Brynn and Becky stole glances at each other as they waited for the woman to return.

Brynn wanted to report back to Wes in detail. They figured the police were doing nothing, but they were wrong. They were on the case. And, from the looks of things, had brought in reinforcements.

"Brynn?" Sheriff Edge walked into the room. "Sandy said you were looking for your phone."

"Yes, Sheriff, I am," she replied. "I've been watching all of this stuff going on here."

He nodded. "I hate these open offices. But we're getting close."

"Is this Wes's case? The murder case? Are you close to finding the guy?"

"Don't get your hopes up. I've seen this happen a lot. These computer criminals . . . let's just say they're smart and wily. We thought we'd gotten close a few times. A lot of stuff just doesn't add up."

"Please let me know if I can help."

He raised an eyebrow. "You can help by going home and taking care of yourself. No more investigating on your part. We've talked about this before."

Becky elbowed her.

"What about my phone? Where is it?" Brynn asked.

"I can't release it yet. I'm sorry."

"Why not?"

"It's a piece of the cyberpuzzle we're trying to put together. We need it."

But I need my phone.

"Maybe you should get another phone, if you're worried about missing calls. It might be a while before you get it back," the sheriff said.

All of my contacts. All of my business information.

"We can go and see about a phone tomorrow," Becky said. "For now, I think we better get you home."

"Good idea," he said, and took his leave.

They walked out of the station and into the car.

"I can't believe I have to get a new phone."

"It's not a big deal. Everything will transfer over," Becky said as she started the car and pulled out of the parking space. "I run my business from my phone. You'll be okay. Don't worry about it."

"Well, that's a relief. But nothing else is, really."

Becky turned out of the lot. "I'm wondering if those guys were FBI?"

"What makes you say that?" Brynn asked.

"Did you see how they were dressed? Not in a uniform."

"I hadn't paid attention. I was focused on what they were saying."

Becky and Brynn laughed. Nobody else would find it funny. But their observations were typical of the sisters. Becky focused on clothing, fashion, and hair. Brynn listened and tried to make sense of it all. Together, they were a good team.

As they drove along, through the village of Shenandoah Springs, Brynn's head pounded and she closed her eyes. The words of the maybe FBI guys rolled around in her head. *Can't get a bead on this credit card. He's messing with us! Jewelry. Cosmetics.*

When Brynn awakened, they were pulling into the driveway and there was a strange car parked in it.

"Looks like we have company," Becky said.

Normally, Brynn would love having company. But for some reason, dread rushed through her.

Brynn and Becky opened the door slowly and crept inside. Voices came from the room that served as an office in the old farmhouse. It used to be a formal dining room, which Brynn didn't need.

The sisters stood in the hallway and listened. A stranger's voice. Young man. Then Wes. "I can't believe you're seeing Chelsea after all this time, dude."

The young man laughed. "She is amazing, if you know what I mean."

Brynn walked in. She wasn't going to stand there and listen to that. "Hello?" Becky was close on her heels.

"Brynn!" Wes stood. "Have you met Roy?"

"A few times, I think," she said, extending her hand. "But not officially. Nice to meet you." Had she met him at the fair? Yes, he'd visited the booth and chatted with Wes.

He sat in front of the computer but turned and shook her hand.

"I called him because Charlie is so backed up. He's a computer whiz, man," Wes said.

Brynn was usually thrilled by Wes's decisions. But this time she wasn't so sure. Roy was dating Chelsea. And, like it or not, Wes was still under suspicion of murder—a murder that had something to do with Chelsea. Brynn needed to figure this out. Her head hurt.

"I think we've got your computer cleaned," Roy said, looking at her and smiling. "We changed your passwords, and I ran an antivirus program. Usually these viruses take hold and most antivirus programs do nothing. But I have a kick-ass one."

Relief washed over Brynn. "Well, that's good." Maybe he was an okay guy. Perhaps it was fine that Wes had called on him.

Wes sat forward. "Yeah, poor Charlie. He's a one-guy shop and things have gotten too busy for him."

"Yet he won't hire anybody. What's with that?" Roy's eyebrows knit. Brynn sensed a story there. Roy must have sought employment with Charlie. Why wouldn't Charlie hire him?

Thoughts pricked at her—*right*—he was also the guy who had left for Richmond, a gaming job that didn't work out, so he came back to Shenandoah Springs to continue to work on farms. Wes had mentioned him more than a few times.

"I have no idea. Maybe he likes to do it himself."

"He's an odd dude. Gives me the creeps," Roy said.

There was nothing creepy about Charlie. At least Brynn didn't think so. "I like him. He saved my butt last week. I wish he could do something to stop it from happening again."

The room quieted.

Brynn wanted to get Roy out of her house. Her head was pounding now, and she needed to take a nap. "How much do we owe you?" He slid the chair back and stood.

"You don't owe me anything. Wes is a friend. I never charge my friends."

She was going to offer him cheese but remembered this was the guy who had said he didn't like cheese at the fair. "Well, that's nice of you. Thank you." What was wrong with her? He was helping them out. Okay. So he was a little strange. But most IT guys were a little odd.

"You're welcome. Well, I need to get out of here. I've a date tonight with my girl," he said, which was an odd thing to say to Brynn. Why would she care about his date with Chelsea? *Weird IT guys.*

"I'll walk you out," Wes said.

Becky, who had been standing there quietly, whispered, "Thank God," when they left the room. "That kid is strange."

"I thought it was just me," Brynn said.

"Did you notice his necklace?"

"No." Once again, her sister noticed something she hadn't.

"It's one of those half heart necklaces like we used to wear in high school."

"Do you mean those things you wore when you were going steady?" Brynn asked.

"Precisely. How old is he? I can't imagine a college kid wearing one of those."

"Well, he's into this relationship, evidently."

"Stupid boy," Becky said.

They walked out of the office and into the kitchen. "It's time for your medicine."

After Brynn downed the pills, she retreated to her bedroom. A nap was exactly what she needed. Even images of Roy's pimple face couldn't stop her from sleeping.

Brynn awoke about an hour later with Romeo on her chest, purring, watching her as if she were doing the most interesting thing ever. "Hello there." Romeo blinked and turned her head. She stroked the purring cat, still frustrated by Wes's case. What could she do to help the police without them knowing? Becky had already given information on the carnie who was an ex-con. Nathaniel gave the police the credit card lead. She invented a story about her business needing a spokesperson and got involved with Chelsea. Then she received the creepy text message. How did this all fit together? If at all?

Becky knocked at her door and walked in. "How are you doing?"

"A nap was just what I needed."

"Good. You have company."

"I do?"

"Chelsea is here to see you."

Brynn sat up and the cat jumped down with a disgruntled meow.

"Take your time. Wes is down there now with her, he's made a plate of cheese straws, and they're visiting."

"Interesting. I didn't think Wes liked her at all. He warned me from her."

"He's too polite to turn her away, I guess."

"Cheese straws? They're worth getting up for." Brynn glanced at herself in the mirror. Okay, she'd just woken up. But a little makeup would help. "I'll be right down," she said.

Why was Chelsea there? Brynn was not thrilled the person she was warned against was sitting in her living room. But then again, she'd not accept orders from anybody on who she could or could not have in her home.

Chapter 36

Chelsea and Wes were sitting in the living room. Chelsea on the couch, Wes on the La-Z-Boy. He had a pained expression when he was being forced to make small talk. Brynn knew it well.

"Hello! So glad to see you, Chelsea!" She took a seat next to her on the couch.

"Hi, Brynn. I wanted to visit Jewel. You said I could stop by anytime."

"Sure. Did you get a chance to see her?"

She nodded. "She's already looking more like herself. You're taking such good care of her. She's a special girl."

"That she is."

Chelsea took another bit of her cheese straw. "These are so good."

Brynn smelled it. And it turned her stomach. *Odd.* She loved cheese straws. But she had to turn her face.

After Chelsea swallowed the cheese straw, she took a sip of water. "I was wondering if you had come to any other solid plans about the spokesperson idea."

"Not really. I'm sorry." A pang of guilt tore through her. She had wanted to figure out how to lure the girl to her house. Get to know her, since all the shenanigans and murder seemed to relate to her somehow. "I'm still recovering and it's difficult to think, sometimes. Plus we've been distracted by a few other things lately." Wes squirmed in his seat. Brynn knew he didn't care for Chelsea. This must be torture for him.

Brynn tuned to Wes. "Wes, if you don't mind, could you please check on those new orders? Since Roy was here and fixed everything, we can get busy with all of that."

Relief washed over his face.

Chelsea sat up. "Was Roy here?"

"Yes, he came to help out with our computer," Brynn answered. "Charlie was so busy and we needed help."

A strange look came over her face. Boredom? Hatred? Brynn couldn't quite say, but she knew it wasn't love or even pleasant.

Wes stood. "So I'm going to check on those orders, boss. Catch you later, Chelsea."

Becky entered the room.

Chelsea seemed to remember her manners then. "How are you doing? What an awful thing to have happened. The man who attacked Wes is crazy. I'm so glad he's behind bars."

"How well do you know him?" Brynn asked.

"We dated a few times. But he got really clingy with me. I don't have time for that. I'm young. I don't want to be tied down." Her blue eyes sparkled. Chelsea had the longest eyelashes Brynn had ever seen. Were they real?

"Well, that's smart," Becky said, and sat down. "I

wish I'd had that attitude when I was your age. Instead, I ended up pregnant and married way too young. I love my daughter; don't misunderstand me. But it would've been nice to have her a little later in life. I missed out on a lot." *Where was Becky going with this?* Brynn wondered. It wasn't as if she were a teenager when she had Lily.

"So is Roy your boyfriend?" Brynn asked.

Chelsea paled. "Where did you get that idea?"

"I'm sorry. I thought he mentioned a date with you tonight, so I assumed . . ."

"Yeah, we're going out, but I don't want a boyfriend. Just don't. He's a little clingy, too."

"He doesn't seem like your type," Becky said.

Chelsea set her water glass down. "I'm sorry. I need to go. I'd forgotten about another appointment I have." She stood. "Please let me know about the spokesperson job when you know more."

"Okay, let me walk you to the door," Brynn said.

"No, that's okay. I can find my way. Bye." She waved her fingers and left the room. Becky and Brynn sat motionless until the door opened and closed.

Becky crossed her arms. "That girl knows something."

Brynn was reminded of Tillie, who'd known something about Nancy's death. She couldn't help but compare the two girls, who were the same age. What Tillie was aware of was deep and dark and serious. Her keeping it to herself weighed heavily on her, which was evident. But Brynn didn't get that sensation with Chelsea, who was polished and, if Brynn was correct in her assessment, was an astute liar. "I imagine she knows a lot."

"Wes doesn't like her," Becky said.

Brynn nodded. "He knows more about her than

he's telling. But it speaks to him being a gentleman. I don't think he likes to talk badly about people."

Becky popped a cheese straw into her mouth and chewed. "So good."

The doorbell rang. "I'll get it," Becky said, and jumped up.

Brynn sat and thought over the strange visit from Chelsea. She said she wanted to see Jewel. Then she asked about the fake position. She also let it drop Roy wasn't her boyfriend. But earlier, Roy said they were a couple and even wore one of those half heart necklaces—which Chelsea did not wear.

She caught herself: Had she stepped back into the strange time capsule of her high school youth? How had she gotten to this place where she was even thinking about high schoolers and their relationships? *Oh, Brynn, what have you become?*

"Hey, look what the cat dragged in," Becky said. It was Schuyler, who'd been so busy with her vet practice, the fair, and taking care of Brynn's morning milking that Brynn hadn't seen her in what felt like forever. Brynn hugged her.

"It's so good to see you."

Schuyler sat down. "I've come with some news. And it's the strangest news you've ever heard in your life."

The three of them sat.

"Can I get you anything?" Becky asked.

"No, and I need you two to keep this to yourselves. But at the same time, I want to warn you because something strange is going on in Shenandoah Springs." Schuyler's amber eyes lit with excitement and worry.

Brynn was growing a bit impatient with the prelude. "Well, spill!"

"I learned this from my brother and it's not been publicly announced yet." Mike was the local fire inspector and had an in with the law officials. "The tractor accident was definitely murder, but not by Josh."

Becky and Brynn waited for the rest of it.

"It was done remotely. Witnesses said they saw Josh flailing around as if he'd lost control. And he had. Someone was controlling the tractor from somewhere else."

"What?" Becky gasped. "Like something from a sci-fi movie! I don't believe it."

"I'm totally serious. It's like a bigger and better technology than the remote toys we had as kids." Schuyler paused.

"We had a little Volkswagen Bug, remember that?" Brynn asked.

Becky nodded. "But that's way different."

"No, it's not. That technology is out there. Now the new tractors have Wi-Fi in them so the farmers don't have to feel disconnected from their families or from the internet, if it's what they want. Evidently, the Wi-Fi is how this person hacked into the tractor. The police don't know who did it, yet, or how far away he or she was. Or how far the technology could even reach. If it doesn't go far, the suspect pool would narrow down to the people on the property right then and there."

Brynn couldn't believe her ears. Someone used Josh and his tractor to kill Evan? Did they know they were doing it? Did they mean to kill? Or was it someone fooling around with technology? She recalled the look of dread on David Reese's face when she told him about the accident. "Have they talked with David Reese? He could probably tell them a lot."

"I assume they have. He's been around. I saw him at the station. He's probably helping the police."

"I told him about the accident and he seemed concerned."

"He should be. He sold Josh the tractor and claimed it was safe and secure. Evidently, it's not."

Brynn asked the obvious question: "Why would a tractor even need Wi-Fi?"

"It's used for all kinds of things, like tracking how many seeds are planted, stuff about the soil. It's collecting information and sending it to a computer at the house. Plus, on a big farm, it's great for communication between the staff."

Gone were the days of yelling across the field and counting the seed yourself. Brynn sighed.

"This is like something from one of those old movies, right? Like where the robots take over the world?" Becky said.

Brynn grinned. "But there's always an evil mastermind behind it. Genius, but flawed. Who could that be?"

"Exactly," Schuyler said. "Who wanted Evan dead and why? Was it specifically aimed at him or was he or she on some power trip to prove it could be done?"

"What about this David Reese guy? Who is he?" Becky asked.

Schuyler shrugged. "Owns the tractor shop. He's not from around here. I don't know him well at all."

"I think he's creepy. When we met, he looked at me as if I were a piece of meat. You know what I mean," Brynn said.

"Just because he's a lech doesn't mean he's an evil genius mad killer," Becky said.

"Yeah, but you know, he gave me the same look," Schuyler said.

"Uh-oh," Brynn said.

"Yeah, I asked him what his problem was. His face got all red and he walked away. Creep." Schuyler didn't broker any foolishness. This guy was lucky she didn't smack him. "My karate training teaches me not to hit someone unless they come at me first."

"You read my mind," Brynn said.

The three of them laughed.

"Okay, but why would Reese want to kill a young summer helper?" Becky said after they calmed down.

"I wondered the same thing," Schuyler said.

Brynn mulled it over and her first thought was too distasteful to mention. Or at least she thought.

"I see the wheels turning in your pea brain," Becky said.

"Nah, it's . . . creepy."

"The whole thing is," Schuyler said.

Brynn paused, trying to gain composure before she spit it out. "What if he likes Chelsea?" Even as she said it, a chill traveled up and down her spine. "What if he wanted to get the competition out of the way?"

"He'd kill a man for a young woman's attention?" Becky's eyes were as wide as the moon.

"David Reese is a creep. But he's too old for her." Schuyler was the voice of reason most of the time.

"How many older men become fixated on younger women?" Brynn said.

"Well, that's random," Becky muttered.

"I don't know," Schuyler said. "But I'm hoping the police come up with someone soon. This creeps me out more than anything else that has happened recently. That you could remotely take over a tractor and demand it run someone over? What's next?" Schuyler said.

Brynn couldn't help but remember all the other

strange technological stuff going on—the ransom ware, for example. She'd always embraced technology. Loved her computer, the internet, the smartphone. But this was all giving her pause. Maybe too many details about her life were on the computer. If someone decided to steal her identity, for example, she now saw how easy that might be. Not that any person in their right mind would want to steal her identity—she didn't have much money; she had a struggling business and property she still owed money on. In fact, now she thought about it, she almost wished someone would steal her identity. *Good luck with that, mister.*

Chapter 37

After their conversation, the women moved into the field for a breath of fresh air. After all the technology talk, Brynn wanted her feet on the earth and her eyes on the horizon. Schuyler wanted to check on Marigold, who was expecting a calf. Brynn was excited, but apprehensive because of poor Petunia and her past grief.

"She's doing great," Schuyler said after examining Marigold. She placed her arm around the cow, who turned and looked at her and blinked. Jewel sauntered up to them, a little hesitant but curious. "Speaking of doing great. Jewel looks good. Gaining weight. She seems to be fitting right in."

"She is," Brynn said. "Any luck finding a home for her?"

"Not yet," Schuyler said, and looked away. It was as Brynn suspected. Schuyler wasn't searching too hard. Could she keep Jewel, along with the new calf? She wasn't sure. But it would be hard for Jewel to go to another strange place, sensitive cow that she was.

Freckles bounded over to Schuyler and nearly knocked her over. "Speaking of gaining weight!"

"I think she's part cow," Becky said as she joined them.

"She might be." Schuyler tussled round a bit in the field with her. Freckles was another one of Schuyler's strays. Brynn had kept her because Freckles and Petunia became fast friends.

Brynn rubbed Jewel's nose, and if a cow could sigh she was certain she would. Her big cow eyes peered at Brynn from beneath the scraggly hair. Brynn worked her way to her neck. "Wait," Brynn said, "didn't she have a collar?"

"Yes, she did," Schuyler said.

Brynn shrugged. "It's gone. Wonder what happened to it?"

"Odd. It's not like a cow can take off her collar." Schuyler rubbed around the cow's neck.

"Right?" Brynn said.

Becky rubbed around her neck, too. "Maybe it got stuck on something and she slipped out of it."

"She was very thin," Schuyler said. "But I don't see that happening."

The three of them looked around. The field had nothing but green grass and flowers. Brynn checked in the barn in Jewel's stall. Nothing. "How odd. A missing collar."

Collars were tagged with important tracking information. It wasn't necessarily the collar Brynn was worried about, but its tag.

"I need to head out," Schuyler said. "I'm on CSA duty tonight at the fair. It's a shame you haven't gotten to go much. Tomorrow is the last night. Perhaps you can attend if you're feeling okay."

Brynn agreed it was a shame. The fair was a culmi-
nation and celebration of her community's farming
work through the year. Besides, it was just good fun.
She didn't want to think about her disaster of a
cheese competition. "I'd like to go. I hope I can."

Had it been two weeks already? Brynn had lost
track of time in her concussed mind. She'd been
concentrating on other things.

"If you find the collar, let me know," Schuyler said.
"Otherwise, I'll have to get new tags for her."

Brynn and Becky walked her to her truck and
watched as she drove away.

"How could a collar slip from a cow's neck?" Becky
asked. Brynn shrugged. "Maybe Wes is aware of this."
She reached into her pocket for her phone and remembered she didn't have one, "Bother! I don't
have a phone."

"That's right. I'll text him," Becky said as they
walked toward the house.

Brynn opened the door and welcomed the cool
air-conditioned breeze on her skin. Brynn made her
way to the couch and lay down. It had been quite a
day. Ransom ware. Monster tractors. And missing
cow collars. What else could happen?

Becky walked into the room and sat on the La-Z-
Boy. "Wes says he doesn't know anything about the
collar, but he and Max will look for it and get back
to us."

"Well, we already looked for it. I don't think it's on
the property."

"It won't hurt for them to look again."

Becky looked weary. She'd been doing such a
great job taking care of Brynn and trying to keep up
with everything. Brynn felt a pang of guilt. She wasn't

100 percent yet. But she was getting better. "Why don't you go home, Becky? I'll be fine. You look so tired."

"Thanks, and no. I'm here for the duration. Everything is fine with Lily. It's summer and she's having a blast. When you're better, I'll happily go home."

"I am better."

"That's what you say, but look at you. It's four in the afternoon and you're lying on the couch. That's not the Brynn I know."

Point taken.

"Sometimes I feel normal."

"Sometimes isn't enough."

Chapter 38

"We've not found Jewel's collar yet," Wes said as he and Max came into the living room.

"The more I think about it the more I wonder if she actually had one." Brynn's head was foggy again.

"Yes, of course she did," Becky said. "I remember it."

"It seems to me the question isn't if she had it, but what happened to it," Max said. "Collars don't fall off of cows' necks."

"No, but sometimes they can slip out of them," Wes said.

"But we've no evidence of it. We've scoured the place. My conclusion is that someone took it." Max sat down on the couch next to Brynn. "This place keeps getting better and better. First our gram dies in a fire, then Wes is accused of murder, plus all of this weird ransom ware stuff going on. Now this? Someone stole a collar from a sweet little cow?"

Brynn's thoughts spun around in her mind. Was this all connected somehow? *Think, think, think.* But the more she tried to think, the worse it became. So frustrating. "Have you heard from the police?" she asked Wes.

"Not recently. My dad is at the station with my lawyer right now." Weariness came over his face and he aged about ten years in that moment. "I don't want to go back to jail. I couldn't survive."

The room quieted. But Brynn's head didn't. "Not going to happen. The credit card incident proved your innocence."

"They suspect he was in cahoots with someone," Max said.

Brynn's heart pounded. "What?"

"It's the most ridiculous thing I've ever heard," Wes said. "But they have to investigate every possibility. A man's life was taken." He quieted. "It's horrible. Logically, I can see why they suspect me. I discovered the body. They thought the gun was registered to me. But now they realize it's not, someone stole my identity, I wish they'd drop it. This whole theory of my working with someone doesn't make sense."

Max let out a frustrated sigh. "Grasping at straws."

"But why?" Becky said. "I mean, I get considering you a person of interest. But it's a process of elimination, right? So eliminating you is as effective as arresting you."

Brynn picked up a pad of paper from the table and scribbled on it: *David Reese. Ian Fellows.* "Does anybody know if Ian has been dismissed as a suspect?"

Wes shrugged. "I have no clue. They don't tell me the details on the other suspects."

"Attempted-murder ex-con. He's got to have something to do with it. Surely nobody in this community shot a young man for no good reason," Becky said.

"Is there ever a good reason?" Brynn shivered, thinking of Wes's own experience getting shot. "How are you doing?"

"The wound is almost healed completely. And that guy is in jail. Some justice is quick." He stood. Brynn noted his jeans were hanging off him. He'd lost a lot of weight. She needed to do more to help prove his innocence. "I'm hungry. I guess if I want to eat, I better make something myself. You lot aren't doing anything but sitting around." He grinned.

Becky stood. "I'll help."

The two of them left the room.

Brynn leaned closer to Max. "I'm so worried about him."

Max nodded. "We all are. It's good his appetite is back. He's not really eaten much. It bothers him so much that people would suspect him of murder. Then there's this whole racist element. It's not as if we've not had to deal with it before. But it really never gets any easier. We definitely stand out here."

Brynn tried to swallow the frustration she felt. But it wasn't going away. What could she do to help? "Live by example" was what Granny Rose always said. Wasn't she doing that? It didn't seem to be enough. She thought of Helen, who was vocal about her suspicions of Wes, as was the guy flinging French fries at the fair. Were they an ignorant few? Or were there more asses in this community than she knew? She understood change came slowly to rural areas. It was a part of the charm. A double-edged charm. One side, she loved the slower pace, fewer people, easier cost of living, and on the other side . . . were remnants of an ugly past. Remnants such as racism, sexism, and complete suspicion of strangers. Brynn tried to understand it, but there was no excuse for it.

None. If people chose to hide their heads in the mountain dirt and not move forward, that was one thing. But to act in such ignorant ways, to judge people on looks, nationality, or gender? Nah, that wasn't going to fly anymore. No matter how deep in the hills you lived. And Brynn would fight it with her last breath.

Brynn tossed and turned that night, even with all the medicine she'd taken that normally made her sleepy. Finally, she rose out of the bed and fired up her laptop. She wanted to look up David Reese. Who was he? Schuyler had mentioned she didn't know him well because he wasn't from around here. Where was he from? Why did anybody assume he could leer at women the way he did and get away with it? Shame poked at her. She shouldn't have bitten her lip. She should've spoken up there and then. She vowed next time she would.

The screen flicked on. *One hour a day*, her doctor's voice rang in her head. Surely this wouldn't even take an hour. She was probably making too much of this. So David was a lech, didn't mean he was a killer. But someone was. Why not him? He had a blog and a website for the tractor business. She clicked on it. Very attractive and professional. About David: "A Norfolk, Va., native, David, and his family, moved to the Shenandoah Valley in 2000 to follow his dream of opening a tractor business." He had a family? Brynn had no idea. Okay, so that made his obvious lechery a bit more sinister. "A graduate of James Madison University, David fell in love with the mountains and vowed to return when he could. He's been top sales executive for seven years in a row; he now makes his home in the most beautiful place on earth, as he likes to call it." Brynn would give him that—it was gorgeous—but the most beautiful place on earth?

Okay, so this was for public viewing and could have been constructed carefully. It didn't tell her much, but she did learn a few things about him. She needed to dig beyond the tractor business. What about Facebook? Twitter?

She clicked on Facebook and yawned. She was getting sleepy. That was a good thing.

All of his settings were private. She'd have to send him a friend request in order to see anything about him. Did she really want to do that? She didn't want to give him the wrong idea. God knows what would become of it. But at the same time, she wanted to view his page. Nah, she'd hold off on friending him. Instead, she clicked over to Twitter.

She keyed in his name. There were three David Reeses—one was definitely not him, as he was African-American. She clicked on one. Not him, either. Then clicked on another. There he was. She scanned his tweets. Mostly about tractors. Very few personal interactions. She clicked on who he was following. Tractor business, newspapers, and several pretty young women. Brynn clicked on one. *Hmmm.* Definitely a model or something, interacting with men on Twitter. But not him. Perhaps he was too smart for that. But yes. He was definitely a man who liked beautiful women and in a creepy way. They were all quite young, as well, which gave credence to her suspicion that maybe, maybe, he had a thing for Chelsea.

Brynn's stomach growled. She shut the laptop and padded downstairs for a snack. She opened the refrigerator and looked for the leftover quiche. "It's over here," a voice rang out. Brynn gasped and turned to see Becky sitting in the dark with the pan of quiche on the table. "You scared me half to death!"

She shut the refrigerator, opened the drawer, and reached in for a fork.

"Sorry. I couldn't sleep," Becky said.

Brynn sat down and plunged her fork into the quiche. "Me either."

"What's on your mind?"

"What's not on my mind?" She shoveled in a bite.

"I hear you."

Bright moonlight streamed in through the window. The sisters didn't need to turn on a light. They sat with silver light beaming in on them and ate the last of the quiche.

"It's been a long time since I've been up at this hour," Becky said. "It's kind of cool. Remember how we used to raid the refrigerator at night?"

Brynn smiled at the memory. "Mom would get so mad the next morning."

"Now I get it. It's hard enough to plan meals, but then add in two teenage girls raiding the fridge when the mood strikes." Becky grinned.

"I wonder if teenage girls still do that?"

"Well, who knows? How many are you acquainted with?"

"I know a few. There's Tillie, thin as a rail. I doubt she eats much at all. Then there's Chelsea, who's not exactly thin, but I bet she watches everything she eats. Her looks seem to be important to her." Saying Chelsea's name brought something to the front of her mind. Something simmered there but didn't quite boil. What was it? Brynn's head felt as if it were full of cotton. Then she remembered. "Chelsea was here, and she spent some time with Jewel."

Becky's head tilted in interest. "Do you think she knows something about the collar?"

"She might." Of course, it made sense. She was the thing Brynn had forgotten. She was what had been picking at her brain, keeping her awake. "She's the only other person who was around Jewel. But the question is why would she take her collar? It doesn't make sense."

"Well, she said she loved Jewel. Maybe she wanted a keepsake." Becky paused. "Teenage girls are often emotional and attached to strange things. Maybe she wanted to keep a piece of her childhood. She seems to love Jewel."

True enough, but still strange. She'd call her in the morning. That would be one awkward phone call.

Chapter 39

Tillie stopped in after tending to the cows the next morning. Wes and she had evidently preplanned a breakfast gathering. Brynn was up and ready to eat, as was Becky.

"Marigold is ready to pop," Tillie said. "I can't wait for a calf!"

"Right? It's going to be awesome," Wes said as he placed a stack of banana pancakes on the table. The smell traveled straight from Brynn's nose to her stomach.

"I'm a little worried," Brynn said.

"I'm sure she'll be fine." Tillie reached over and patted Brynn's hand. "I've seen so many cows and horses giving birth. It's not pretty, but it's amazing."

"Well, there's that. But I'm worried about Petunia. Her emotional state. I mean, she lost a calf and had such a hard time with it."

"Well, she seems fine now."

"But what if it brings up memories?"

Becky placed a dish of fresh whipped cream on the table. Wes put a tiny bowl of crushed walnuts next to it. Brynn took another sip of coffee. She was aching to get back to her daily life.

"It might." Becky sat down. "But we'll deal with that when it happens."

"She and Freckles still seem to be the best of buddies." Wes sat down and reached for the pancakes.

"Where are your dad and Max?"

"Sleeping in this morning. These early hours don't suit them." He dropped a pancake on his plate and passed the stack to Tillie. He reached for the whipped cream and plopped it onto his pancake.

"Oh my God, this smells so good. Like a banana dream!" Tillie leaned over her plate. She passed the stack to Brynn, who loaded her plate with two pancakes chock-full of banana and spices. Cinnamon. Nutmeg. She then passed it to Becky, who by that point was almost drooling. "I want to put the whole thing in my mouth!" She put whipped cream on top and sprinkled walnuts on it. Her amber eyes were lit with excitement.

Brynn savored the first bite, which was, indeed, a banana dream. The fresh whipped cream was a perfect complement. With each bite, Brynn's head seemed to clean more. Walnuts were brain food, right? "I think I may be getting enough fortitude to make the phone call to Chelsea."

"Why would you be calling her?" Tillie's voice held disdain. Wes looked up from his plate and Becky stopped shoveling pancakes in.

"Oh, I forgot to mention to you-all. I suspect she took Jewel's collar."

"What? Why would she do that?" Tillie tucked back into her pancake.

"It's missing," Wes said. "We've looked all over the place. Why do you think she took it?"

"When we came home the other day, she'd already been here, and she was visiting Jewel. She's the only other person besides us around her. Deductive reasoning."

"Yes, but why take a cow collar?" Becky reached for more whipped cream.

"I've no idea. But as you said last night, she's attached to the cow and perhaps wanted a souvenir."

"I don't buy it at all," Tillie said. "Take a lock of fur, not a collar."

"On the one hand, your reasoning makes a world of sense. On the other hand, what's the MO?" Wes took another bite.

"Oh well. Let's chalk it up to one of the weird things happening lately." Brynn's attention shifted to her pancake, deciding not to think too hard about Chelsea and her motives. It was a cow collar. They'd get another one. If Chelsea took it, let her have it. No, she'd not call. It would be too awkward. More awkward even than the fake job she'd made up to lure the girl in. A pang of shame tore through her. She was a teenager. Brynn had no right to do that.

But still. No harm done. And, even more important, Brynn was still convinced Chelsea was involved with the murder of Donny Iser. She didn't pull the trigger. But she knew something. It was too coincidental—the tractor accident had to do with her boyfriend; then the shooting victim was another one of her boyfriends. Sounded like another suitor was offing all his competition.

Wait. People didn't really do that, did they? It was too crazy of a thought to share with her friends and sister at the breakfast table this morning; that was for sure.

"I'm blown away by the whole tractor thing," Tillie

said. "I mean, who knows if it was intentional? And how will they prove it?"

"I'm assuming it was. I'm also surprised more of this kind of thing doesn't happen, with the technological capabilities we have. I guess the FBI has a special cybersecurity unit checking into this. Should be a better way to prevent such things from happening," Wes said.

"Agreed. I love technology," Becky said. "I love all the apps. The ease of banking and e-mails. But since my visit here, I've been considering going back to the old-fashioned way of doing things. The whole ransom ware thing is crazy. Now this remote tractor killing."

"All true," Wes said. "But we know it wasn't a computer who pulled the trigger and killed Donny. If only, maybe I'd have a bit more hope."

Tillie reached out and grabbed his hand. "Wes. It's going to be okay. I promise."

Such compassion in her voice. Such hope. But Brynn's stomach turned. How was any of this going to get better?

After breakfast, Tillie left and Wes gave Brynn the chore of fulfilling orders. "Take it slow."

"I think I can manage." She refrained from rolling her eyes. She had a concussion, but she was still alive and getting better every day. She wasn't an invalid.

"I'm going out to the barn to check on some things and I have an appointment with my lawyer in a bit, so I won't see you until later. Hopefully, I'll be back to take you to the last night of the fair."

"You better be," she joked.

"Becky should be back soon. You won't be alone long. Everything okay?"

Becky had gone out with a grocery list. It would be the first time Brynn had been left alone since she'd gotten the concussion. "I'll be fine," she said.

Brynn was alone with her boxes, cheese, linen, and raffia, along with all the labels and paper she needed to send the orders out with. There were fifteen. She could handle this with one arm tied behind her back.

All the orders were for the same cheese—Buttermilk Creek Farmstead, a mild white cheese, already wrapped in a special packing material to keep it cool during shipping. Brynn wrapped each hunk in linen and placed her label on it. Then she wrapped raffia around it, cut it, and tied a sloppy bow. *Nice.*

Romeo came sauntering into the kitchen and rubbed up against Brynn's legs. "Hello, kitty." The cat meowed back. "Poor girl, named a boy's name. The worst name ever." Brynn was not a fan of *Romeo and Juliet* and really didn't like the name Romeo. At all. "Perhaps we should come up with another name for you." She sat down and watched Brynn's every move, as if she were doing the most fascinating thing ever. Such is life with cats.

About halfway through, Brynn took a water break. She sat down and looked out her kitchen picture window. There were her three cows along with Freckles and Jewel, all hanging out together, which Brynn loved to see.

Becky entered the house with her arms full of groceries. Brynn stood and took some bags from her. "How's it going, Brynn?"

"Okay. I'm about halfway through and haven't keeled over or anything."

"Well, that's good news. I'd have been here sooner, but there was quite a crowd at the grocery store. I didn't realize that many people lived here, let alone all converged on a Thursday morning at the local grocery store. God." She opened the fridge and placed eggs inside. Brynn usually got her eggs from the farmers' market, but things had been a little crazy with the fair, the murder, and her concussion.

After the groceries were put away, Brynn returned to her packing. Becky helped. "I love your labels. Did I ever ask you why they call the farm Buttermilk Creek?"

"I don't think so. But the answer is not that interesting." Brynn laughed. "You'd think in an area rich with history the name would have some interesting story attached to it. But it was named after a German family whose last name was Buttermilch, which sounds like 'buttermilk' to the untrained American ear. So after years, it became Buttermilk."

"Well, it's perfect for your farm, isn't it?"

"It is," Brynn said as she wrapped a hunk of cheese in linen, then stuck a label on it.

"How are you feeling? It's almost time for another dose of meds."

"I'm okay. I'll probably take a nap before the big show tonight."

Becky laughed. "Me too. I'm not much of a night owl. I like being in bed early."

"Same."

"When we were teenagers, we'd never had said such a thing."

"No. We were so cool then," Brynn said, and she boxed up her package.

Becky sighed. "If only we were as cool today . . ."

"If we were, we'd have more energy," Brynn said. "I don't have enough to be that cool."

"Ain't that the truth?" Becky cut a piece of linen and handed it to Brynn.

Brynn took in the tableau—she and her sister, separated by distance and a few years, working together, as if time had slipped away. She blinked back a tear. Becky had picked up and raced to her side when she was hurt. She left her daughter, her life, in Richmond and came to make sure Brynn was okay and to help. "Thank you for coming here."

Becky's head tilted, and she leaned forward. "Where else would I be right now?"

"Home with your daughter, your work. Our parents."

Becky sighed, looked away, and blinked. She looked steadily at Brynn. "Don't make too much of this. I needed a break from all of it. Your concussion was a great excuse." Straight-faced. A twitch in her cheek. Then she exploded in laughter.

Chapter 40

The fair was everything Brynn had remembered from the previous years. The skies were darkening when they arrived, so the strung lights and carnival rides lit the place. She tried to view the grounds with fresh eyes as she had done last year. But it was difficult, realizing the underside of things. How much work it took to put the fair together. How behind some of these friendly faces a strong current of racism was hidden. How a young man had tied to kill Wes. She was trying not to be paranoid as they strolled through the crowds and she noted people taking a second look at Wes and Max. They could be looking at them because they were handsome young men. That made sense. That is what she'd choose to believe.

The organ music from the merry-go-round played in the background and the scent of buttered popcorn mingled with candied apples clung to the air.

They sat at a picnic table and watched people go by. A mother with a baby in the stroller and another wide-eyed child holding her hand. A group of preteens looking cool and disinterested in the fair. Couples holding hands.

The skies were a dark blue-black beyond the lights, with stars starting to come into view. Brynn was glad to be here, even with all the chaos.

"How are you feeling?" Becky asked, and then bit into a hot dog.

"You've asked twelve times. I'm fine." And she was. She felt stronger than she had in a long time. "Things keep going like this and you'll have to go back to your awful life."

Becky grinned.

"We're going on a few rides." Wes leaned across the table. "I love the Ferris wheel." For a moment, Brynn thought she glimpsed the boy he used to be—or even maybe still was.

"I'll go with you," Nathaniel said. He was not letting his son out of his sight. Brynn realized he had seen the onlookers glancing Max's way as they strode through the crowds. Wes, Max, and Nathaniel took off to ride the Ferris wheel.

David Reese came up to their table. "Well, hello, ladies. I don't believe we've met." He turned to Becky and eyeballed her as if he were looking at a piece of meat

"My sister, Becky," Brynn said. "Becky, this is David Reese. He sells tractors."

"Oh," Becky said. "Like the freaky robot tractor that killed that boy?"

He paled. "Uh. Listen, I'm sorry. I've got an appointment. Catch you ladies later." He took off.

"Not if I can help it," Becky muttered under her breath.

Brynn's stifled laugh came out. "It's not me, is it? There's something way off about him."

"I'd say." Becky stuffed the last of her hot dog into her mouth.

Brynn watched as a mother with a stroller attempted to navigate the grassy fairground. A group of preteens sauntered by trying to look as uninterested as possible in the rows of fair games and rides around the corner. The *ding-ding-ding* from a game caught at least one of the girls' attention. One of them stopped to talk with a tall young man wearing cowboy boots. Brynn recognized him. It was Roy.

Roy strolled through the crowd. He stopped and talked with someone, then started to make his way past Brynn, then stopped. "Ms. MacAlister? Do you remember me?"

"Of course I do."

"Have you seen Chelsea?" Roy asked. "I was supposed to meet her an hour ago. It's not like her to be late and she's not answering her phone."

A chill traveled through Brynn. With all the sinister events of the past few weeks, this might be cause for concern. "I've not seen her. Have you, Becky?"

"I don't think I have."

"Have you called her parents?" Brynn asked.

"That's what I'm going to do next. I'm heading into the craft building to get away from all the noise. I don't want to worry them, but at the same time . . . it's not like her."

"I think they'd appreciate it. Who knows? Maybe she's with them." Brynn recalled when Tillie was missing. She was so thankful it had turned out okay. But these days, you couldn't be too careful—there was a freak accident and a murder in their own little community. "She may have gotten sidetracked."

"Let us know," Becky said. Her eyes were wide with

worry. Every parent's nightmare. A missing child. Brynn could read her sister's thoughts.

Let's hope that's not the case, she thought.

As Brynn watched him walk away, something else occurred to her. "Maybe she's out with another boy."

"I thought about that, too. Hopefully she stood him up. Could be that's all it is."

"Too bad for him. But at least she'd be okay."

Wes found it hard to imagine Chelsea and Roy were dating. Brynn didn't like to judge people based on their looks. But Roy was an average-looking young man, with a bad complexion. Chelsea was unusually beautiful—like breathtaking. When she walked into a room, your eyes couldn't help but land on her. It was almost as if there were an angelic glow around her.

"I'm going to find the bathroom," Brynn said, and stood.

"Need help?" Becky asked.

"I think I can manage."

Brynn walked slowly through the grass and around the corner of the craft building to find a bathroom. There were David Reese and Roy at the end of the building. Roy was gesturing. David's hands were on his hips. "What's wrong with you, old man?" Brynn stopped in her tracks. A crowd started to gather.

"Look, boy. You need to move on."

"Don't tell me what to do. Where's Chelsea?" He pushed David. Hard. David stumbled and almost fell. His chest puffed. "I told you I don't know where the little slut is."

Roy plunged into him. The next thing Brynn knew, the two of them were on the ground, rolling around, punching, pulling hair. She stepped forward and tried to help break it up.

"What's wrong with you two?" She reached for Roy and tried to pull him off.

"Step aside, Brynn." She turned to see Sheriff Edge, who pulled Roy off of David with one yank.

"Gladly!" Brynn's heart thudded in her chest. What was going on here? Why did Roy think David knew Chelsea's whereabouts? Why was he so angry at David? Why would David even concern himself with young people in the valley? He was a grown man.

"Okay, everybody!" the sheriff said in a loud, forceful tone Brynn had never heard come out of him before. "Move along! Nothing to see here!" Another officer grabbed David and put his hands behind his back, then took him away.

The sheriff still held Roy. "Let's you and me take a walk."

Okay. Things seemed to be under control here. The crowd was dispersing and Brynn still needed to find the bathroom. She turned to run into her sister. "We really can't take you anywhere," Becky said.

Chapter 41

Brynn nearly collapsed into bed that night. She wouldn't admit it to anybody else, but she had to admit it to herself—going to the fair exhausted her. She was getting better, but long outings sapped energy from her.

Even though she was bone-tired, she tossed and turned, recalling the argument between David Reese and Roy. How odd. Why would Roy presume David knew where Chelsea was? And had they ever found her? She whispered a prayer that the young woman was safe and back home, where she belonged.

She rolled over onto her stomach, which usually helped when she wanted to fall asleep. Romeo jumped on the bed and settled herself on Brynn's lower back, purring. The purring worked its magic and Brynn nodded off.

She awakened to the scent of frying eggs, which always stirred her. She untangled herself from her quilts and made her way downstairs, surprised to see Willow at the breakfast table.

"I talked her into staying," Wes said.

"He can be very persuasive," Willow said, smiling. Brynn leaned down and hugged her. "So good to see you."

"It smells heavenly, doesn't it?" Becky said. "He's making an omelet, with all of the fresh veggies from the garden."

"Well, from other people's gardens. We only have a small one. Don't have time to do cheese and gardens, Not this year, anyway." Wes placed the platter of eggs on the table.

"How are the girls this morning? I miss them."

"They're fine. I'm sure they miss you, too. That Jewel is gorgeous. She's looking so healthy. You should be able to find her a new home soon."

Brynn's heart sank at the thought.

"Have you ever found her collar?" Becky asked to nobody in particular.

Wes sat down. "No."

"Collar?" Willow asked. "Was her collar missing?"

"Still is."

"No, it's not. I'm sure I saw it on her this morning." She took a bite of eggs.

Brynn's head spun. "What? Her collar is back?"

Becky's eyes widened. Wes stood. The three of them left the table.

"What? Where are you all going?" Willow said, her mouth half full.

Brynn kept moving. "Going to see the collar."

"What's the big deal?" Willow said, staying with her food. "I'm not sure what's going on here, but I'm hungry," Brynn heard before she left the house, still in her pajamas and slippers.

The three of them rushed to the gate. Freckles spotted them and ran over as they opened it. "Hey, girl," Brynn said, patting her but moving toward Jewel, grazing peacefully, ignoring them until the three of them got closer. She looked up, blinked.

"Well, ain't that something," Brynn said, for there stood the cow with a collar around her shaggy neck.

"How did that happen?" Becky said what they were all wondering.

Wes shook his head in disbelief. "Someone must have taken it and then put it back on."

Astonished, Brynn's breath was ragged. "But why would someone do that?"

The three of them stood staring at the cow as if she held the answers. She batted her big eyes and turned back to her breakfast.

Wes walked over to her and gently removed the collar and examined it. "It looks like the same collar, but I can't be sure. I wasn't paying much attention to it before."

Becky and Brynn looked it over, too. Brynn held it up to the sky and noted the wobbly inseam. "I think there's something inside."

"Let's take it in the house and cut it open," Wes said. "We can always get her another collar."

When the three of them came into the house, Willow was on her second helping of eggs. "If you-all aren't going to eat, I am. These biscuits are amazing." She looked up. "What are you doing bringing that filthy collar in here?"

"We suspect there's something inside of it."

She dropped her biscuit. "What?"

Wes reached for a knife and a pair of scissors. "Let's take it into the living room."

All of them, even Willow, followed Wes into the living room. He spread the collar out on the coffee table.

Brynn's head was spinning. A missing collar returned, with something inside. This had to be one of the strangest things that had ever happened to her—and plenty of odd things had happened since she moved to Shenandoah Springs.

He gently took the knife and cut open the underside of the collar. What was inside? Jewels? Drugs? Brynn knew about the drug problem here and everywhere. She was expecting to see cocaine or something inside of the collar.

Wes turned it upside down. Little square pieces of plastic fell onto the table.

Becky's mouth dropped. "What the heck is that?"

Wes frowned. "Computer chips."

Brynn had held off calling Chelsea because she was so young and really, if she had taken the collar, what proof did they have? She didn't want to be accused of harassing a minor. But if Chelsea did take it, would she have brought it back last night when she was missing—with those computer chips inside?

Looks like she would have to call her. She dreaded it.

"Are you thinking what I'm thinking?" Becky said.

Brynn shrugged. "I have no idea."

"Those computer chips must hold valuable information."

"Yes, but I was thinking . . . Chelsea must have been the person who brought it back. What would she know about computer chips?"

Wes's head titled. "Plenty. She's dating a brilliant computer guy, and she's in the tech program at school."

As they sat in silence, each with their own thoughts, Brynn's stomach growled. Loudly. "Sorry."

"You better get something more to eat."

"I always think better on a full stomach. I didn't get a chance to finish my eggs."

"We all do," Wes said. "This is crazy, right?"

"Can we see what information is on the chips?" Becky asked as they gathered around the breakfast table to finish eating.

"I'm not sure, but I'll look into it. I can always call Roy."

Brynn wondered if Roy was even available, assuming he might be in jail for assault. She kept her thoughts to herself. The eggs were getting cold.

Chapter 42

Brynn's trembling fingers picked at the numbers on the phone. She needed to get her phone back—or get another smartphone. And why was she so nervous? Chelsea was a teenager. She was no danger to her. And yet Brynn was certain she'd taken Jewel's collar and brought it back, which meant she knew something about these computer chips, or whatever they were. Also, she didn't like the idea of harassing a teenager. She hung up the phone. Maybe she should talk with Chelsea's parents first.

Her thoughts rolled over and over in her brain as she recalled everything the family had been through with the accidental murder and the crazed tractor.

Perhaps it was best to directly ask Chelsea and then, depending on her reaction, Brynn would go to her parents.

"Are you going to make that call or what?" Becky walked into the room.

"Yes, I was mulling over how best to approach it."

"Directly is best," Becky said. "I'm running to the market. Are you okay to be alone for about an hour?"

Brynn nodded, staring at the phone as if it would move at any minute. Who knows. With all of the strange technology goings-on, tractors controlled remotely, ransom ware running through the community's computers, chips in a cow's collar, perhaps the phone would start to dance at any moment. Brynn smiled.

"Are you okay?" Becky said. "You've got a weird smile on your face."

"I'm fine. Go to the market and I'll call Chelsea. I'll have an answer by the time you get back."

Becky left the room muttering to herself.

Which made Brynn smile even wider.

She picked up the phone and dialed Chelsea.

"Hello?"

"Hi, Chelsea, it's Brynn. How are you doing?" She tapped her fingers on her knee. Still shaking slightly.

"I'm doing well. I'm going shopping for school clothes later. That's one of my favorite things to do."

Brynn's stomach wavered. Chelsea was so young. She took a deep breath.

"Hey, I've got a strange question for you."

A pause. "Okay."

"Did you take Jewel's collar?"

Another pause. "Come again?"

"Someone took Jewel's collar and I think it was you."

"Her collar is missing?" She sounded flustered.

"No. You brought it back last night. Your boyfriend was looking for you at the fair and couldn't find you. You were here, replacing the collar."

"Look, I have no idea what you're talking about," she stammered. "I didn't take anything and I don't have a boyfriend. I told you that." She paused. "Is this some kind of joke?"

"No. I wish it were." Brynn didn't believe a word Chelsea said. It had to be Chelsea. She wouldn't admit it. But why? "Are you in some sort of trouble?" She recalled how oddly Tillie behaved when she was in a perceived trouble. Chelsea knew something about all this and felt like she couldn't say anything.

"I'm sorry, Brynn. I've got no idea what you're talking about. Why would I do any of that? I need to go. My mom is waiting for me." She clicked off.

That was that. Did she really imagine Chelsea would spill her guts? Well, she had harbored a tiny sliver of hope.

Here she was dealing with the odd creature known as a teenage girl again. She and Tillie had gotten close. But Chelsea was a different creature altogether. Tillie was solid, knew what she wanted, even though God knows she had family problems. She had the weight of the world on her shoulders at one point and she ran away.

Chelsea was slippery. Brynn couldn't say if she even liked the girl. On the face of it, Chelsea was the all-American teen queen, right? Beautiful cheerleader, prom queen, and so on. When she walked into a room, all eyes glanced her way.

Well, none of this mattered. Chelsea wasn't going to confess. Brynn understood she'd done it. She was perplexed as to why. Maybe that's the question she needed to focus on. They needed to find out what information was on those chips.

Wes walked into the house. Brynn recognized his footsteps. Max was with him.

"Brynn?"

"In here!"

He entered the room, looking flushed. "Did you just talk with Chelsea by any chance?"

A tingle traveled up her spine. How did he know? "Yes, why?"

He handed her the phone. "She Snapchatted about it."

"She what?" The phone screen had a picture of Chelsea with words going across the screen. "Some old lady just called me and accused me of stealing a cow collar. Really, lady? Get a life. Lol."

A pang of hurt tore through her. She'd get a life all right. One that started with a visit to Chelsea's parents.

"She's such a bitch," Max said. "I'm telling you something isn't right with her."

"Yes, but she's a minor. I need to be careful. I'm going to talk with her parents," Brynn said. "In the meantime, we need to find out what's on those computer chips."

Max nodded. "Agreed."

"We should take them to the cops," Wes said,

Brynn thought about it. They were so busy working on the murder case. Would they care about computer chips and her cow's stolen collar?

"Let's find out what's on it first, then go to the police," Brynn said.

"Sounds like a plan," Wes said.

Chapter 43

"Would you like to help me wash cheese?" Brynn asked Becky.

"Pardon?"

"I have a cheese cellar in the basement and it's time to wash the cheese. I think I can manage alone, but I thought you might like to help."

The two of them proceeded to the basement, which smelled of cheese, just the way Brynn liked it.

As she scrubbed the rinds of the old cheese, Brynn couldn't get Chelsea off her mind.

"Have you heard anything about Wes's case?" Becky asked.

"He's not said much." Brynn moved on to the next cheese.

"His dad is still here, so I'm assuming he's not been cleared yet."

"I don't understand what's taking so long."

"Right?"

"Maybe it's because of the fair. Now it's over, the police'll have more time to investigate. I hear there was a lot going on this year. It's a shame, really. It's usually such a lovely fun event. This year? Well, it seems like it's been cursed."

"That's for sure," Becky said.

Brynn was almost finished with her row of cheese and wearied, which she didn't want to admit, but she had to if she was ever going to heal. "After I'm done with the row, I'm going to lie down."

"Are you okay?"

"Just tired. It's so frustrating. One minute I'm fine and . . . and the next minute I'm exhausted."

"That's typical with a concussion, unfortunately."

"We can finish up here, later," Brynn said as she put away her cleaning brushes. "I need my bed."

Later, as Brynn drifted in and out of sleep, she heard voices downstairs. Or was she dreaming?

Her eyes wouldn't stay open long enough to figure it out.

Later, she padded down the stairs and heard those same voices.

"Look, Brynn is recovering from a concussion. I'm not sure when she'll be down," Wes said with force.

"Like I said, we'll wait," another voice said.

Brynn walked into the room to find Josh and Hannah sitting on her couch. Becky stood with Wes.

"Josh? Is everything okay?"

His face reddened. "You tell me, Brynn. What's this nonsense I hear from my daughter?"

"Now, Joshua—" Hannah started.

He held up his hand to silence her. "My daughter is no thief."

"Okay," Brynn said, and sat down. She looked at Wes. "Did you explain what happened?"

Wes nodded.

"I've no idea what happened to the collar or why it was put back. Any of that. But you need to stop hounding Chelsea."

"Wait a minute. I've not hounded her. I asked her once if she did it. That's all."

"That's not what I hear," Josh muttered.

Brynn was still half asleep but was taken aback by this side of Josh. He'd always been so polite and mannerly. Evidently, Chelsea was a sore spot.

"She does tend to exaggerate," his wife said.

"She's sixteen, for God's sake," he replied in her defense.

"No offence, Josh, but sixteen-year-olds realize the difference between a lie and the truth," Becky said. "In fact, my six-year-old knows that."

There was an awkward pause. Brynn was at a loss for words, humiliated and angry.

"I'm sorry, Josh. I won't bother her again." It was all she could say. Though she swallowed her anger. If these were *her parents* and she'd been accused of something, her parents would get to the bottom of it—usually by taking the adult's side. She had had to prove her innocence on more than one occasion. But it was clear in Josh's eyes Chelsea could do no wrong. Was this some kind of new parenting?

He nodded. "Fine. And I think you owe her an apology."

Anger traveled from the tiny bit in the center of her chest to encompass her entire body. Josh was a pillar of this community, the president of the CSA, and had been through a lot recently with accidentally killing a young man. And she was new here, didn't want to make any enemies. She opened her mouth, but nothing came out. Her eyes met her sister's, and her mouth was also agape.

"Come on," Wes said. "Someone stole the collar off one of the cows and Chelsea had been here spending time with her. Brynn had every right to ask her if she took it."

"If I were you, I'd watch myself," Josh shot back at him.

His wife stiffened. "We should go."

"Good idea," Becky said. "I'll show you out."

Brynn and Wes sat in silence for a few moments. Brynn could hardly believe the attitude Josh had given Wes. She'd never have considered that of him. *People surprise you,* she heard Granny Rose's voice ringing in her ears. *Cows rarely do. Treat them well. Be kind to them and they will be kind to you. People? Now that's another matter.*

Was it any wonder Brynn preferred cows to most people?

Becky came back into the room. "I just have to say it." Brynn and Wes looked at her.

"What the heck?" She flailed her arms around. "Why are they sticking up for Chelsea rather than trying to figure out what her problem is? Or if she did it? Like whatever happened to real parenting?"

"I know my dad would always stand by me. But in a situation like this . . ." He grinned. "He'd grab me by the ear and assume it was me and question me until I could convince him otherwise."

There was nothing worse than the disappointment in people who turned out not to be who you thought they were.

"I don't even want to imagine what my parents would've done," Becky said. "Once I got in trouble at school and I was punished at home, too."

"So, I don't know about you, but I'm beginning to

get a more clear picture of why Chelsea is so screwed up." Wes pulled out his phone. "I've been trying to call Roy about our chips and there's no answer. Maybe he's still in jail for assaulting David Reese. I'm going to call Charlie. Let's find out what's on those chips. I hope it's going to clear up some of this."

Chapter 44

As Brynn drifted off to sleep that night, she made a mental note to rise early and try to work with the cows the next morning. She wasn't certain whose turn it was—Schuyler's, Tillie's, or Willow's—but she thought it would be a good time to see how much of it she could handle. Gratitude swam through her. Her friends had taken such good care of the place. Becky had taken such good care of her. It was time to try to stand on her own again. If she could.

She thought through the events of the past few weeks. Everything had been going so smoothly. She and Wes had settled into a routine for the business. They got along so well. She hadn't obsessed about Dan, her ex, in months. She was looking forward to the fair and the cheese contest. Then everything went to hell. Other than her friends stepping in to help, there were a few others things to be grateful for. The young man who shot Wes was in jail—swift justice. And the police knew Josh didn't kill the other young man on purpose.

But the person who killed Donny Iser was still at large. He had been shot point-blank with a gun registered to Wes. Why Wes? Of all people. Was racism at work here?

Brynn shuddered beneath her quilt.

The next morning, she rose from her bed, dressed, and headed for the barn. Tillie was finishing the milking. She turned to Brynn. "You startled me. Good morning!"

"Good morning, Tillie. How's it going?"

She nodded her head. "Good." She paused, tilting her head. "Why are you here?"

"I want to slowly get back into the routine. You know? I'm tired of being so useless."

Tillie blinked. "It must be hard for you." She lifted the milk and poured it into the container. "I heard Charlie's coming by today to look at those chips."

Brynn drew in the scent of the clean barn. Home. "Yes, it should be interesting. Did he tell you about Chelsea's parents?"

Tillie stiffened, looked away, and looked back at Brynn. "Yeah." She shrugged. "I don't understand what's going on there." She walked over and opened the barn doors and the cows filed out into the steamy morning. Jewel stopped at the door, as if girding her loins for the heat.

"You don't know her well at all, right?"

"Nah, not really," she said, watching the cows march off into the fields. "But I do think she's trouble. She always has been. Boys. Booze. I remember she got caught stealing jewelry or something once."

"Stealing doesn't surprise me. I'm still certain she stole Jewel's collar. Do you want to come in for breakfast?"

"Yeah, sure."

"I don't know what Wes is cooking up, but I bet it's something delicious."

They walked together back into the house. Cool. *Thank God for the AC.*

The scent of cinnamon and berries and something else filled the house. He was making more of the blackberry breakfast bread. Brynn nearly swooned.

"Where've you been?" Becky asked, pulling out two loaves from the oven as Wes set the table.

Brynn took a seat. "The barn. I want to try getting back into the swing of things. I plan on cleaning the make today."

Becky and Wes exchanged glances. "We've already cleaned it. You don't need to worry about it," Becky said.

This was the second time they've steered her away from her make. She missed her work space. The smell of it, the touch of it, and even missed cleaning it. Cleanliness was such an important part of making cheese.

"If you insist," Brynn said, distracted by the blackberry breakfast bread being sliced in front of her. It was still warm and a little sloppy, but that made no difference to any of them. Brynn slathered fresh butter from her own cows onto the bread. Was she drooling? She hoped not.

Wes poured them each a cup of coffee and sat down. "Charlie will be here at nine. I can't wait to see what he says about those chips."

Tillie set her coffee cup down. "That guy knows his stuff. Brilliant."

Becky snorted. "Well, let's hope so. He seems to be the only expert around for miles. I tried to find someone else and couldn't."

"Well, there is Roy," Wes said.

Brynn picked up her coffee and drank it. *So good.* "In jail for assault."

"What were they fighting about, anyway?" Tillie asked.

Brynn paused. "They were fighting about Chelsea. Roy told me he was worried because she didn't show up for their date and he accused David Reese of not telling him where she was."

Silence permeated the room.

Tillie swallowed her bread. Her amber eyes were as wide as saucers. "That's gotta be one of the weirdest things I ever heard."

Wes smiled. "Right? Why would David Reese be aware of anything about Chelsea?"

Brynn chilled, even as she held her hot coffee and sipped from it. "Perhaps you could find out, Wes. When Roy gets out of jail, you should ask him."

Wes nodded as she shoved a piece of blackberry bread into her mouth.

"I had a crazy thought." Becky reached for another slice. "What if it's Charlie who's creating all the havoc with the computers? I mean, he's the expert. We trust him. But what if he's sabotaging computers for the business?"

"He'd lose his business if he was caught. It seems like a desperate thing to do. I don't think he needs to do that. He's busy and successful. Why would he risk it?" Wes sliced more bread.

Brynn's brain clouds seemed to clear for a moment. "But you might be on to something, Becky. And Wes? You said 'desperate.' Who's so desperate they'd try ransom ware on most of this small community?"

Tillie cleared her throat. "Might not be the reason. Hackers do it just for the challenge. They're not really motivated by money."

"It seems awfully risky to ruin people's lives for the thrill of it," Becky said.

"That's part of the 'fun' of it," Wes said, with air quotes around fun.

Brynn glanced at the clock. She suddenly couldn't wait for nine. She had a few observations to make. She recalled what she'd learned about figuring out whether people were telling the truth or not. And she figured it was time to practice a bit more on Charlie.

Chapter 45

Charlie Calloway was hunched over some contraption, flipping the little chips into it and looking over a laptop screen hooked up to the whole thing.

"Hmmm."

Brynn tried to look over his shoulder, but Wes blocked her view. "What?"

He didn't reply, just kept clicking and watching. Wes whistled as he looked over the screen. "Holy smokes."

Brynn stood on her tiptoes. "What?" She tried to look around Wes. She poked him.

"Oh, sorry, Brynn." Wes moved out of the way.

She squinted at the information on the screen. It didn't make any sense to her. "What is it?"

"It's a list of IP addresses," Wes said. "And their passwords."

"It looks like it's everybody in about three Virginia counties," Charlie said, looking up from his contraption. One of his eyebrows lifted. "Where did you get this again?"

"We told you. It was in Jewel's collar."

"Hunh-huh. I see. Let's not get into why it was there." Charlie paused. "This is valuable information. Let's check over the next chip here and see what it has on it." He moved some stuff around, *clickety-click.* He intently stared at the screen.

"What the heck is that? Code?" Wes asked.

"Yes. Give me a minute. Be quiet, please."

Wes looked at Brynn and their eyes locked. What had they stumbled on?

Charlie mumbled.

Brynn rolled her eyes at Wes. Why wouldn't he just get on with it?

"This is code for remote commands. I can't quite tell you what it is . . . looks like . . . I don't know. I can't tell. But it's definitely a code for remote commands."

Remote? "Could it be the remote code for a tractor?" Brynn asked.

"It could be. I can't say for sure because of the way it's been designed. I've really not seen anything like it."

The room quieted. Brynn's thoughts raced. One chip held the information for someone to hack into the community's computers. Another held code that might have been used in a murder. God only knew what the other chip held. Brynn clenched her hands into fists. Did she want to know?

"Next," Wes said, breaking the silence.

"Uh-huh," Charlie said, clicking, moving stuff around, gazing at the screen. He eyed Brynn. "I'm going to have to ask you to leave."

"What? Why?" Brynn wasn't going anywhere. This was her office, her house, and they found the chips on Jewel, who wasn't quite her cow. But whatever.

"If I'm right about this code, it's going to take us to an illegal site. I don't want to make you uncomfortable."

"What? What do you mean? Adult?"

"Porn, Brynn," Wes said. "Do you want to be here?"

Brynn's face heated. "Certainly not." She left the room and moved into the kitchen, where Becky sat drinking a cup of tea and flipping through a magazine.

She looked up at Brynn. "What's wrong? You look like . . . I don't know . . . sick. Do you want some tea? I made a pot of Earl Grey."

Earl Grey. Brynn was comforted, albeit slightly, at the mention of her favorite tea. She sat down and her sister poured. "Why are you here and not in the office with the guys?"

"One of the chips might have porn on it. They asked me to leave."

Becky's eyebrows rose. "Oh!"

"They found all sorts of things." Brynn lifted the steaming tea to her nose and drew in the scent. She remembered Granny Rose. She remembered Nancy. Women she kept in her heart. Women who knew good tea. "The IP address of everybody in Shenandoah Springs."

"What's that?"

"Computer and internet addresses." Brynn waved her hand around. "Private information so someone can hack into all of our computers."

Becky stared at her, as if she were speaking Greek.

"Plus they found codes that might have something to do with Josh's tractor. The remote commands."

"Wow. Okay," Becky said, and set her cup down. "Why was it in Jewel's collar?"

"To hide it."

"I get that, silly. But why Jewel? Why didn't they throw the chips into the river or something?"

"Because they wanted to be able to get them back," Wes said from the doorway. Becky and Brynn turned to face him. "We're unraveling something big here. We're finding the tractor incident and the ransom ware incidents were done by the same person—or people."

"What about the other stuff?" Brynn said. "Was it porn?"

Wes looked away, but he nodded, embarrassed. "Yes. And we're familiar with the other person."

Brynn's heart raced. "We are?" Who did they know that could be in porn?

Becky sat forward and slammed her hand on the table. "It's Chelsea, isn't it?" Brynn's mouth dropped open. Why would Becky jump to that conclusion?

"I'm afraid so," Wes said. "Chelsea's in a film and it's . . . well . . . Disgusting."

Brynn wanted to cry. Why would such a young beauty who had everything do such a thing?

"She looked completely stoned. Like half the time she wasn't even awake."

Sickness waved through Brynn. "Do you mean she was forced into it?"

He shrugged. "I've no way of knowing at this point. All I know is what I saw." He paused. "There's one more thing. It has to do with my case. The guy in the film with her? Donny Iser."

"Well, that's good news," Becky said as Brynn tried to catch words racing so quickly through her mind. "Another reason for someone else to off him and not you."

"What would that reason be?" Brynn said.

Becky shrugged. "The heck if I know. But if you're

going to be in a porn flick, you don't exactly attract the right kind of people."

Something about that statement struck Brynn's funny bone, and she giggled. The three of them laughed.

Charlie walked into the room. "I've called the police and canceled my appointments for the rest of the morning. This is going to take some time."

In less than thirty minutes, Sheriff Edge, a deputy, and two people Brynn had never seen before were gathered in her office. They were introduced as FBI special agents. They worked in tandem with Charlie as Brynn and Becky brought them coffee and leftover breakfast bread. One of the agents was a gorgeous young woman named Rita and Brynn couldn't get enough of watching her setting up the hidden surveillance cameras, imagining what her life was like as an agent. Smart. Young. And the world at her feet.

Several hours later, Brynn and Becky sat in the living room. Tired but wired, Brynn attempted to relax. A small headache jabbed at the back of her head. She downed another aspirin and hoped for the best.

Wes and Max, who came over when he saw the sheriff's car, entered the room. "They're almost done in there."

"Amazing to watch. I wish Dad could be here. He had a Skype meeting and couldn't miss it," Max said, sitting down in the La-Z-Boy. "Wow, this place? I don't get it, Wes . . . do you really want to be here?"

"Absolutely," Wes said immediately, and sat down next to Brynn on the couch. Brynn warmed. She wasn't going to lose him. Unless his dad made him leave after all this murder trial ugliness.

Sheriff Edge walked into the room with the others. "So, any idea why the chips were hidden in a cow collar? In particular on your cow Jewel?"

"She's not my cow. I'm fostering her. And I have no idea. All I know is Chelsea recognized her and said she always really loved the cow." Brynn's heart sank. "She knew the woman Jewel belonged to and had visited the cow often."

"Can we talk about the timeline?" Rita, the FBI agent, stepped forward, with a notebook in hand.

"Certainly," Brynn said, and repeated the story.

The doorbell rang. "That should be my lawyer," Wes said, and left the room.

His lawyer? What was he doing here? Brynn's head spun. This was getting to be too much. She wanted to crawl under her quilt, wake up tomorrow, and everything would be back to normal. No ransom ware. No computer chips. No porn and no murders. She drank water and tried to calm down.

"Good news," Wes said. "They found the person who's been using my credit card information!"

The lawyer, short, plump, and bald, stepped forward. "Yes, but the bad news is this person just started using it. He purchased it from someone. Quite a market out there for stolen credit cards. But"—Wes's lawyer slapped him on the back—"it'll be a matter of time before the guy will crack and tell us where he purchased it. Once that's done, we'll be looking at the person who purchased the gun in Wes's name and he'll be let off."

"Thank God!" Brynn said.

"We've got even more news for you," Max said. "Let's go in the office. I'll fill you in. Other stuff is going on in here."

The lawyer nodded and the two of them left.

Brynn wondered what that was about but turned her attention back to the FBI agents and Sheriff Edge.

"The case is building," said the sheriff. "We've got loads of information. But a lot of things still don't add up."

"I'll say," Brynn said.

"But you're in the middle of it. Like it or not." He sat down next to her.

The hair on the back of Brynn's neck prickled. "Me?"

"Your cow. Your assistant. Like it or not. You're in the middle of it."

"We have a theory they will be back to get these chips," Agent Rita said.

Brynn's heart nearly left her chest. "Back here?"

"Well, you-all need to stop them. We don't need porn computer people coming here, let alone killers!" Becky exclaimed.

"Calm down, please," Sheriff Edge said. "If it was Chelsea who stole the collar and put it back, she's hiding information. But she's aware you've been alerted to the collar and will have to come back to get it."

"We'd like to set up more cameras. We've ordered a special one to place on the cow."

"What? A camera on Jewel?" Brynn wasn't sure she liked the sound of that. What if it was dangerous?

"Chelsea is a teenage girl. She's shown no signs of violence. But she's gotten involved in something we don't quite understand yet. We need to catch her in action. It's the quickest way to figure it out. She's a minor and can hide behind the law. Unless we have proof," Sheriff Edge said. "And who knows? Maybe it's not her."

"In any case, we need to find out," Agent Rita said.

She turned to Brynn. "You've got no problem with surveillance on your property, do you?"

"No, as long as my animals aren't hurt by it, I don't care," Brynn said.

Rita smiled. "Good. We need to keep this quiet, of course."

Brynn nodded. "Of course."

Sheriff Edge sat forward. "We figure it will happen sooner rather than later. Today. Maybe tomorrow."

Why did this make Brynn so nervous?

"You won't even know we're here."

"What? You'll be here?"

He nodded. "We'll be stationed around the property. Like I said, you won't realize it. And the neighbors won't know it. In about an hour, a van will pull up in your driveway. It will be a cable business van. They will install all the cameras. And that's the last you or your neighbors will actually see of us."

"This sounds like it could be dangerous. I don't like the sound of it at all," Becky said. Brynn agreed.

"Believe me, the only danger will be to the person who comes for the collar. And it won't be because we'll shoot him or her. It'll be because the law will be enforced." He paused, drew in a breath. "We never involve civilians in dangerous situations. It'll be fine."

Intellectually, Brynn accepted every word he said. But her body didn't, as her stomach wavered and she felt dizzy. It wasn't the concussion dogging her again. It was fear and disgust. These were children, albeit teenagers, in porn films and getting killed.

Chapter 46

"Okay, so this is kind of freaky," Becky said later as she and Brynn cleared away the dishes from the dinner table. "Like we won't know when we're being watched."

"But it's only outside and in the barns. It's not in the house. I can live with it." Brynn opened the refrigerator to put the butter inside. But Becky was right—it was freaky. Brynn tried not to focus on that. She'd focus on feeling safe and happy that the FBI and police were on her property. What could happen, other than good things?

Nathaniel was making decaf and fussing with the coffeemaker.

"Do you need help?" Brynn asked.

"Nah, I think I've got it."

"Well, I'm glad this is all coming together. And the best part is this may completely exonerate Wes," Brynn said. She examined the table, giving it one more good swipe. Clean.

She'd told Schuyler not to bother coming tonight, she'd take care of the cows herself. But she was already bone-tired. A little fresh air would do her good. But first, coffee and a little respite. She joined Wes and Max in the living room. She sank into the La-Z-Boy chair and relaxed, knowing the police were working hard on this crazy collar thing and Wes might be completely let off. She closed her eyes—for a moment, she told herself—and drifted off.

She was shaken awake. The room was dark. Her heart stopped. Becky stood by the chair. "You better go to bed or you're going to be sore in the morning."

"But I—"

"We took care of your girls. No worries."

Brynn made her way to her room, arms, legs, and head heavy, as if she were treading through water. She lay down in her bed, without changing her clothes. It was too much right now. Exhaustion went through her. The day had left her spent, physically and emotionally.

The idea of Chelsea involved in porn broke her heart. She couldn't help but wonder how the girl had even gotten involved with something like that. It would all come out, eventually. Her parents were going to be heartbroken. Even if Brynn didn't like their parenting, albeit it was none of her business, she hated to see families ripped apart and she was afraid it would happen.

Those computer chips held so much more than information. They held people's lives.

She rolled over on her side, her head aching. This concussion thing wasn't for sissies.

She was awakened by a sound. Freckles barking. Commotions. She pulled herself out of bed and looked at the clock: 5:30. But what was going on? She slipped her shoes on and headed for the barn.

The steamy morning air met Brynn with a whoosh.

Freckles was barking wildly and barely acknowledged Brynn when she opened the barn door. The lights were dim, and all Brynn saw was shadows.

"Look, lady, I'm telling you. I'm with the FBI."

Brynn turned and saw Schuyler sitting on top of one of the FBI agents.

"Then what are you doing here?" Schuyler said. "In the barn?"

"I was checking out our camera."

Brynn stood without making a sound and watched the scene unfold, trying to make sense of it in her hazy morning brain. "Schuyler?"

"Brynn!"

Freckles still barked. "Down, girl," Brynn said. "Why are you sitting on that poor man?"

"Caught him sneaking around here," Schuyler said, her amber eyes lit with anger.

"Look, Brynn, can you call your friend off, please? Tell her who I am." His voice was muffled because his face was pushed into the barn floor. Tiny Schuyler had gotten the best of an FBI agent.

A bubble of laughter erupted from Brynn. "I'm sorry," she said. "Schuyler, you're sitting on an FBI agent." One she herself had just met that day.

"I am?" Her face fell. "Are you sure?"

Brynn nodded and helped her off the man, who stood, wobbly, and rubbed his chin. "You've got a mean right hook, lady."

Schuyler folded her arms. "What's going on here?"

Brynn filled her in. "I'm sorry. We should have told you." She turned to the agent. "I thought you said we'd never know you were here."

"Yes, but then I saw her. I didn't know who she was. I thought she was our collar thief. I guess I startled her."

Schuyler's arms were still folded. "You should get some ice for your jaw. You're going to be sore."

He stood trying to regain composure and pride. "I'll be fine."

"Schuyler has a black belt," Brynn told him.

His eyebrows lifted. "I'm not surprised." He smiled. "Would you like an FBI job?"

Schuyler walked back toward the cows. "Not on your life, buddy."

He looked at Brynn, who shrugged.

"She's a vet," Brynn said, as if it mattered. The air was bristly with emotion. She was trying to calm it down with small talk. Which rarely helped.

"A redheaded black belt vet? I think I'm in love," he said under his breath to Brynn, and grinned.

Brynn laughed. "You have no idea." She paused. "Schuyler, are you coming for breakfast?"

Schuyler placed the milking cups on the cow. "The O'Reilly's need me this morning. I have to run. But thanks."

Brynn looked at the agent. "How about you?"

"Thanks, but I'm off duty and heading home to catch some sleep and try to find a little of my pride."

"That shouldn't be too hard," Schuyler clipped. "I mean, you're a man and they are generally full of it."

He looked at Brynn, shook his head, and grinned even harder. "I better get outta here before I ask her to marry me."

Brynn laughed and headed into the house for breakfast.

* * *

Breakfast was almost normal. Almost. Between intermittent chuckles about Schuyler kicking the FBI agent's ass and conversation about computer chips and Wi-Fi, Brynn wondered if things would ever get back to normal. Was there a normal to get back to? Since she moved to the valley, things had been crazy. Deadly crazy.

"We've gotten more orders in," Wes said as he cleared away the table. "Do you think you can handle it? I've got another meeting with my lawyer this morning."

"Yes, I hope it's a meeting where he tells you the charges have been dropped," Nathaniel said.

"Me too, Dad, believe me. But I don't want to get my hopes up." He'd lost weight, and from the circles under his eyes, Brynn understood he wasn't sleeping well.

"Your mom wants you to come home with me," Nathaniel told him again. How many times had Brynn heard that? She bit her tongue. It wasn't her place to interfere.

"I know. But I like it here. I'm staying here." He opened the refrigerator and placed the butter and milk inside.

"You are so stubborn."

"Humph. I wonder where he gets that from," Max said as he placed dishes in the sink.

Brynn smiled. Healthy family banter. But she knew there was a serious undertone to it. Wes was at an awkward age—old enough to make his own decisions, but not quite old enough to be completely independent. It was an awkward time for everybody as children grew into adults.

Brynn loved being a part of a family and deeply desired her own. If she was honest with herself, she still did. It wasn't too late for her, she knew. But she didn't have the time for a relationship, let alone a child. A relationship. She hadn't thought about her ex, Dan, in a while, and when she did she wondered if she'd ever be able to trust another man, after the way he'd cheated on her. Thank the universe she didn't marry him and have kids with him.

"I'd like to clean the make today. How much milk do we have in the stores?" Brynn wiped off the table.

Becky and Wes glanced quickly at each other, then looked at Brynn. "One thing at a time, Brynn, okay? Let's get these orders filled and see how you do," Wes said.

"It sounds like a great idea," Becky said. "Don't overdo it."

Something was definitely going on with the make. What were they hiding from her? Well, she'd sneak over there later—if she could sneak away from all the prying eyes.

She shrugged. "Okay."

"I've already cut the cheese. It's in the office. It needs to be wrapped and packaged. All of the invoices are printed out." Wes flung a towel over the sink. "Are you ready to go, Dad?"

He nodded. "Let's roll."

Wes, Max, and Nathaniel left and Becky and Brynn moved into the office/dining room, where Wes had laid out everything. They busied themselves for most of the morning, until the doorbell rang. Brynn made for the door. When she opened it, it took a moment to gather herself—for there stood David Reese, the sleazy owner of the tractor store. "David? What can I do for you?"

Becky came up beside Brynn.

"I heard you have a cow needing a home and I've

been looking for one," David said. "Is she a good milker?" Sweat beads formed on his brow. Another scorcher of a day.

Brynn was torn between her normally polite self— she should invite him in for a glass of water or iced tea—and the bad vibes he gave her. No. She couldn't invite this man into her house.

"I'm sorry?"

"Your little Highland cow, Jewel. I'm interested in taking her off your hands." His eyes flitted between Brynn and Becky. *No way in hell.* This man would never get his hands on Jewel.

"Oh, Jewel." Brynn and Becky stepped outside. "Well, she's still not quite well enough for adoption."

"I agree," Becky said. "She's getting there, but not quite."

He shuffled his feet around, tucked his thumbs in his jeans, his gut hanging over his belt. "Can I take a look at her?"

Brynn's instincts were kicking into full gear. At first she thought, *No, I want him nowhere around her.* But then she remembered the FBI were watching. She felt safe. To a point.

"Okay, well, all the girls are in the pastures," Brynn said, heading toward it. The pasture was so much better than the house. So. Much. Better.

Becky followed along, stiffly, with her arms crossed. She didn't like the scene any more than Brynn did. He was a cad. Brynn was glad Roy had hit him. And Brynn was a nonviolent sort.

She opened the creaky gate, and they all walked through. Freckles bounded over to them, barking at David. "Freckles!" She continued barking, baring her teeth. Brynn crouched down. "It's okay. Freckles, sit down." The dog whined but sat down.

"She doesn't like men," Becky said.

Petunia looked up from her grazing. Buttercup and Marigold walked off in the other direction. Jewel stood in place as David approached her. She mooed loudly and took off in the other direction.

He turned to look at Brynn quizzically.

"I'm sorry. I should have warned you. She's shy."

"Yeah, I see that."

"And you can see she's not ready for adoption. I'll be happy to give you a call when she's ready."

"I've got cash. I'd like to take her today," he said.

The hair on the back of Brynn's neck bristled. "What? She's not mine. She belongs to Schuyler. I can't take your money."

"You can give the money to Schuyler. It's more than a fair price." His hands balled into fists and rested on his hips. "I need that cow."

"I wish I could help, but she's not mine to sell." She hoped her voice held enough gravity. What was his problem? Why did he want Jewel so badly? As the wheels spun in her brain, it hit her with a bang. He knew about Jewel—and the collar. Was he there for the computer chips?

He pulled out a fistful of cash. "I'd like to give this to you and take the cow."

"Look," Becky said. "The cow is not for sale, David. You need to take your money somewhere else."

"Well now," he said with a strange evil grin. "I can tell you're not from around here."

"What's that supposed to mean?" Becky asked, with her arms still crossed.

"Look, David, you better go. We're busy with orders and I've got a business to run. When Jewel is fattened up and healthy, I'll let you know."

He glanced around the hilly fields, as if he was searching for something. Was he checking to see if they were alone? *Two against one, bucko, don't even think about it.*

"Okay, then," he said, and stomped off. "You'll be hearing from me."

"I hope not," Becky muttered as he walked away.

Becky and Brynn stood on the grassy hill and watched as David drove off. He actually had a trailer attached to his truck—so confident Brynn would take his money.

"What is his problem?" Becky said.

"Think about it. He knows something. He knows those chips were in Jewel's collar. That has to be it. Otherwise, him coming here, offering me money for Jewel? It makes no sense."

"You're right! That has to be it. And he's the guy who sold Josh the tractor, right?"

Brynn nodded. "He is. Where's an FBI agent when you need him?"

Chapter 47

Brynn's hands trembled as she poured herself a glass of iced tea. Adrenaline coursed through her. *Of course!* It all came to her. It made sense on one level—but not on other levels. David had the power to pull it all off, and he was certainly interested in Jewel. But why would he involve himself in this? That was the question. A man with a good business, wife, and family and, from the looks of things, an average guy.

Becky walked back into the kitchen and sat at the table. Brynn drank her iced tea, looking out over the field where the cows and Freckles were.

"Do you think the surveillance crew caught that conversation?" Becky asked.

"I'd hope so." Brynn frowned. "I've been thinking about this. What would prompt David Reese to be involved in this? Family guy with a good business."

"What do you mean?"

"Why would he risk it? What would be the reason?"

"Don't be naïve. Guys like that are a dime a dozen.

Just because he looks like he's an upstanding citizen doesn't mean he is. Remember how he looked at us. He's a lech, if nothing else. So he's not all that great. Besides, it happens all the time. Pillars of the community, clergy, you name it. We're talking about child porn here."

Point taken. "Okay, I hear you. But why would he want the cow?"

"Who knows? He's not up to any good, for sure."

Brynn took a long sip of her sweet tea. "This tea is great. Did you make it?"

"Yes, I did. I thought about using your fresh mint, but I didn't get a chance to go and pull some out of the garden."

"I like it the way it is."

A knock at the front door interrupted their conversation. Becky stood and left the room to go answer it.

"Come on in," she said, then brought one of the FBI agents back into the room.

"Ms. MacAlister. We wanted to ease your concerns. We heard the conversation and are checking him out. How well do you know David Reese?"

"Not well. I met him at the fair this year. And I saw the fight."

"Fight?" The agent's head tilted.

"Yes, there's was a young man who actually hit him at the fair. Roy. I don't know his last name."

"What was the fight about?"

Brynn explained the fight to him. He didn't seem to be surprised or affected by it. He remained calm and cool as you'd expect from an FBI agent.

An FBI agent was in her home.

"I'm with the cybercrimes unit. We don't see much of that kind of action," he said. "But that's good information to have." He stood awkwardly in the kitchen, shifting his weight.

"Would you like a glass of iced tea?" Brynn asked.

"No thanks, I need to get back to my station. We wanted to let you know we're watching and we saw and heard all of it."

Brynn should feel better than she did. A sense of protection. But uneasiness sat in her guts. *The FBI was watching her place.* "Thank you. Do you know how much longer you'll be here?"

He looked surprised. "We'll stay until we figure this out." He paused. "I know it's unfortunate. We respect that and are trying to stay out of your way."

Brynn's stomach settled a bit. "Okay."

The agent took his leave.

Brynn sat quietly and finished her tea. An ominous, prickly sensation swept through her. Was it because the FBI was here? *Oh, calm down, Brynn; you've done nothing wrong. Okay, so you've got a little illegal imported cheese in the cellar.* But that's not what they were here about.

"Who'd have thought the FBI would take such an interest in this case?" Becky said.

"Cybercrime is an FBI issue. Especially when it involves entire communities."

"If you think about it, it's a wonder more of this stuff doesn't happen. We're all online. All of our important information is online. Banking. Taxes. Everything."

"Right. I don't like it. I've been considering going off the grid."

"I get that. But what a pain that would be, right? I'll stay online and take my chances. Change my password frequently." She paused. "And I've no money, so who would want what I have?" Brynn laughed. "It's funny because I've yet to make a profit. It's just looks like we're successful."

"Well, I don't even have that." She grinned. "I never thought I'd think that was a good thing."

Brynn knew her sister had it rough. After her husband died, there wasn't much. Becky worked hard as a beautician and made decent money, but as she was a single mom, it never was enough and it certainly wasn't secure.

But what Brynn was doing was risky, too. If the cheese business did not start to earn, she'd have to start again. She wanted to succeed, but there always seemed to be problems to keep her away from her business. Like Nancy's death. Like the murder and accident and cybercrimes going on now. Her concussion didn't help any of it. Sometimes when she closed her eyes at night she saw the whole scene over and over again in her mind's eye. Wes on the floor, in pain. And all of the blood. Then blackness.

Who would've imagined a cheese contest would wind up with a half-crazed young man shooting an innocent man? Who knew she should have hired security? She would next year. If there was a next year. She'd poured more money into the cheese contest than she should have. How would they recoup their losses? She felt she needed to return the application fees to the contestants. It was the right thing to do.

In the meantime, there was work to accomplish. She'd only washed about half of the cheese in the cellar the other day before she'd gotten too tired.

"You want to help wash some cheese?" Brynn asked Becky.

"Sure. We can't have dirty cheese."

"Keeping the cheese clean is important," Brynn said as she stood.

"I remember Granny Rose going on about it."

"Remember the time a friend of hers died and she always said it was because she ate dirty cheese?"

Becky squinted her eyes. "I sort of remember it. But cheese is really like milk gone bad or something. It's amazing more people don't die from it."

"No, it's not milk gone bad. It's milk transformed into something else. Food. With different flavors and nuance. People don't die from it because cheesemakers are very careful, very clean. Well, at least most of us are. But you can bet the wrong mold on cheese would definitely kill someone."

Every cheesemaker's nightmare. Brynn shuddered and crossed herself. Just to be on the safe side.

Chapter 48

Brynn cranked up the Dolly Parton tunes and she and Becky finished washing the cheese. She was happy to complete the task without needing a nap. She shut the music off and they headed upstairs to search for lunch. But Freckles' barking interrupted her.

She ran out of the house, searched for the reason for the barking. No cars. Nobody walking along the driveway or road. Did Freckles have an animal cornered? Brynn hoped not. She wished Wes were here.

But she and Becky rushed to the barn.

"Freckles!" she said. "Heel."

The dog kept barking at the barn. Was one of the FBI guys inside? She opened the door. And the dog stopped barking but gave a low growl.

"Doesn't seem to be anything in here," Becky said.

Brynn crouched down and petted Freckles, trying to calm her down. "It's okay, girl. Look around. There's nothing in here."

The dog's fur was stiff with fear or something. Brynn hadn't ever seen anything like it. "Hush, now. It's okay."

Brynn stood and looked around herself. A tingle traveled through her. Freckles didn't behave like this. She'd seen or heard something—even if it was just a groundhog.

An odd scent crept into Brynn's nose. The barn didn't smell right. What was she smelling? Then it left as quickly as it came. Was it soap? Perfume?

"Have you been wearing perfume?"

Becky shook her head. "I smelled it, too. I don't think it was perfume. Cologne. A man's scent."

Brynn froze. There was someone in the barn. That person was gone. It must have been an agent. That must be it. "One of our friends, no doubt."

Becky shrugged. "Let's hope."

The dog was still unsettled even though she was quiet. Freckles had made friends with all the FBI guys. And they all had snacks for her. Was there a new guy who didn't know about Freckles? Some misunderstanding?

There certainly had been a lack of communication with Schuyler—although it was partially her fault.

She heard a foot thump. The dog growled. A click.

"Call your dog off or I'll shoot her."

Brynn looked at Becky, eyes wide. She turned to face David Reese—holding a gun.

"What?"

"Call your dog off or I will shoot her. Right now."

Brynn crouched next to the growling, barking dog. "It's okay," she said to Freckles, trying to calm her. The dog whined. "It's okay," Brynn kept saying, trying to make her voice soothing, but with each breath her voice became more and more scratchy and trembly.

Becky stood quietly, eyes watching the gun and

David. "If you put the gun away, the dog will probably stop barking."

"No chance of that, Becky," he said with a sinister expression.

"What do you want?" she asked while Brynn was calming the dog.

"I think I made that clear earlier."

"This isn't about a cow; come on," Becky said.

"If you want her, take her," Brynn blurted. "Just get outta here with that gun."

He stood with the gun pointed at them. "Well, now you're talking some sense. But, you see, now I've got two more problems. You and your fine sister."

Becky folded her arms.

The man was unaware of FBI agents stationed throughout the property. They probably were outside right now. Brynn felt a little braver, a little more secure.

"Why are we a problem?" Brynn asked. "Take the cow and go. Do you think I care about that cow?" *Oh, but she did. She did.* If she and Becky got out of this alive, she'd never let anything happen to Jewel. She knew right then and there she was keeping her. He'd never get out of there with Jewel. Where were the agents?

"I need some time. So I'm going to ask you two to stand back to back," he said, pulling out handcuffs. "By the time anybody finds you, I'll be in Mexico."

Where was the FBI? How long were they going to let this continue? *Hello? FBI? Rita? Where are you?*

Becky and Brynn stood back to back, and the dog sat and watched as Brynn told her to be quiet over and over again.

"What exactly is going on? What do you need with the cow? Why are you going to Mexico?"

"I don't need the cow," he muttered as he hand-cuffed the sisters together. "I need the collar."

Brynn knew then he must be behind everything. But she didn't know why. "The collar was stolen a few days ago. But it was returned yesterday. Go ahead and take it. I can get another collar. Why do you need to do this?"

"Like I said . . . I need time . . . to get out of the country."

"But why?" Brynn persisted. "I don't understand."

He didn't respond. He set his gun down and exited the barn and left the door open a bit. Brynn assumed he was looking for Jewel. She wondered if Jewel would let him near her. A jolt of fear hit her. What if she did and he discovered nothing in the collar? Becky must have thought the same thing. "Holy smokes, Brynn, there's nothing in that collar." Her voice trembled as she whispered to her.

"I don't think Jewel is going to comply."

The sisters sat on the barn floor, back to back. Brynn looked at the camera on the ceiling corner, stared at it, willing the agents to come and help them.

What were they waiting for?

She eyed Freckles, who was in the same position. But unhappy about it. Such a good dog.

"Argh!" Brynn heard from outside. "Jesus! Help me!" David yelled.

But of course, Brynn and Becky couldn't help him. Who knew what was going on out there?

Rita, the FBI agent, came out of the darkness. Where did she come from? How long had she been there?

"Thank God!" Brynn whispered.

Rita took a key and uncuffed them. "Be quiet. You've got to see this."

Brynn and Becky looked out the door.

David Reese was on the ground with three Red Devon cows surrounding him. And Petunia poked him with her horns. Red patches of blood spread on his shirt.

"Ouch, God help me!" David screamed.

Brynn and Becky walked over to him. "I'm not sure about this, but I don't think God's going to help you now," Brynn said.

She pulled Petunia away, glanced around for Jewel, who was sitting in the corner of the field shaking. Brynn ran to her; the agent stepped in and handled David Reese.

"Jewel?" The cow sat motionless, trembling. "Jewel? Sweetie?" She rubbed her nose for several minutes and finally the cow's eyes opened and she blinked at Brynn. That was a good sign. Jewel was going to be okay. He'd probably come after her and the other cows stepped in between. Brynn's heart exploded with pride. *Watch cows. Ha!*

Chapter 49

Wes and Max bounded onto the scene. The agents were quietly taking David away in an unmarked car. Handcuffed and withdrawn, he stared out the window as they drove off.

"What the heck is going on?" Wes asked.

"He's just been arrested," Brynn answered. "He was behind the tractor accident and the ransom ware. He wanted those chips, and he threatened us with a gun."

"A gun?" Wes's voice leveled up a notch. "Are you okay?"

Brynn nodded. "We're both okay, but it could have gone really bad. Thank God the FBI agents were here."

"Did they take the gun?" Max asked.

"I'm not sure," Brynn replied.

"The last time I saw it, it was in the barn," Becky said.

Wes and Max raced to the barn. Becky looked at Brynn and shrugged. Then it dawned on Brynn: the reason Wes was so interested in the gun. Was it the gun he'd been accused of buying and killing Donny

Iser with? Was David Reese the killer of Donny as well? Brynn's heart raced.

Wes exited the barn holding the gun. An agent came up beside him and took it from him, examined it, and smiled at Wes. Suddenly Wes's expression changed. Relief washed over him.

He walked over to Brynn. "That's the gun they thought I killed Donny with. David Rees had it. I never imagined him a killer."

"None of us imagined you one, either," Brynn said, and wrapped her arms around him. He dropped his head on her shoulder and stood there for several moments. When he lifted his head, he wiped away tears. "It's over," he said. "It's over."

Rita, the agent, walked over to them and asked if they wanted to go inside to talk.

"Of course," Brynn said, hoping she would straighten out the mess in her head. What had David Reese been thinking? What was his ultimate goal—other than money, of course? Why would he have killed that young man? And why did he try to frame Josh for killing the other one? And why was he trying to frame Wes? So many questions. Brynn wanted them all answered, but she knew some of them might never be. Human behavior was often unexplainable, unfortunately.

After they situated themselves in the living room, each with a glass of water or iced tea, Rita cleared her throat. "Do you have any questions?"

"Where do we start?" Becky said after a few moments.

"I can tell you a few things you probably are unaware of and we can move forward from there," Rita said. "We've been watching Reese for quite some time. But not for cyber issues, per se, for porn issues.

He runs several underground porn sites, using underage teenagers."

Chelsea!

"He befriends them, gives them gifts, good drugs, and then drugs them, uses them in these flicks."

"That's the most disgusting thing I've ever heard," Becky said.

Wes and Max sat with their mouths open.

Brynn's head was spinning. So the flick they found of Chelsea? She was drugged. She must have been trying to keep it quiet. So David Reese had her under his thumb. And Roy must have been aware of it.

"One young girl came to us, confessed in a way, and reported the circumstances. She was afraid for her life. He'd threatened her to keep her mouth shut or he'd tell her family, everybody she knew, and so on. She suspected he'd killed young men who she had an interest in."

"Was this Chelsea?" Wes asked.

"I'm not at liberty to tell you that. But he's ruined many young women's lives. This girl is bringing him down."

Brynn hoped it was Chelsea. It would redeem her in Brynn's mind. After all the nonsense with the collar. *Wait. If it was Chelsea, were her parents in on it? Is that why they behaved the way they did?* She hoped so.

"Those chips were valuable to him because they link him to cybercrime and he's going down." Rita looked at Wes. "That gun, however, links him to the murder of Donny Iser. We don't have a confession. But I'm certain it won't matter. His crimes are so deep, he'll be in prison a long time."

"I hope so," Brynn said. "This has all been too much. Why was he trying to frame Wes, of all people?"

"He's also a member of the KKK."

"What!?" Brynn's heart couldn't take much more. "Do you mean there's a chapter around here?"

She nodded. "It was disbanded several years ago. He's been trying to start it up again."

"Whoa," Wes said, eyes wide.

"After this incident, I don't think they will be a problem," the agent said, smiling reassuringly. She drew in a breath. "David had an obsession with Chelsea. He was trying to off all of her boyfriends, who he thought were his competition."

"Why did they hide the chips in Jewel's collar?" Becky asked.

"We have no idea, but maybe we'll find out, eventually." She drew in air. "I know this has been rough on you. But we figured he'd act quickly, and he did. Allowing us to watch your place was helpful. Thank you for complying and for keeping it quiet. It wouldn't have worked otherwise."

Brynn warmed. It didn't matter that she didn't have all the answers right this minute. She had the most important one: Wes would be completely exonerated, and he'd be free to live his life. She blinked away a tear. "Thank God," she said.

Becky reached over and held her hand. "It's going to be okay."

Wes glanced at Brynn and quickly looked away. So young, any display of emotion embarrassed him. She smiled. "You're a free man, Wes." Tears now were streaming down her face. The agent handed her tissues.

"Well, good. We've got a lot of work to do around here," he said with a hint of cracking of his voice, as his father's arm went around his shoulders.

Chapter 50

By the next day, there were no traces of the FBI or their surveillance cameras. Brynn learned the arrest and events were all over the news. But she chose not to turn on the computer or watch TV. She'd lived it and didn't want or need a review.

She was surprised people were still hanging around, not that she minded. Not at all. But Wes's family didn't seem like they were about to leave anytime soon— and neither did her sister. Brynn was getting stronger every day, but she enjoyed Becky's company. So she wasn't about to complain.

She'd missed having her sister close by. True, Richmond wasn't on the other side of the country. But it was far enough away that Brynn couldn't just visit for the day, carefree, popping in whenever.

"Brynn, there's something I need to show you in the make," Becky said.

Uh-oh. They'd been keeping her away from the make since her concussion. She figured they were trying to spare her something. Something that would have stressed her out or upset her.

"Okay," Brynn said, getting up off the couch. Romeo leaped down, too. The cat had been snuggling up next to her in a near-perfect round ball. "Sorry to disturb you, Romeo."

She and Becky walked outside into the humid, hot day. "Whew, it's awful out here," Brynn said. "What's in my make?"

"It's a surprise." Becky led the way and opened the door.

Brynn stepped into the make and blinked her eyes. "Surprise!" the voices of a crowd rang out. She blinked again. Who were these people? They looked vaguely familiar.

Wes stepped forward. "Welcome to your cheese contest. We decided to reschedule it and hold it here."

Brynn's face heated and mouth dropped, but something in her chest bloomed.

"We couldn't let the contest be ruined by a bunch of crazies," Becky continued. "So these are the folks from the first contest. And it's just as official."

"Next year, we'll have it at the fair, no problem," Wes said.

"With security, though," Brynn responded.

He laughed. "Of course."

The crowd spread as she walked through her make—the place where she created her cheese. The long tables now held other people's blocks of cheese, with their tags explaining the cheese. It looked beautiful!

Willow stepped forward. "We didn't suppose we'd surprise you." She smiled. "But we managed." Brynn hugged her. Willow was so much better than at the start of this mess. Brynn said a little prayer to the universe that she'd be okay after witnessing the tractor "accident."

Beyond where Willow stood was Schuyler—and she was with a date. Maybe. Was she?

"Hey, Schuyler, were you in on this, too?" Brynn walked over to her and hugged her.

"We all were. Wes didn't give us a choice."

Brynn eyed the guy next to her. He waved like he knew her. *Wait.* Was he—

"Do you remember me, Brynn? I'm Deacon, the FBI agent Schuyler knocked down." He grinned. "Told you I fell in love."

Brynn laughed and Schuyler elbowed him. "I told you to stop saying that."

He shrugged.

Wes interpreted. "Enough with the socializing, ladies. Let's get the show on the road. Here's the first cheese. You start here. And I'll start on the other side."

"Bossy!" Schuyler said.

"You gotta be around here," Wes answered.

Brynn drew in air. It smelled so cheesy in her make that she could have sworn she'd died and gone to cheese heaven. And then the first cheese she tasted was the cheddar she adored. She doubted any of the others were quite as good—but she was willing to keep an open mind.

Cheese after cheese. Some better than others. Others way worse than most. What she would expect. For many of these cheesemakers, cheese was a hobby they were just starting to pursue. It made her heart glad some folks were as enamored with cheese as she was. It was so easy to go and buy cheese from the store or farmers' market. It took a special sort of person to feel inspired enough to try it on their own. And Brynn was surrounded by them.

The cheddar won, hands down, with a Parmesan coming in a close second and a Swiss third. Many honorable mentions were given and the next thing she knew she was signing people up for classes. Not in the plans. Not yet. But it would be okay with just this small group of people—as long as the list didn't get any larger. And the income was much needed.

After the event, Willow and Schuyler and her date and Wes, Nathaniel, and Max stayed to clean up. Brynn's sister pulled out a bottle of iced champagne and Wes passed out glasses.

Wes stood on a crate. "Friends and family, we have much to celebrate here tonight. The first ever Shenandoah Springs cheese contest was a success. Finally. After a bit of a rocky start."

Brynn's face burned as she tried to hold back tears.

"We are all together. Healthy and free. Thank you all so much." Wes's voice cracked. "Thanks so much for standing by me during my rough patch."

"Hear, hear!" Brynn said as she raised her glass. Never had a toast meant so much to her.

The next day Brynn received a dozen yellow roses. She choked up when she read the card. It was from Chelsea and her family, thanking her for her discretion and apologizing to her for the way they behaved.

I'm so sorry to involve Jewel, but I thought it would be a great hiding place for the chips. I didn't know he'd been spying on me and saw

me do it. I've made terrible mistakes I hope to
never make again. But I thank you and hope
you will forgive me.
    Chelsea

Brynn held the card to her chest. *We all make horri-
ble mistakes. It's what we do after that matters.*
She pulled out her new cell phone and called
Chelsea to invite her and her family to dinner.

Chapter 51

Two Months Later

Brynn watched the photo shoot in the crisp autumn air, with the colorful Blue Ridge Mountains as a natural backdrop. Chelsea spun around and the photographer ate it up, camera clicking. Petunia stood next to her and she even seemed to be enjoying it. Chelsea ran her hand along Petunia's nose and the cow lifted it in obvious pleasure.

"Perfect! Daughter of the Stars!" Mick, the photographer, said.

It was the name of Brynn's new award-winning cheese, the cheese that Wes sent off to a contest without telling her, a contest in which she came in first place and won enough money to launch the cheese into national markets, while still keeping her focus on the local, artisanal market. Branching out was always in the plan, just not so soon.

"She's doing a great job," Wes said about Chelsea as he came up beside Brynn.

Brynn never thought to hear kind words about

Chelsea coming out of Wes's mouth. But after everything that had gone down, he'd stopped talking
about her.

A gust of wind prompted Brynn to pull her sweater
in closer. "I hope it's not going to rain. She's perfect
for the job." And the situation made Brynn's lie seem
like less of a lie. Granny Rose always said one lie led
to another and that it would always come back to bite
you. She was right, most of the time. This time, Brynn's
lie led to a plan.

When she found out that Wes had entered her in
the contest, she imagined what she'd do if she won.
Daughter of the Stars cheese was a new cheese she
crafted when moving to the Shenandoah Valley. "Shenandoah," as close as anybody could tell, meant "Daughter of the Stars." At least it has been interpreted that
way for generations.

Hiring Chelsea became a plan, not a lie. She was
Daughter of the Stars personified.

"It's amazing how far we've come in a few months,"
Wes said.

"True." She still didn't want to think about Wes
being accused of murder, nor any of the other weird-
ness happening at that time for which David Reese
was responsible. The ransom ware. The remote-
controlled tractor. And worst of all, the murders.
Thank goodness he'd be in prison probably for the
rest of his life. *Good riddance to bad trash.*

As Brynn had read over the article in the paper
about him, she wondered how many young people
had been affected by his hideous porn scams. They
would never know. Most victims would not step forward. No victim had—except Chelsea, who was made
of sterner stuff than anybody had given her credit
for, including Brynn.

"Are you ready for a break?" Wes asked the photographer. "Lunch is ready."

"We're almost there," Mick said, turning to them and then back to Chelsea, smiling, emanating wholesome energy and goodness.

"What's next, boss?" Wes said.

"Lunch?" Brynn grinned.

"You know what I mean. This has fast-tracked your business. What other plans do you have?"

Brynn thought about it for a few minutes. Wasn't this enough? More than enough? A few years ago, she just imagined this farm, this business. Now it was real—and more successful than she imagined.

"We've got plenty to deal with right now," she said. "We've got the new calf coming along and we've got Jewel. I might like to experiment with cheese from a Highland cow."

The wind picked up even more and dark clouds moved quickly across the sky. Shadows moved across the mountains, in a play of light and shadow that Brynn had come to love.

"I read that their milk is high in butterfat," Wes said. "It'd be fun to experiment now that she's fattened up so nicely."

Jewel had indeed fattened up and her coat had taken on a bit of a sheen. It was almost hard to believe she was the same frightened, half-starved cow that Schuyler brought to her a few months back.

"We should."

"That's a wrap!" Mick said as he sauntered over to them. "I've got some great shots. I'll e-mail the proofs. But in the meantime, look at them here." He held up his camera for Brynn and Wes to view the screen. He flipped from one photo to the next, then stopped on a perfect picture: Chelsea smiling straight at the camera, Petunia looking straight at the camera, and the sunlight hitting them both just so.

"Perfect," Brynn said. The only thing that would've made it more perfect was if Becky were there. But she was back in Richmond.

Later, with all of them sitting at the kitchen table consuming pimento cheese sandwiches and tomato soup, contentment washed over Brynn. She didn't think she'd ever heal completely from Dan and his cheating on her, but she could honestly say she was happier now than she'd ever been.

Even with the bad events that had happened after she moved to Shenandoah Springs, including the latest murders, she knew this was the place for her and her cows. Maybe it was the place for Wes, too. Maybe he'd outgrow it. Chelsea certainly would.

A serenity washed over Brynn. Maybe she'd spend the rest of her life doing what she'd always wanted to do. She'd dug her heels in and made this home. She'd been here almost a year and she'd realized she hadn't really embraced the place—with all of the strange events and murders right after she moved in. It was almost as if she hadn't exhaled into her new life. Ridiculous. After all, it's such a small community. What were the chances of any more murders?

She took in the scene. Food on the table. Friends gathered around. Her cows in the field. She was home. Finally.

Acknowledgments

Thanks so much to Mary Sproles Martin and Jennifer Feller for being such great beta readers. Very special thanks to Jill Marsal, literary agent extraordinaire. I'd also like to acknowledge my daughters, Emma and Tess, two lovely young women who make me proud and inspire me every day. A big hug to the team at Kensington—Elizabeth May, Larissa Ackerman, Lauren Jernigan, Alexandra Kenney, Kristin McLaughlin, and Tara Gavin. A shout-out to my favorite bookstores and people Kelly Justice of Fountain Bookstore in Richmond and Mary Katherine Froelich of Stone Soup Books (now online.)

More big hugs to my review crew, who receive advance copies to review through my newsletter. And the Cozy Mystery Review Crew does a great job. Thank you!

A special word of thanks to Aimee Hix and Dru Ann Love, who are very supportive of me. I'm grateful for your friendship.

I worked for an IT company briefly and picked the IT guys' brains frequently. Special thanks to Thomas Kinsinger, Stephen Shilling, and Peter Fitch.

Mostly I want to thank my readers. I can't tell you what a joy reading has been to me. I love the whole experience of opening a book, the sound of pages turning, the scent of paper, and being drawn into another world. It's an honor that readers choose to spend their time in my happy little book worlds. I'm grateful.

XO,
Mollie

Recipes

Whole Wheat Banana Pancakes

Ingredients
1½ cups whole wheat flour
2½ teaspoons baking powder
1 teaspoon ground cinnamon
2 tablespoons brown sugar
1 small ripe banana, mashed
1 cup milk
2 eggs
1 teaspoon vanilla
3 tablespoons melted butter

Directions
In a bowl, whisk flour, baking powder, ground cinnamon, and sugar. Set aside. In a mixing bowl, add in mashed banana, milk, eggs, vanilla, and melted butter. Mix well. Add flour mixture into banana mixture and mix until just combined. Don't over-mix. (If your mixture is too thick, thin out with a bit of water.) Coat a griddle or nonstick skillet with canola oil and preheat to medium heat. Pour approximately ¼ cup batter on heated skillet. Cook until bubbles form and flip over. Cook approximately another 3 minutes. Repeat until batter is gone.

Cheese Straws

Ingredients
½ cup butter, softened
2 cups shredded sharp cheddar cheese
1¼ cups all-purpose flour
½ teaspoon salt
¼ teaspoon cayenne pepper

Directions
Preheat oven to 350 degrees F. In a large bowl, beat butter until light and fluffy. Beat in cheese until blended. Combine flour, salt, and cayenne; stir into cheese mixture until a dough forms. Roll into a 15x6 inch rectangle. Cut into thirty 6-inch strips. Gently place strips 1 inch apart on ungreased baking sheets.

Bake until lightly browned, 15–20 minutes. Cool 5 minutes before removing from pans to wire racks to cool completely. Store in an airtight container.

Tortilla Breakfast Treat

Yield: 1 treat

Ingredients
1 whole wheat tortilla
2 ounces fresh soft white cheese (honey/cranberry
    walnut goat cheese optional)
½ Fuji apple, thinly sliced
1 tablespoon honey

Directions
Spread thin layer of cheese on half of tortilla, top with apple slices, and drizzle with honey. Fold tortilla in half.

Place quesadilla in a greased, heated skillet and cook on each side for 2–3 minutes, until tortilla is lightly browned.

Lemon Dill Cucumber Sandwiches

Ingredients
6 ounces Neufchâtel cream cheese, softened
2 tablespoons Greek yogurt
Zest of ½ lemon plus the juice of ½ lemon
½ teaspoon vinegar
½ teaspoon sugar
1–2 tablespoons dill
Salt and pepper to taste
1 loaf of your favorite bread
1 cucumber, peeled and sliced

Directions
In a bowl, put in the cream cheese, yogurt, lemon zest, juice, vinegar, sugar, and dill. Mix with a wooden spoon until smooth and season with salt and pepper to taste. Cut the bread in half or into quarters depending on the size you want. Spread the mixture on each half or quarter of the bread and put 2–3 cucumber slices on top of each piece.

Blackberry Breakfast Bread

Make this quick and easy blackberry bread recipe with fresh summer blackberries, or use frozen blackberries to get a taste of summer any time of the year!

Ingredients
2 cups all-purpose flour
½ cup sugar
1½ teaspoons baking powder
½ teaspoon baking soda
¼ teaspoon salt
2 eggs, lightly scrambled
1¼ cups milk
¼ cup butter, melted
1 tablespoon pure vanilla extract
1 cup blackberries (fresh or frozen, thawed), lightly
   mashed

For the topping
3 tablespoons all-purpose flour
3 tablespoons brown sugar
3 tablespoons cold butter

Directions
Combine flour, sugar, baking powder, baking soda, and salt in a large bowl.

In a small bowl, whisk together eggs, milk, butter, and vanilla.

Pour wet ingredients into dry ingredients, and mix until just combined.

Fold in mashed blackberries.

Pour batter into lightly greased 9-by-5-inch loaf pan.

Place flour, brown sugar, and butter for the topping in a small food processor. Pulse until all ingredients are combined and mixture looks like coarse crumbs.

Evenly sprinkle topping over unbaked bread.

Bake at 400 degrees F. for 45–60 minutes, until the top is brown and a toothpick inserted in the center tests clean. Check bread after 40 minutes and loosely cover with aluminum foil if the top is getting too brown.

**Keep reading for a special excerpt of the first book
in the Buttermilk Creek Mystery series!**

An udderly murderous holiday . . .

CHRISTMAS COW BELLS
A Buttermilk Creek Mystery

Mollie Cox Bryan

**The first novel in Mollie Cox Bryan's brand-new
mystery series, set in the Blue Ridge Mountains, will
keep you guessing until the cows come home. . . .**

Christmas is a time for new beginnings, so after
her big breakup Brynn MacAlister takes the gouda
with the bad. With her three Red Devon cows, she
settles in bucolic Shenandoah Springs, eager for a
new life as an organic micro-dairy farmer and
cheesemaker. Then her dear cow Petunia's bellows
set the whole town on edge. But it isn't until Brynn's
neighbor Nancy dies in a mysterious fire that her
feelings about small-town life begin to curdle. . . .

It seems some folks were not happy with Nancy's
plan to renovate the Old Glebe Church. But is a fear
of change a motivation for murder? As a newcomer,
Brynn can't ignore the strange events happening just
on the other side of her frosty pasture—and soon on
her very own farm. Suddenly Christmas doesn't feel
so festive as everyone demands she muzzle sweet
Petunia and Brynn is wondering if someone wants to
silence her—for good. . . .

Look for *Christmas Cow Bells*, on sale now.

Chapter 1

Sometimes a place reaches deep inside of you, flows through you with light and warmth, and fills you with a sense of belonging, a sense of home. Brynn MacAlister's first view of the Shenandoah Valley from the Blue Ridge Mountains—a blanket of green, yellow, and brown rolling fields and farms spread for miles into the mists—had grabbed her with certainty. The village of Shenandoah Springs, a blip in her view, was small and tattered but oozed charm, tucked in the valley between the mountains and the town of Staunton, Virginia. She and Dan had figured this was the area for them to grow their dreams: a micro-dairy farm to support their cheese-making. Some dreams fade, such as her marriage plans with Dan, but Brynn was determined to make a go of the cheesemaking and dairy farm.

"Yoo-hoo!"

Brynn would know that voice anywhere.

She opened the door for her closest neighbor, who was dropping by for tea, and then quickly shut it against the cold December wind.

Nancy held a plate of scones, wrapped in plastic. "My grandmother's recipe, straight from Scotland."

Brynn took the plate. "Thanks so much. The kettle is on." She led Nancy back to her favorite spot in the house, a kitchen nook where the table sat beneath a window with a view of her rolling backyard pasture and three Red Devon cows. Three cows were just enough for her to handle on her own. Maybe too much.

Nancy settled into her seat, and Brynn poured the tea. Earl Grey was the tea they had first bonded over in the grocery store, and then realized they were neighbors, both new to town, both into local, artisanal food, and both into farming, as were most of the residents of Shenandoah Springs.

"How's it going with the renovations of the church?" Brynn asked.

"Things are going well. It was difficult to find contractors. They acted interested until I told them I was turning the old church into a farm shop. I don't get it." She stirred sugar into her steaming tea and set the spoon on the saucer. "I had to hire contractors all the way from Lexington."

"Strange. Your plans support the local community. It's too bad." Brynn sipped from her tea.

"The locals are all lovely," Nancy said. "But they do have some strange ways."

Brynn hadn't been in Shenandoah Springs long, but she agreed with Nancy. Most locals had roots that stretched back generations, and they didn't feel the need to make new friends. Still, Brynn thought it would just take time to get acquainted.

"I thought I'd be doing something for the local economy by offering farmers a place to sell their goods every day, rather than just one weekly farmers' market.

I plan to sell produce, beer, wine, and even crafts. I just met a weaver who makes the most astonishing rugs and things." She paused while taking sip of her tea. "But I don't know. I sometimes get the feeling they either don't get what I'm doing, or don't support it."

"Why wouldn't they?" Brynn said. "You're doing a wonderful thing for the area. Once it's up and running, it will be a mad success. I know I can't wait to see my cheese on display at the Old Glebe Market."

Nancy cracked a smile. The crinkles around her eyes seemed to smile, too. Her big, droopy brown eyes reminded Brynn of a puppy. She wasn't sure they were good enough friends for her to mention that.

"How's it going with you?" Nancy asked. "I take it Petunia is still giving you trouble."

Brynn's stomach fluttered. Was it that bad? "Yes, unfortunately. I know she's loud. The vet said cows have a strong maternal instinct, but she should get over the loss of her calf any day now."

Petunia had given birth to a stillborn calf a week ago. Each morning, the moment she left the barn, the cow ambled right to the hillside where her calf lay, buried beneath an old oak tree, and bellowed through the day. To make matters worse, she wasn't eating right, and she wasn't getting along with the other two cows, Buttercup and Marigold, both docile and sweet. Marigold was the shyest cow Brynn had ever known. Yesterday, when Petunia came into the barn, she kicked over a bucket with a stubborn deliberation Brynn had never seen from her cows—and it scared Marigold.

"I'm worried about her." Brynn picked up her cup of tea and drank in the strong brew.

"Perhaps you should call that hunk of a vet to come

over again," Nancy said, with one white eyebrow cocked. "I may be old, but I ain't dead, honey. That man is something else."

"He's okay," Brynn said. "But he's a good vet, and that's all I care about." It had been almost a year since she caught Dan cheating, and she had no interest in men at this point in her life. She couldn't imagine trusting one long enough to have a relationship. Not even the vet. Besides, he was married, which didn't seem to concern Nancy.

"Boy, that Dan did a number on you. You're young, and there's plenty of time to find a new love," Nancy said. "But then again, my husband's been dead for years, and I've yet to find one man anywhere near as good as him."

Brynn's face heated. "Let's eat the scones." She unwrapped the plate and cinnamon wafted. She lifted a scone to her lips and bit into it. "Mmm." She couldn't speak because her mouth was full. "So good!" she said after she swallowed.

"Grandma Sadie wasn't kidding around when she baked. She used real butter, real eggs and sugar, and the freshest cinnamon she could find." Nancy bit into her scone. "I followed her recipe to a *T*."

"It makes a difference," Brynn said and took another luscious bite.

"I'm glad you like them. Now let's talk about that cow of yours. You need to do something. I can hear her all day long. And I'm not the only one."

Brynn dropped her scone. What did Nancy think she could do about it? Poor Petunia was in mourning. Dr. Johnson said she was depressed, and it would run its course.

"I'm sorry, Nancy. I'll call the vet again."

"Can't you muzzle her? I mean it sounds cruel, but at least it'd be peaceful."

Brynn's heart broke at the thought of muzzling her sweet Petunia—and because her new friend didn't realize that she adored her cows. She'd no more muzzle them than she'd muzzle a person.

"No, Nancy. I can't do that." She took another sip of tea, even as her stomach soured.

Chapter 2

One of the many reasons Brynn and Dan had decided on Shenandoah Springs for their own farmette and cheesemaking hub was its active Community Supported Agriculture program. Residents bought shares and received locally grown or sourced goods once a week.

Brynn and Dan had responded to an ad in *Mother Earth News*: "Be a part of our farm community revitalization in the heart of the breathtaking Shenandoah Valley of Virginia. Land is cheap, and the community practices organic, healthy, artisanal farming. We have a very active CSA and farmers' market."

They were both living in Richmond, with her family, until they could figure out their next step. When they found that Buttermilk Creek Farm was for sale at a reasonable price, it seemed like kismet. Buttermilk Creek was the small creek that ran through the property, though nobody seemed to know why or when it was named. But the name added to Brynn and Dan's sense that it was the perfect place for them to grow their dreams. Brynn decided to keep it, rather than come up with a new name.

Brynn first fell in love with cheesemaking as a chemistry student in college. She'd taken the class on a lark because she needed the credit. But there was something so magical about the way milk turned to cheese, even though she understood the chemistry behind it. She couldn't get ideas for cheese out of her mind. Throughout the rest of school, she experimented with making cheese. After she graduated from college, she searched for cheese school, much to her parents' dismay. They'd paid for a degree in chemistry. Where was this cheesemaking thing coming from?

Brynn briefly considered Murray's, a high-end cheesemaking school in New York City, but just as quickly dismissed it. She wanted a place with cows. A place that she could see and control the cheese-making process from the start. She found St. Andrews Creamery, which is where she met Dan. He had the same mindset for wanting to control the cheese-making process from start to finish, which meant knowing exactly what your cows ate and how the food affected the cow's health and the flavor of the cheese. "All organic" and "grass fed" were not just buzzwords. They were a way of life. It took time and care to create good cheese—why wouldn't you want to know your cows and see that what they ate was the best for them?

Not only was there an artistic and healthy element to Brynn's way of handling cheese and cows, but there was also a spiritual one that seemed to be in development at all times. She realized happy cows give better milk—just like Granny Rose had always said. She was always experimenting with what made them happy—music, a scratch behind the ears, a rubbing of the nose, and speaking to them as if they understood her. Sometimes she swore they understood her more than most people do.

And, when she tended her girls, a sensation she described as spiritual often came over her. She felt at one with the universe, like she was taking part in something bigger than herself.

Dan used to tease her when she expressed this sentiment to him. Yet, he understood that happy cows make better milk and cheese.

But Brynn didn't want to think about Dan. Or the dreams they shared. Not today. Not ever. She needed to stay present as she drove to the fire hall.

Brynn had volunteered to help box the products for the CSA, and she'd brought along tiny linen-wrapped wedges of her Buttermilk Creek Farmstead Cheese to introduce to the locals.

As she arrived at the fire hall, a meeting place which doubled as the center where they held bingo on Thursday nights and square dancing on Saturday nights, she heard raised voices inside. She stopped awkwardly at the door, apprehensive, not knowing what to do with herself. She pressed on and opened it.

A large man with a Jack Daniels ball cap shadowing his face cleared his throat. "It's an old church, and it should be preserved, that's all I'm saying."

"But it's just sitting there," a woman said. "It'll be restored to its former beauty, and it will be a great place to sell our products."

"But that's what the fire hall is for! I'm just saying, people come from out of town and think they know what's best for this community. I don't like her or her ideas."

Brynn tried to pretend not to hear him talk about Nancy, but as she set her box of cheese down, it landed with more of a thud than she wanted. All eyes were on her.

The woman who had been speaking in Nancy's defense stood. "Hi, Brynn. How's it going?" Willow Rush was an organic vegetable grower. "What do you have there?"

"Cheese, what else?" She tried to lighten things up with her tone. She felt as if she'd walked into a hornet's nest, instead of a working meeting of the CSA. She moved along and inspected the boxes, brimming with organic, local, and artisanal products. Baggies full of winter greens, like arugula, rocket, kale, bok choy, collards, mustard, and turnips, along with brussels sprouts and small cabbage. "The brussels sprouts are almost too pretty to eat."

"Thanks," Willow said, beaming. Long and lean, mocha-skinned Willow had the freshest face Brynn had ever seen. And she had been the biggest help since Brynn had moved here.

A large, young man came into the room carrying jars of applesauce with ribbons on them. He placed them in the boxes, and, as he moved by Brynn, she smelled the strong scent of apples, nutmeg, cloves, and cinnamon—scents that always comforted her. She recognized him as a part of the O'Reilly family, who own the orchard near her place. He turned his gaze toward her. He had the iciest blue eyes she'd ever seen.

The man wearing the Jack Daniels cap also looked at Brynn. The shadow lifted from his face as he looked up. "Hello. I don't believe we've met." He extended his hand as he stood. "I'm Tom Andrews."

"Good to meet you," Brynn said, although she wasn't too sure about that. He was clearly a man with a temper, and his face was still red from his machinations. "I'm Brynn MacAlister. I'm living at the old rectory with my cows. Buttermilk Creek Farm. I'm a cheesemaker."

"Nancy is your neighbor then. I don't know what that woman's doing," Tom said. "I wish she'd go back to where she came from!"

Brynn's mouth dropped as she tried to search for the right thing to say. She wanted to defend Nancy, but she didn't want to make enemies.

"Now, Tom," someone said from behind Brynn. "Now is not the time. We need to get work done here today and decide about raising our membership fee in the new year."

Brynn turned to face the person who'd spoken. It was Josh O'Connor, the president of the CSA and a honey farmer. He held a box full of small jars of fresh honey—some still had bits and pieces of honeycomb in them. Brynn's mouth watered. She made a mental note to seek out that honey, for both herself and for her sister, Becky, who loved honey.

Josh placed his brimming honey jars in the boxes.

Brynn followed suit with her cheese.

"Besides, you'll scare away our newest member." He looked at Brynn, and his green eyes twinkled as if in acknowledgment of Tom's mischief.

Brynn looked away. "No worries. I'm not so easily scared away."

"Don't pay any attention to me, sweetie, I'm just an old guy with old ways," Tom muttered.

It had been a few years since a man had called her sweetie, other than Dan. It raised her hackles, but she stopped herself from telling him it was unacceptable. Just this once. If he said it again, she'd inform him. She was nobody's sweetie—and certainly not his.

A few more people entered the room. They made

introductions, and Brynn was certain it would take her months to remember all their names. But she would remember their products. Lavender. Radishes and rutabaga. Persimmons. Apple butter. And to top it all off, the local Christmas tree and pumpkin farmer brought miniature Christmas trees, which gave the boxes a festive flair.

She reached into a box and held up one of the tiny trees. "Adorable."

"Thanks," the man standing next to her said. "It's a great way to use up scraps on the farm, and people seem to like them. I'm Kevin." He extended his calloused but warm hand.

"Okay everybody. Listen up. We have a decision to make," Josh said, after clearing his throat. "Some of us think we need to raise prices. We're barely earning out."

"But earning out is just one of our goals," Willow said. "We wanted to support the community by offering healthy products and exposing them to what we're producing. More people have ordered from my website since I joined the CSA."

Which reminded Brynn that she needed to find someone to do a website for her. She planned to sell her cheese online and ship it. But first she had to find someone to create the site—she was not technologically astute.

"I say we give it another year before we raise prices," Kevin said. "You know the local economy isn't that great. If we raise prices now, I'm afraid we'll lose subscribers."

Mutters of agreement sounded from around the table, where they had gathered in a deluge of earthy-colored flannel shirts and wool sweaters.

"Tom?"

"Well, I suppose you're right. It's just that I sometimes feel like we're giving our products away for nothing. I'm still teaching, so we're doing okay, but if we were just trying to survive by our greens and such, we'd never make it. I wonder how some of you are doing it."

Willow spoke up. "We all have other gigs, Tom. You know that."

The group decided to table the issue until next year. After the meeting, they loaded the boxes into Willow's truck, as it was her turn to make deliveries. If a member had a truck, they took turns. Brynn had thought about getting a truck, but she hadn't followed through yet. A pang of regret plucked at her. There were a lot of things she needed to follow through with, but she had no time. Maybe Dan was right. Taking care of three cows on her own was too much for her, even if she was just milking one of them. But she could manage the cows—it was the rest of her life that fell away.

"How's that cow of yours?" Willow said. "Is she still giving you problems?"

"Unfortunately, yes," Brynn said.

"I have a friend who specializes in acupuncture and herbs for animals. She's a vet of sorts."

Acupuncture? Herbs? Petunia was too valuable to mess around with New Age pseudomedicine. "I don't know if I'd trust any of that."

"I know what you mean," Willow said. "But she's got a great track record. It might be worth a shot."

"Complete and total mumbo jumbo," Tom said. "What your cow needs is a muzzle."

Chapter 3

Brynn didn't expect people to understand how she felt about her cows. She was a cheesemaker, not a farmer. She didn't see her Petunia, Marigold, and Buttercup as "agricultural," but more as a part of the team it took to make the artisanal cheese. The reason she owned cows was because she'd become a freak with wanting to control every part of the cheese-making process—right down to what the cows who gave her the milk were eating.

She tossed and turned that night worrying about sweet Petunia. The cow had been blessed with such a sweet personality, a church at the edge of town had asked for her to be part of the local living nativity scene. Brynn thought it was an excellent way for the community to get to know her and her cows. But Petunia was mourning her calf. And her grief was taking longer than the vet said it would, so it worried her— and it broke Brynn's heart. And it was starting to annoy the other two cows, who were avoiding Petunia. Somehow, she fell asleep, jolted awake by sirens screaming a few hours later. She glanced at her clock:

3:03 AM.

She stuffed a pillow over her head, but the sirens were getting closer. The girls would be frightened and on edge. So she untangled herself from her quilt and slipped on her jeans and sweater. She padded down the stairs, realizing the sirens were close indeed. As she peered out the window, several fire trucks were flying down the road—toward the Old Glebe Church. She looked off toward it and saw flames.

"Oh my God!" She rushed outside, and then went back inside as the cold smacked her with an icy grip. She reached for her coat and slipped on her boots.

While struggling to get her coat on, she raced toward the church, over the hilly field connecting her property to the church property.

She almost tripped over several clumps of field grass as she made her way, heart racing as she came up over the small hill where the church came into view. Flames engulfed the old building.

She continued to run across the field toward the church, now surrounded by fire trucks and ambulances, along with several cop cars with red lights flashing.

Where is Nancy?

As she moved closer, the fire's blistering heat enveloped her and the flashing lights shot through her eyes. She squinted, examining each person she saw. The firefighters were hosing off the place, and the police had gathered in a corner. The ambulance was lying in wait.

Where is Nancy?

She ran toward the group of police officers. "Where's Nancy?"

One of them turned toward her, yelling over the roar of the fire. "Excuse me?"

"Where's Nancy? The woman who lives here?"

"And you are?" He pulled her over to the side. "I'm Brynn, her neighbor. I live right over there," she said. *As if that makes a difference.*

The officer took in a breath and released it. "We don't know if she's inside."

That can't be right. "Do you mean she didn't call?" Brynn's heart was pounding in her ears.

"It was called in by another neighbor, up the road," he replied, still yelling over the noise.

A firefighter unraveled another fire hose about ten feet from Brynn. Tufts of wiry red hair sprang from the bottom of his fire helmet. His partner was the same large young man from the CSA meeting. The one who smelled of apples. The one with icy blue eyes. "Well, she's inside." Brynn tried not to scream.

"Where else would she be?"

"Our guys are inside. If she's in there, they'll find her."

Brynn took in the blaze. It was destroying the old church, the place Nancy wanted to renovate to make into a market, the place she lived in, the place she'd always dreamed of.

A great gust of wind blew smoke in Brynn's eyes and burned her throat.

The cop reached for her and led her farther away from the smoke and fire.

Her head was spinning, her heart was pounding, and a stream of hot salty tears ran down her face.

"Calm down, okay?" the officer said, in a gentler voice. They were now farther away from the noise of men yelling, engines roaring, and fire consuming the church. "We don't know anything yet."

"There's no way she could survive that fire!"

"You never know. I've seen people survive fires all the time. Sometimes they're hospitalized with smoke inhalation, sometimes with burns. But it happens."

Brynn's stomach was churning now. She gasped for air. How could this happen? Nancy was always so careful.

A wave of sick came over her, and she turned to wretch, dizzied, as her knees wobbled.

The officer held her up as her knees resisted. The flames blurred as she fell forward onto the officer.

"Can I get oxygen over here?" she heard him say.

Another firefighter ran up to her, with a sooty, sweaty face and kind blue eyes, and he scooped her up in his arms right before she passed out. Her last thought was: *So many blue eyes around here.*

When she came to, Brynn was in a warm ambulance with a cheerful paramedic. "Hi Brynn," she said, smiling. "You'll be okay. You passed out."

Brynn took the oxygen mask off. "What about Nancy? The woman who lives here?"

Her smile vanished. "She was just taken away. Zach Flannery, the guy who carried you over here, said they're taking her to Augusta Medical, weirdly enough. She's burned, but not badly, and suffered a lot of smoke inhalation."

"Will she be okay?"

"Let's hope so." The paramedic looked at her watch as she held Brynn's wrist. "You're good to go. But take it slowly, okay?"

Brynn tried to sit up, and it turned out, the paramedic was right. She dizzied and lay back down.

The paramedic smiled. "Let's try again, shall we?" Brynn sat up and inhaled.

"That's better. Now, can we give you a lift home?"

Brynn nodded. "Thank you. I live at the old rectory, next door."

"I've always loved that place," she said. "The way it sits tucked in that long driveway against that green field and the hills."

"Yes, it's lovely, but I'm sure I've got three upset cows to deal with."

"You're the cheesemaker, right? I'm Casey, Doc Johnson's daughter."

It was a cliché, but certainly true about small towns: everybody was either related or knew each other. In a community like this, it was difficult to be a newcomer, and it would be even more difficult to keep secrets, Brynn imagined. Everybody would be all up in everybody's business.

"Nice to meet you, I'm Brynn MacAlister." She coughed. She tamped down the fear creeping into her guts about her girls. They must be nervous, with all the commotion from the fire. Petunia would need milking, and they all would need to graze.

The vehicle's engine started, and they crept along the road.

When Brynn stepped out onto her driveway, the rank scent of the charred building invaded her senses. She tried not to think about the fire as she made her way to the barn. Cows were sensitive creatures. Her Granny Rose always said to approach them only with happy thoughts in your head. To some it might be a silly superstition, but Brynn had learned to take her granny's advice about everything. She wished she had done so when saying yes to Dan's marriage proposal. She remembered Granny Rose's words vividly: "It's not that I don't like him. I just don't think he's good enough for you. And he's not husband material."

Brynn had inwardly scoffed. Husband material. Who talked like that these days? Funny expression—but exactly right. Finding her fiancé with a woman named Jolene had just added salt to her gaping wound. Dolly Parton was Brynn's personal country music guru, and she'd not been able to listen to any of her music since. Her stacks of albums and CDs sat unplayed.

After milking and letting the girls out, she'd head over to the hospital to check on Nancy. At the very least, Nancy would be heartbroken. Brynn was certain the Old Glebe Church, which had been sitting there since 1835, was in ruins.

But, ultimately, it was just a building, old or not. Nancy, on the other hand, was still alive, and Brynn was eager to see and comfort her—and find out what the heck happened.